Willow House

Willow House

Linda Eschler

iUniverse, Inc.
New York   Bloomington

Willow House

Copyright © 2009 by Linda Eschler

This is a work of fiction. All of the characters, names, incidents, organizations, and dialogue in this novel are either the products of the author's imagination or are used fictitiously.

iUniverse books may be ordered through booksellers or by contacting:

iUniverse
1663 Liberty Drive
Bloomington, IN 47403
www.iuniverse.com
1-800-Authors (1-800-288-4677)

ISBN: 978-1-4401-2711-3 (pbk)
ISBN: 978-1-4401-2712-0 (ebk)

Printed in the United States of America

iUniverse rev. date: 3/25/2009

Introduction

This is the story about Jack, Evan, and Madison Bloom, three siblings from Shreveport, Louisiana.

The Bloom children grew up working in the family seafood company, which their father Zachary Bloom had taken over when his father passed away. He said he was always told the business would be his someday, and though he loved the seafood industry, he realized that at least one, if not all, of his children might not feel the same way, so he made sure they all had the opportunity to go to college.

Jack is the eldest of the three, and the most serious in nature. He is tall, and has dark brown hair and dark eyes like his father.

Evan is the middle child, and though he is also tall, his hair is a lighter brown than Jack's, his eyes are green, and he is anything but serious.

Madison is an exact replica of her mother when she was her age, or so her father always told her. She is average in height, has blonde hair, and dark blue eyes. Her personality is a combination of Jack's and Evan's, and though the two of them love to tease her, it's apparent they both adore their sister.

None of the Bloom children look even remotely alike, and Evan loved to take advantage of that when they were children, by telling anyone who would listen, that he was in fact, an only child until his parents adopted Jack and Madison.

Chapter One

It seems that a great aunt, on their mother's side, passed away, and the three

Bloom siblings were her only survivors so she left them a house in Ocean Springs, Mississippi that had been in the Bienvenue family for generations.

The old aunt lived in South Carolina so it was assumed that this was a vacation cottage. Jack, being the eldest of the three, said he barely remembered her, so of course; the other two didn't remember her at all.

Both their parents were deceased, and they knew of no other living relatives they could speak with about Aunt Margaret.

Jack said he did remember going with his mother to South Carolina once to see her aunt Margaret, and when they left, his mother seemed very upset, and from that day on, he never heard her name mentioned again, that is until today.

"I don't get it," said Madison, "a great aunt, that we didn't even know, left us her summer house and we are not even allowed to show our respect by at least going to her funeral."

"Hey, I agree," said Jack, "but the attorney said that she had already been cremated, and did not want a memorial. Her only request is that the three of us to go to the cottage within two weeks of her death. He said there would be a letter there, explaining everything we needed to know."

"This is kind of eerie, don't ya think?" said Evan. "After all, she is dead, so why would she be so mysterious."

"Maybe it has something to do with her last visit with Mom," said Madison. "Jack, you did say that Mom was pretty upset when the two of you left?"

"She was, but when I asked her what was wrong; she just said she didn't feel well. I can't even say I actually saw Aunt Margaret, because her cook took me into the kitchen for milk and cookies before she came downstairs to meet with our Mother, I heard them raise their voices a few times, and the next thing I knew, Mom was dragging me out of there."

"That is strange," said Evan. "If they were not even speaking to one another, why in the world would she leave us a house? Maybe it's a rat's nest, and she wants to punish her descendants from the grave."

"You always did have a morbid imagination, Evan," said Madison. "Must have been caused from Jack scaring you so much when you were small."

"Or it could have been from you dropping him on his head so many times," said Jack.

"Come on Guys, let's get serious," said Evan. "What do you say we leave Friday?"

"Sounds perfect to me," said Jack. "What about you Madison?"

"I don't know, Jack. You know we do run the family business, and one of us has always been here."

"You're right, Maddie, but Jimbo has been has been with us for nearly twenty years, in fact, he helped Pop teach me the business. We all grew up working in the family business. I think it would do us good to take a couple of weeks off together. You know Mom and Dad haven't been gone that long, and I think they would like it if we spent some time reminiscing. That is if Evan can tear himself away from all his women."

"Hey, watch out Jackie at least I date."

"That's not fair," said Madison. "Jack is still healing from his breakup with Carrie."

"What about you, Maddie?" said Evan "what's your excuse for not having a boy friend?"

"I've had plenty of boyfriends Evan; I just haven't met the right one so yet."

"How would you know, you never go out with any of them on a second date?"

"You know Evan, I should have dropped you on your head a few more times."

"That's enough," said Jack. "Are we leaving Friday for the summer house or not?"

"Sorry, Jackie," said Madison. "I guess we do all need to get away. I'm game, what about you, Ev?"

"I'm sorry too, Jack and I agree with Maddie; I think Mom and Dad would like to see us take a family vacation together. The last one we took together was when they were alive. I say let's do it."
"Great," said Jack "now all I need to do is talk to Jimbo and fill him in on our plans."

After Jack left the room, Evan put his arm around Madison, and said he didn't mean to tease her that much about her boyfriends and he would try and be a little more compassionate. Madison just smiled and said he wouldn't be being true to himself, if he stopped being so obnoxious.
"And on that note, I will leave you to dream about your next victim, er, I mean date."

Chapter Two

By the time Friday rolled around, Madison was getting pretty excited. She had never really been to the Mississippi Coast. Family vacations were always spent in Florida, and though her mother was from Ocean Springs, she never took them there. She said she had no living relatives left there, and she didn't need to return to her hometown in order to remember her childhood. Madison had the feeling that her mother's childhood was not a very happy one, so she never asked her too many questions about it. She always thought that someday her mother would open up to her about her past, but that day never came because both her mother and father were killed in a car wreck, less than a year ago. She still had a hard time believing it, because they were only in their fifties, and still so full of life. *This really will do all three of us some good,* she thought. *Maybe we can learn a little more about our mother.*

Evan was at home, waiting for Jack to pick him up. Jack had a beautiful red van that everyone called the fire truck, but they both figured it was the only vehicle big enough to hold Madison's luggage, so the plan was for Jack to stop for Evan, and pick Madison up last, so that they could both haul her luggage out to the van.

God, this is going to be strange, thought Evan. *Our father's parents died when he was a young man and he had no other living relatives. Our mother's parents had also passed away when she was young. As far as he knew, Jack and Madison were his only living relatives. He knew that it was very important to his parents that their children remain close, and he always assumed it was because they never really had much of a family.*

Jack began honking the horn, and that brought Evan back to reality. He was glad though, because he was thinking about how violent his parent's deaths were. They were told they went off a bridge into the water, but their bodies were never found.

On the way to pick up Madison, Evan asked Jack if he had spoken to the Police Chief recently.

"Not recently, Evan, why do you ask?" "I just think it's strange that they never found Mom or Dad's body, or anything that belonged to them."

"They did find the car, Evan, and you know they said the river current could have taken them away."

"I remember that, Jack, but it just seems they would have surfaced somewhere. We were all in shock for so many months that none of us was thinking very straight. I just don't believe we were told the whole truth."

"I agree Evan, just don't say anything to Madison about it. She and Mom were so close, and she is just now starting to heal a little."

"I won't say anything, for now, Jack, but I do think you and I should start a little investigation of our own when we get back from this vacation."

"I think so too, it hasn't quite been a year, so it shouldn't be too hard to research the, so called, accident."

"You don't believe it was an accident, do you Jack?"

"I don't know what I think, Evan, the police ruled it accidental, but my gut says that there was someone else involved."

Chapter Three

"It's about time the two of you got here," said Madison, as the two men got out of the van. "I've been waiting out here for half an hour, in fact I was just about to call and find out what was holding the two of you up."

"Wow, you really must be in a hurry to see the rat's nest," said Evan, as he and Jack started loading Madison's luggage.

"I am excited about this trip, Evan, this is an opportunity to see where our mother was raised, and maybe meet some of the people who knew her when she was growing up. We know all there is to know about Dad. We live in the same city he grew up in, and everyone knew and loved him, but we have never met anyone that knew our mother."

"That's true, Ev," said Jack. "This could prove to be a very enlightening trip. Now, if you two morons are ready, we need to hit the road. It's about a six hour drive, and I would like to get there before dark."

"I don't know, Jack," said Evan, "are you sure you want to see this place in the daylight? I'd hate to see you go blind at such a young age."

As Jack pulled off, Madison started laughing at Evan's remark, and said "what if they all went blind when they saw the summer house? They could tell everyone they were the blind leading the blind."

"Not funny, you two," said Jack. "But I do wonder if maybe the house blinded Aunt Margaret. We know she was an old bat, and that could be where the saying "blind as a bat came from."

"That was much worse than our jokes, Jack," said Madison.

"You don't know if Auntie Margaret was blind."

"We are all sick. Ya know that don't ya?" said Evan. "Mom always said that all three of us got Dad's sense of humor. I remember that sometimes she would have to calm Dad down. She would walk in on all of us ragging each other, or just acting like idiots, and she would say, "Now, John, you know you need to set a better example for the children, after all, you are the role model for the boys, and Madison is beginning to act just like them." Then dad would say, "You're right, sweetheart. I promise to start acting more like an adult."

"Yeah, but as soon as she left the room," said Madison, "he would start acting crazy all over again."

"Mom knew it too," said Jack. "She always left the door open when she left the room, and I could always see her shaking her head and laughing herself. We really did have a lot of fun growing up, didn't we?"

"Hey look," said Madison, "the next exit is Ocean Springs. I can't believe we are here. It's really not a bad trip, wonder why Mom and Dad never brought us here."

"Guess we are about to find out," said Evan. "Maybe the whole town is a rat's nest, like the summer house."

"Alright now, knock it off and help me with directions," said Jack. "We are about to enter Ocean Springs"

Chapter Four

"According to the directions the attorney gave us," said Madison, "all you have to do is turn left at the next traffic light, and the summer house is the last house on the right."

After driving about a mile down the road, Jack made a comment that he had passed all the houses on this road, so they must have missed it, but as he pulled off the road to turn around and go back, Madison said she thought she saw something pretty far down the road.

"You could be right," said Jack. "I did see a sign that said *No Outlet*, so that could be the last house on this road."

"Yeah, I saw that sign too," said Evan, "but I didn't want to call it to Madison's attention. You know, with her shopping addiction and all."

"No Outlet," said Madison. "That is about as old as your underwear."

"So is what you just said, Maddie," said Evan.

By this time, Jack had reached the end of the road, and pulled into the driveway of what looked like a huge antebellum home. "This can't be the summer house," said Evan. "No, but I have to turn around somewhere, and since the gates are open, and there are no cars in sight, the owner's will never know that we trespassed."

"This is the address of the house we inherited," said Madison, as Jack rounded the circular driveway.

"I doubt it," said Evan. "You always were a little cross eyed."

"I'm serious," said Madison. "This is the right address, but there is no mention in our copy of Aunt Margaret's Will, that the house had a name. This house is called Willow House."

"And rightfully so," said Evan. "There must be at least a hundred willow trees surrounding the house which seems a little strange."

"Why would that seem strange? asked Madison, "The house is called Willow House, after all."

"Yes, but did you notice any willow trees anywhere else along the way?"

Before Madison had a chance to answer, Evan burst out laughing.

"We must have inherited the servants quarters' over on the far end of the property. What a dirty trick old Aunt Margaret played on us. She must have really been upset with Mom the last time she saw her. Well if she thinks that we are going to be the servants to whomever lives in the mansion, she is just wrong."

Just then, someone in a maid's uniform came out of the mansion, and began waving for them to stop.

"Look, Maddie, she just can't wait to turn her uniform over to you, not that I blame her, it is an awfully big house, for one little old Magnolia to clean all by herself."

"Well, if that's the case, then I guess that fella behind her in the Butler's uniform, can't wait to relinquish his position to you, Ev."

"Don't make me hurt the two of you," said Jack. "Oh, don't worry, Jack," said Evan, "I see that there's a Rolls Royce parked in the driveway, so I'm sure the driver is chomping at the bit to turn his keys over to the driver of this big ole fire truck."

Jack stopped in front of the mansion and got out of the van. By this time, the woman in the maid's uniform was standing directly in front of him.

"Mr. Bloom?" she asked. "Yes, I 'm Jack Bloom, and you are?" "My name is Beatrice, Mr. Bloom. "I am the head housekeeper. This is my husband, Franklin, who is the Butler, as well as the Driver, and this is Martha. Martha is the only other member of our staff at this time so she does the cooking and helps with the housework."

As Franklin gave a slight nod, Jack said that it was very nice to meet all of them.

"Maybe someone could show us to our quarters now," said Jack.

"I apologize, Mr. Bloom, I'm sure you, Mr. Evan, and Ms Madison are very weary from the drive, and could use a nice long bath. I'll have Martha show you to your quarters."

As Jack and Evan began to unload the luggage, Franklin stopped them in their tracks.

"Please, Sirs," he said, "your luggage will be taken care of."

"I like it here already," said Evan. "But shouldn't we have parked a little closer to the servant's quarters?"

Chapter Five

"I don't understand any of this," said Madison, as Martha led them up a Marble stairway that appeared to look like the one in Tara, from Gone with the Wind. "Why would a Great Aunt, that we never knew, and obviously wasn't close to our Mother, leave us her mansion?"

"Why the hell was she living in South Carolina, when she had a mansion like this one, here?" asked Evan.

"She probably married someone from South Carolina, and had to move there," said Madison.

"You really think someone actually married the Wicked Witch of the South?" asked Evan.

"You're a moron, Evan." said Madison. "The name on her Will was Margaret

Montgomery. Mom's maiden name was Bienvenu, and Margaret was the sister to our Grandfather, Bienvenu. If she had not married, the name on her will would have been Bienvenu."

"So she was married, once, or maybe even more than once, it doesn't really matter, because they probably never lived to tell about it."

"Sorry to interrupt, Sir," said Martha, "but I need to know if you will all be staying in the same wing, or will you each require a wing of your own?"

"I think one wing is quite sufficient," said Jack, as they followed Madeline up to the second floor.

"Very good, Sir," said Martha, as she reached the top of the stairs. "Ms. Madison, your room is the first door to the left, and Mr. Jack, and Mr. Evan, your rooms are the next two doors adjacent to Ms. Madison's room."

As Martha opened the door to Madison's room, she said the other two rooms were identical in every way except color. She said that Ms. Madison's room was done in pastels and the other two in more masculine colors.

"As you can see, you each have your own private bath, and balcony, and should you need anything whatsoever, just push the number one button on your phone. Cocktails will be at five p.m. and dinner will be served at seven p.m.., unless otherwise requested."

"That sounds perfect, Martha," said Jack. "But can we have a tour of the house before then? We have no idea where cocktails are served, let alone where the dining room is."

"Certainly, Sir, Franklin will meet the three of you downstairs in the foyer at five p.m. and that should give you time for cocktails and a short tour before dinner. The grounds are rather large, so you might want to wait until tomorrow for the full tour."

"That sounds wonderful, Martha, thank you for your help."

After Martha left, Madison said she could not believe how big her room was.

"I've never even stayed in a hotel room this big."

"Hotel room?" said Evan. "My house isn't as big as this room. But I don't understand why the doors to each of our rooms are so far apart."

"*Duh*," said Madison, as she seemed to disappear through a wall. "You two have got to come see this."

It seemed that they were so overwhelmed by the size of the room; they didn't notice there was no bed.

"Of course," said Evan, as he followed Madison's voice, "this is a suite. We are such hicks. That was the living area, and this is the sleeping area."

"Correct, Mr. and Mrs. Hick," said Jack. "Now, I think we should let Maddie unpack, since she has so much more than we do, and go settle into our own rooms, excuse me, *suites.* We shall pick you up on our way downstairs for cocktails, mum."

"I shall be waiting, kind sir," said Madison, giggling as the two brothers left her room.

Chapter Six

As Jack, Evan and Madison descended the marble staircase, Madison made a comment that she hoped they didn't expect them to be dressed for dinner, because all she brought were casual clothes. "I didn't expect anything like this," she said

"Hey, we own this place," said Evan. "We could be nude if we wanted to."

"But of course Jack and I would never want to," said Madison. "And you better not even consider it, ever."

"Good evening, Franklin," said Jack, as they neared the bottom of the staircase.

"Good evening, Mr. Jack, Mr. Evan, and Ms. Madison. Please follow me and I will take you into the parlor for cocktails. We can take a short tour before dinner."

"That sounds great," said Madison. "I can't wait to see this wonderful house."

"Hey, did ya hear, old Frankie?" whispered Evan. "We have a parlor? I wonder if we have a dungeon, as well?"

"Just ignore, Mr. Evan," said Jack. "We sometimes wonder if he really is a member of this family."

"Oh, Mr. Jack," said Franklin, as they entered the parlor, "only Bienvenue descendents are supposed to be here. And if you're not sure that he is…."

"I'm just kidding, Franklin, my brother may act like a red headed stepchild sometimes, but I assure you, he is a descendent of the Bienvenue family."

"Very good, Sir," said Franklin, with no expression whatsoever. "Now what will you have to drink, Ms. Madison?"

"I'll have a glass of white wine thank you.

Very good, Madame, and you, Mr. Jack and Mr. Evan?"

"I'll have a vodka martini," said Jack.

"And I shall have a Bushwacker," said Evan. "Oh, never mind, I'm sure you don't have a Bushwacker machine, so I'll just have what Jack's having."

As Franklin handed everyone their drinks, he asked Evan if he knew where he could purchase this machine that made the Bushwackers he requested, and again, Jack told him that most of what Evan had to say was nonsense, so he should not take him too seriously, but Jack knew that he was going to have to take Evan aside and calm him down, otherwise he would have to tell everyone that he was actually dropped on his head when he was a baby, and to just ignore everything he said.

"Now, if everyone is ready," said Franklin, "we shall start the tour."

The first place he took the three was to the kitchen, which looked like a restaurant kitchen. He explained the history of when the kitchen was actually added to the house, because during the period that the house was actually built, kitchens were not attached to the main house, because if there was a fire, there would be no risk to the rest of the house.

"Very interesting, Franklin," said Madison. "And if I may ask, when was this house built?"

"I believe it was built in the middle eighteenth century, by Tempest and Bedelia Bienvenue, your great grand parents

"We don't really know anything about our mother's side of the family Franklin."

"I'll fill you in as best I can Miss Madison. "Tempest Bienvenue was a real terror. He and his wife Bedelia, had one son, named Rene`. Rene` grew up and married Juliette, and Rene` and Juliette were of course the parents of your mother, Camille."

"Were you employed here when our mother was a little girl?"

"We do need to get on with the tour, Ms. Madison, if that is okay with you. It is nearing dinner time, and it seems that we have fallen behind. Perhaps we can discuss your heritage another time."

"Of course, Franklin, we have plenty of time, don't we?" said Madison, who noticed that Franklin seemed taken aback when she questioned him about her mother.

Chapter Seven

After dinner, Franklin asked the Blooms if they would like an after dinner drink in the parlor, and Jack said he thought that would be very nice, and he also mentioned there was supposed to be a letter for the three of them from their Aunt Margaret.

"Yes, there is such a letter, sir; I shall bring it to the parlor."

After everyone was settled with their after dinner drink, Franklin went to get the letter, and as soon as he left the room, Jack asked the other two if they noticed the look on Franklin's face when he mentioned Aunt Margaret's name. It was if the very sound of her name terrified him."

"I was wondering why his hair stood up, and his eyeballs seemed to pop out when you said her name," said Evan. "I wanted to say it again just to see his hair stand up again, but then I remembered that he wasn't very fond of my humor."

"I noticed too, and I also noticed that he did not want to discuss our mother with us," said Madison.

By this time, Franklin was back, and he had a large manila envelope with him. As he handed it to Jack, he asked if there was anything else they needed.

Jack took the envelope, thanked him, and said that they would not need him the rest of the evening.

After Franklin left the room, Jack said he felt as if he were about to open Pandora's box.

When Jack opened the envelope, there was another sealed envelope inside, with a letter attached to it. It was from Aunt Margaret. The letter contained the following:

If you are reading this letter, then you are the only living relatives of Tempest and Bedelia Bienvenue. By now, you know that you have inherited Willow House, but what you do not know is that you have also inherited the curse it brings.

Previsions have been made with a local bank, to take care of the upkeep of Willow House.

Inside this envelope, is a map that will guide you to a treasure that has been hidden here since Tempest Bienvenue died.

Should you decide to leave before you find the treasure, you will not be allowed to return, and the house, along with the treasure, will be passed on to your descendents.

Obviously I never found the treasure, however I did find the curse, and I was never allowed to return to Willow House.

My Niece Camille left long before I, and wanted nothing to do with her inheritance. I, on the other hand, felt that I was cheated out of what I deserved, but I have no choice now except to pass the treasure or possibly the curse on to you.

"That sounds like something out of a really bad horror movie," said Evan.

"It really does," said Jack. "But I do wonder why our mother never told us about this place, and why she and Aunt Margaret had a falling out when I was a little boy."

Chapter Eight

After breakfast the next morning, Madison and the boys decided to take a walk down to the beach, so they could have some privacy to talk. Madison said that she felt as if someone was watching her inside the house, and she wanted to make sure that no one heard what she was about to say.

As the three neared the water, they noticed all you could hear were the birds singing. The smell of Magnolias was in the air, and Madison commented that she could not imagine anyone not wanting to live here.

"Just look around you, boys," said Madison. "I can't get over all these massive oaks, and have you ever seen so many Willow trees?"

"At least we know why Aunt Margaret didn't live here," laughed Evan. "They ran her off."

"Who ran her off?" asked Madison. "See, this is the part I don't understand. She says in her letter that she wasn't allowed to return to Willow House, but if she was the only other Bienvenue left, besides us, who was keeping her out?"

"I don't think anyone was keeping her out, Maddie," said Jack. "I think she was just convinced that there was a curse, and she was afraid to come back."

"She was probably a fruitcake," said Evan.

"Well I don't doubt that, Evan," said Maddie. "But why did Mom never mention this place, and why did she always change the subject when we mentioned her family? She said that one day she would tell us everything we wanted to know, but I guess she didn't think that she would be gone so quickly."

Jack said that he thought that they should start on their treasure hunt right away, and Madison and Evan agreed.

"We just need to keep mum about our plan," said Evan. "Wouldn't want old Frankie following us around. I think he knows much more than he is letting on."

Jack and Madison started laughing, and Evan said that he was not kidding.

"Just take a look at his eyes the next time you see him," he said, "they seem to follow you no matter where you are in the room."

"That's because he's looking at you, Bozo," said Madison. "He's not a painting on the wall."

"Well, all I know is that there is something not quite right about that boy" said Evan. "and I don't mind telling you that I slept with my door locked last night."

"That's enough," said Jack. "We need to get started on this treasure hunt. I don't really care if we find anything or not, but I'm hoping we can uncover some information about our mother's childhood."

"We might be better off not knowing," said Evan. "It must have been pretty bad, for her not to share that part of her life with us."

"That's true, but she's gone now, so we are not hurting her, and besides, if any of us ever have children, we need to be able to tell them all about their Grand Parents," said Madison.

"Well, considering that you're not even dating anyone right now." said Evan.

"Don't even start with me, Evan, let's just open the map and start our treasure hunt."

Chapter Nine

Franklin and Beatrice stood staring out the window at the three figures sitting under a tree near the water.

"I was hoping that we were through with the Bienvenue family, once and for all," said Beatrice. "But we could still have their children to deal with."

"There won't be any children, if they never leave here," said Franklin.

"You mean if they decide to join their ancestors?" asked Beatrice.

"Of course not, Beatrice, I meant if they just never leave. You know there is no set amount of time allotted for them to find the treasure, if indeed there really is a treasure. No one has found it so far."

"Just look at them down there," said Beatrice, "thinking they are so smart that they will be the ones to figure out where the treasure is hidden. I just wish I could hear what they are saying."

"I don't understand why anyone would have a problem finding the treasure," said Madison, as she stood up and looked around the grounds of Willow House. This map is simple enough for a child to read."

"Exactly," said Jack, "so why hasn't anyone found the treasure?"

"I give up Jack, why hasn't anyone found the treasure?" said Evan.

"Because it's a setup; either there is no treasure, or the map is a fake."

"But what would be the purpose of a fake map?" asked Madison. "Who would have anything to gain by no one finding the treasure?"

"Franklin and Beatrice, for one. If we found the treasure, then the mansion would be ours, and we could do what we wanted with it. They could be out of a job, and a place to live if we decided to sell it, but as long as no one finds the treasure, they continue to have their security."

"And of course, one of the stipulations, in the original will of Tempest Bienvenue, is that the property would be passed down to the surviving relatives, and that they could come and stay as long as they like, but once they leave, they cannot return, unless they find the treasure, which would then mean they owned the property free and clear."

"Sounds to me like great grand daddy Tempest is the one that faked a map, insuring that the property would never leave the hands of his ancestors," said Evan.

"But why would he care if the property gets sold or not, he is dead, after all," said Jack.

"Maybe," said Madison. "Then again, maybe he still resides in Willow House."

"Here we go," said Evan. "Maddie is letting her very wild imagination run away from her again."

"Just think about it, guys, just suppose that our great grandfather, Tempest died in this house, and his spirit has never crossed over. Wouldn't it make sense that he would never want the house to leave the hands of his family?"

"Sure," said Jack, "if he knew beforehand that his spirit would never leave the house, or that he would even die in this house."

"Maybe he was sick and he didn't know that he was going to die in the house, and if he was as much of a terror as Franklin implied, he could have made a fake map just to make sure that no one ever owned the property, just in case his spirit decided to stay here."

"Now you're reaching," said Evan. "But I do think you are

on the right track. What if he made a fake map, so that no one else would ever be able to own this property after he passed away, he obviously left enough money to pay the taxes, upkeep, and Franklin and Beatrice's salary for many years, and if no one ever found the treasure, then he would remain the *Lord of the Manor*, so to speak."

"I don't know, Evan," said Jack. "I think that Franklin and Beatrice have the most to lose, and if there really is a map, then maybe they destroyed it, or kept the treasure for themselves."

"I've got an idea," said Madison, "let's go have lunch in one of those rustic little restaurants on the water, and maybe we can find out what the local gossip is about the Bienvenue family."

Chapter Ten

"This is such a wonderful little town," said Madison, as they entered the *View* restaurant. "I just can't imagine why Mom never talked about it."

Jack asked the hostess if they could dine out on the deck, overlooking the water, and after they were seated; he told Madison and Evan not to mention they were staying at Willow House. He said they could probably find out more by playing dumb.

When the waitress approached their table, they all ordered a draught beer, and Jack said they would like to look over the menu. He noticed there were several other groups dinning on the deck, and since the waitress seemed to know them, he assumed they were locals, so he pretended to be interested in moving to Ocean Springs, from New Orleans. He introduced himself to a group at the table next to ours and said he was an investor, and was interested in purchasing Willow House for a summer retreat, and that Evan and I were his brother and sister, and also his associates.

"Welcome to Ocean Springs," said one of the men sitting at the table.

"My name is Joe Bailey, and this is my wife Angie. Angie has lived here her whole life. I'm originally from Louisiana myself, but I can tell ya'll that living in Ocean Springs is like stepping back in time. It's so relaxing, and a great place to raise children."

"Wow," said Madison. "You sound like the welcome wagon."

"He really does, doesn't he?" said Angie. "But he does love it here. My family has been here since the early eighteen hundreds, and I could never see myself living anywhere else; in fact, we bought this restaurant from my uncle a couple of years ago."

"I'm sorry Angie, I didn't realize you were the owners, I thought you were customers since you were sitting at the table."

"No problem Madison, we were just taking a little break and chatting with some of our regulars."

"So, Joe, do you think that Willow House would be a good investment?" asked Jack.

"I doubt that Willow House is for sale Jack."

"Are you sure Joe, for some reason I thought that all the family died and the estate was being sold?"

"I don't think so," said Joe. As far as I know, the old aunt that owned it passed away, but her sister's children own it now."

"Jack, I wouldn't waste my time with Willow House," said Angie. "It has stayed in the Bienvenue family since it was built. For some strange reason, no one ever sells it. No one in the family ever lives in it, but they never sell it either."

"I heard there was a curse on the old estate," said someone at another table. "I'm sorry to interrupt, but I couldn't help but overhear your conversation. My name is Andre Bergeron, and I have lived here all my life. I went to school with Camille Bienvenue. She lived in the old estate until she graduated, then she left town. I never saw her again, that is until about a year ago. I saw her and her husband in this very restaurant."

As Jack, Evan and Madison heard Andre say that he saw their mother and father in Ocean Springs a year ago, they knew they had to tell him who they were, so Jack asked if they could join him at his table. He told him that Camille was their mother, and that she and their father were killed in a car wreck almost a year ago.

Andre said he was sorry to hear it, and that it must have happened right after he saw them. "If you don't mind me asking, why are you pretending to be tourists?"

"I'm sorry," said Madison, "it's kind of personal."

"I understand, it's just that I really thought a lot of Camille, in fact, I had a huge crush on her in high school, but she wasn't interested in anyone or anything in this town. I guess that is why she left so fast after graduation. Just let me know if I can be of some help. I 'm a pretty trustworthy guy, and if you don't believe me, just ask my completely trustworthy son."

Just then a young man appeared and Madison was at a loss for words. This has to be the most mesmerizing man she had ever seen, she thought. He had huge dark eyes that caught your attention right away, and there was something very familiar about him. She could hardly take her eyes off of him, and when Mr. Bergeron introduced him as his son, she felt as if everything was happening in slow motion. She extended her hand and as he touched her fingers with his, she felt a strange tingle throughout her entire body.

Evan kicked her under the table, and that seemed to bring her back to reality.

"I'm pleased to meet you, Mr. Bergeron." said Madison.

"Please, call me Andy,"

As Jack and Evan introduced themselves to Andy Bergeron, Madison regained her composure.

Andre told Andy they were investors, and were quite interested in Willow House.

Madison quickly corrected Mr. Bergeron, and said that it was okay if his son knew who they really were, and that they would really appreciate any information they could share with them about her mother's family.

Andy said that he didn't really know that much about the Bienvenue family, and most of the stories he had heard seemed to be very far fetched, in fact, they were more like ghost stories.

"What do you mean ghost stories?" asked Jack.

Andy quickly explained that when he was growing up, he and his friends would sit on the beach and tell ghost stories, and one in particular seemed to stick in his mind. He said that even though no one lived in the Bienvenue house, there were always lights going on and off, and many folks claimed to see the figure of a man and a woman pass by the windows now and then.

"Occasionally a few of the kids would venture onto the front porch, but usually a strange noise or a shadow would scare them away; frankly it always intrigued me, and I've always wanted to see the inside. Unfortunately I was never invited, in fact, I don't know of anyone that has ever been inside that house, with the exception of the family."

"Well I'm sure we could arrange a tour for you while we are in town," said Madison. "Give me your card and I'll give you a call tomorrow."

Chapter Eleven

"It was easier to get rid of Margaret" said Franklin," since there was only one of her, and all she was interested in was the treasure, but there are three of them and they seem much too curious about their ancestors."

"Well you can understand why, can't you?" asked Beatrice "Camille hated it here and who could blame her. She never wanted to come back here, let alone allow her children to come here. She never told them about her horrid old grandfather or this house."

"Still, we need to see that there visit is as short as possible, these three are pretty clever and if they find the treasure, well I don't have to tell you what will become of us."

The rest of the afternoon, the Bloom family explored Ocean Springs and they all admitted that they would love to relocate there.

"I feel as if I am at home in this town," said Jack.

"I agree." said Evan. "It's the most peaceful feeling I have ever had, and of course we all know why Maddie has taken such an interest in this town."

By this time the three were pulling into the driveway at Willow House and Madison just shook her heard and smiled at Evan.

"Oh, Evan," she said, "I'm sure if you hang around Ocean Springs long enough, someone will notice you too."

Before Evan could answer Maddie, Jack interrupted and asked if it looked like there were lights on in the attic.

"Looks that way," said Evan, "but so what if there are lights on? Franklin or Beatrice is probably looking for something."

"Like what?" asked Madison. "When Franklin took us on a tour, he said there wasn't much reason to go into the attic because it was empty, remember? He said they didn't keep anything stored there because the floors were much too unstable."

"That's right," said Jack, "he did say there was some roof damage from a hurricane and a leak caused a lot of damage in the attic that was never repaired."

"Yeah, a hurricane named Camille, no wonder mother left; they named a hurricane after her."

"What doesn't make sense is why they never had the repairs done," said Jack, "especially since there seems to be ample money to take care of the house, not to mention insurance."

"Good evening, Bloom family" said Martha, as the three entered the mansion. "Did you have a pleasant day?"

"Yes we did, thank you," said Madison. "Martha, do you know why the attic floors were never repaired after Hurricane Camille? After all, it was nearly forty years ago and our mother was still living here at that time."

Before Martha could answer, Franklin entered the room and said that he would be happy to explain it to the three of them during cocktail hour.

"I feel as if we were dismissed," said Evan, as the three of them started upstairs to freshen up before dinner.

"Maybe he just didn't want to get into it until he had the time to explain." said Jack.

"Or maybe he just needed time to think of something to tell us," said Madison.

"There goes that devious little mind of yours," said Evan. "Though this time I tend to agree with you."

"See you two at five," said Jack, as he disappeared into his room.

"Sis, do you seriously think that there is something Franklin

29

and Beatrice are keeping from us?" asked Evan. "Or do you think maybe they are just eccentric."

"Oh I believe they are eccentric, all right, but I also believe they are hiding more than one thing from us."

"That does it then, we gang up on them tonight and beat the truth out of them."

"See ya at five Guido," said Madison, as she opened the door to her room. "Don't forget the rope."

Downstairs, Franklin and Beatrice were discussing what they were going to tell this much too curious Bloom family.

Franklin thought they should just stick to the original story about the hurricane damage and say they never had it repaired because they didn't need the attic, with all the other storage rooms they had on the property.

"They won't be satisfied with that, Franklin; they must have seen the lights on in the attic when they came home. They want answers, and if they stay in this house long enough, they may just get them, and we cannot let that happen."

No, I'm afraid that if the Bloom children don't leave soon, we will have no choice but to make sure that they meet the same end their parents did."

"What are you talking about, Beatrice; their parents were killed in a car crash. You are scaring me a bit with that crazy talk."

Chapter Twelve

"Franklin," said Madison, "we thought we would like to sit on the front porch and have our cocktails, and we would like for you and Beatrice to join us. After all, this has been your home for many years, and we would like to get to know you better."

"Very well," said Franklin. "Beatrice is a little under the weather, but I will be happy to join you."

Madison said she was very sorry Beatrice wasn't feeling well, and she hoped she could join them another time.

"Franklin," said Jack, "you seemed a little nervous when we asked you if you were employed here when our mother lived here, and we never did get an answer."

"I'm sorry, Sir, it's just that Willow House has never been a house that was filled with children's laughter because your great grandfather Tempest would not allow it. He ruled with an iron fist, and no one dared defy him, not even your grandfather Rene` dared to cross him."

"Your grandmother Juliette begged Rene` to take her and your mother away from Willow House, but he said he was born here, and it was here he must die."

"Your mother of course hated it here as much as, Juliette, her mother.

I always believed that your mother would be the first Bienvenue to leave Willow House, and I was sure that when she did, she would take Juliette with her, but sadly, Juliette died in a fire in the attic, and after that, no one was ever allowed in the attic again.

I'm sorry for not telling you the true story it's just that it was such an upsetting time for all of us. You see, I cared very deeply for Juliette because she was the only light in this house; that is until your mother came along."

"Franklin, dinner is served" said a rather harsh voice, and as everyone looked up, they saw Beatrice standing in the doorway.

"Beatrice," said Franklin, "I thought you were not feeling well."

"Well, I'm feeling much better now, and I'm sure that our guests are quite hungry."

"Oh, we are not guests," said Madison, in a tone that said, *you need to remember who owns this house,* "and by the way, I'm very glad that you are all better."

Madison later told Jack and Evan that though she had softened towards Franklin, there was something about Beatrice that she just didn't like.

"Taking over as lady of the manor already?" asked Evan.

"Maybe, it never hurts to practice."

"You two do know," said Jack, "that if we don't find the treasure by the time we leave here, we don't own jack."

"Please, Jack," said Evan, "leave the jokes to me. It just doesn't suit you."

"You're right Evan, you are the jokester in the family."

"This is getting downright scary," said Madison. "Jack is always the one to stop our bickering back and forth, and suddenly he is joining in. This house must be affecting all of us."

After dinner, Madison told Franklin that she would like to invite a guest for dinner tomorrow night.

"You and Beatrice and Martha can take the night off, if you like" said Madison. "The boys and I have decided to have a barbecue and that is something we can handle all by ourselves."

Franklin began to protest, saying they didn't need a night off and they would be glad to help in any way they could, but Madison insisted they take some time for themselves.

"We may be here for quite some time, Franklin, and we

certainly don't want to wear the two of you out, after all you are not used to having three extra people to take care of."

"Yes, but Miss Madison we are enjoying having family around for a change and I believe that Beatrice would agree."

"And speaking of Beatrice, where did she disappear to?"

Franklin seemed a little shaken as he looked around and realized that Beatrice was nowhere in sight. He then made some lame excuse about Beatrice having a relapse of whatever ailment she had suffered earlier.

Madison was beginning to believe that Beatrice had something on Franklin and was using it to keep him quiet.

"Franklin, I would like to speak to you alone sometime, just you and me; no Jack, no Evan and no Beatrice. Please keep this between us Franklin, okay?"

"Yes, Miss Madison, I will indeed keep this between us," said Franklin, and for some reason, Madison believed him.

Chapter Thirteen

After dinner, Madison called Andy and said she would like for him and his father and mother to come to Willow House for a barbecue the next evening.

Andy quickly accepted the invitation and said he would check with his mother and father to see if they had any plans of their own.

"I think it would be safe to count them in though, I can't see my mother turning down an opportunity to finally be inside Willow House."

Andy suddenly realized how shallow that sounded.

"My mother is a really terrific person, Madison and I know she is going to love you."

"I'm sure she is Andy and I don't blame her for wanting to see inside Willow House. If it were me, I would probably have found a way to get inside long ago, but then my brothers always tell me that I'm a little too nosy for my own good, and speaking of my brothers, I'm sure they will be grilling enough food to feed everyone in Ocean Springs, in fact, I would love it if Joe and Angie would come."

"Madison, my dear, I will do my very best to make your wishes come true," said Andy, "though I'm not sure they will be able to leave the restaurant at the same time."

"Then I will let you go for now, after all, you are on a mission, and for some reason, I believe you can be very persuasive."

"Yes I can be very persuasive and you must never forget that."

Madison laughed and said that she looked forward to seeing

him and hopefully his mother and father and Joe and Angie tomorrow evening.

Evan walked in right after Madison hung up the phone and asked Madison if she had raided the wine cellar.

"Your eyes look kind of glazed over and you have this really stupid grin on your face. Oh wait a minute you were talking to that Andy fella weren't you? That explains the big ole grin on your face, but the glazed eyes, well, I still think you…"

"You can't bring me down tonight, Evan, so give it up."

"But you didn't let me finish what I was about to say."

"Who are you two plotting against?" asked Jack, as he came down the stairs, "and what were you about to say?"

"It's not important, Jack," said Madison. "Why don't we have an after dinner drink in the gazebo?"

Jack poured everyone a glass of Brandy, and as the three walked toward the beach, Madison said that she needed to discuss the menu with them for tomorrow night.

"What menu?" asked Jack, as they neared the gazebo. "It's a barbecue. You know what we always have at our barbecues, ribs, potato salad, baked beans, French bread and the famous Bloom bread pudding."

"What famous Bloom bread pudding?" asked Evan. "You stole that recipe from Emeril and claimed it as your own."

"I didn't steal it. I made a few subtle changes in the recipe and therefore it became my very own."

"Back to the menu," said Madison. "I think we should grill some Angels on Horseback for appetizers."

"What's this, we?" asked Jack. "You have never grilled anything in your life."

"Oh, and Evan, you can be the bartender," said Madison, pretending she didn't hear a word that Jack said.

"I think we should talk about Franklin and Beatrice," said Jack. "Franklin didn't seem too happy about being excluded from our barbecue."

"He's probably scared to death of Beatrice," said Madison

"Well, so am I" said Evan. "She gave me the stink eye earlier today."

"You two should be ashamed of yourselves, Beatrice hasn't done a thing to you and here you are making fun of her."

"We are not making fun of her, Jack." said Madison.

"I am," said Evan.

"Look, we agreed that we would stick around for a week or two at the most so that we could learn more about our mother's family, so if we expect to get any information out of the staff, we have to try and win at least one of them over. What about Martha, has anyone even thought about questioning her?"

"Beatrice never leaves Martha alone for one minute Jack; I wouldn't be surprised if she kept her tied up when she isn't working."

"Okay, so go to her room and untie her. See what you can get out of her about our mother."

"I swear that Evan is becoming a bad influence on you Jack, and on that note, I am going to bed. See you two at breakfast."

Walking back to the house, Madison began thinking that it might not be a bad idea to pay a little visit to Martha. The problem was that she didn't know exactly where her room was.

Chapter Fourteen

Just as Madison entered the front door of Willow House, she heard what seemed to be raised voices coming from somewhere upstairs, so she decided that this would be a good time to do a little snooping, but before she was halfway up the stairs, she heard a door slam. She immediately ran back down the stairs and hid in the storage closet just under the staircase.

Wow that was close, thought Madison, as she heard footsteps pounding on the staircase overhead.

"Just where do you think you are going, missy?" came an all too familiar voice.

"I'm leaving this dreadful place as quickly as possible." said another very familiar voice.

Madison realized it was Martha trying to leave Willow House, and that Beatrice was trying to stop her.

"You're not going anywhere, missy," said Beatrice. "Just remember what happened to the others."

"But they are not like the others," said Martha. "especially miss Madison."

"What are you talking about Martha, the others never settled in like these three have and now suddenly Miss Madison wants to have a party?"

"There have never been outsiders in this house you know that, only descendents of the Bienvenue family. Who knows what could happen."

"That's what I'm afraid of, Miss Beatrice."

"Just trust me, Martha. Have I not always protected you? You do understand that if you leave Willow House, I cannot guarantee that you will be safe."

"But who would want to hurt me, Miss Beatrice?"

"Who do you think, Martha? No one leaves the employ of Tempest Bienvenue and lives to tell about it."

"But he's dead, Miss Beatrice."

"Is he really, Martha? Besides, if you do leave, who knows what might happen to Franklin."

"Well good evening, Beatrice, Martha."

Madison recognized this voice as that of her oldest brother Jack and realized he must have walked in on the conversation.

"Is there anything wrong Beatrice?"

"No, Sir, Martha received a call earlier from her aunt in Gulfport, Mississippi. Seems that she had a terrible fall and needed Martha to come and care for her for a few days until her daughter could make it down from Memphis."

"Oh, that's too bad, Martha, may I drive you there? I noticed when I was looking at a map of the Mississippi Coast that Gulfport was very close to Ocean Springs."

"That won't be necessary," said Beatrice. "You see, I just came downstairs to stop Martha from leaving. Her Aunt just called back and said that her daughter was flying in tonight so she would not need Martha after all."

"Oh, well then I'll help you bring your bag back up to your room. Martha."

"Oh, no sir, I can manage."

"Miss Martha, you know a true southern gentleman would never allow a lady to carry her own bag. Now give me that, and show me the way to your quarters."

That was pretty clever, thought Madison, *Jack will be able to tell me where Martha's room is and from what she heard tonight, Martha is the one that can help her find out what Franklin and Beatrice is hiding from them.*

"Hey Evan, are they gone?" whispered Madison as she eased out from under the staircase.

Evan seemed to jump at least three feet off the floor as he turned to see Madison tiptoeing toward him.

"What the hell is wrong with you, Maddie? You scared the living sh…"

"Now, now, Evie, don't forget your manners. You are a true southern gentleman, are you not? Just like Brother Jack."

"Well what do you expect when you jump out like that? You just caught me off guard."

"Listen, Evan, we need to talk." said Madison as she pointed toward the front door.

Evan could see, by the look on her face, that she was very serious, but before he could reply, Jack appeared at the top of the landing and as he descended, Evan and Madison both put their finger to their lips and motioned for him to follow them outside.

As they all reached the front porch, Jack wanted to know what was going on that had them acting so secretive.

"Jack, you and Evan will never believe what I overheard tonight"

"Oh, we can hardly wait, Nancy Drew," said Evan.

"Just knock it off, Evan, I'm afraid the three of us could really be in danger if we remain here."

She then began telling them what she overheard while she hid under the staircase, and both Jack and Evan had to admit there might be much more to Willow House than they thought.

"What do you think Beatrice meant when she said she would make sure that our gathering never took place Jack?"

"I don't know, but now that we know her intentions, we can beat her at her own game."

Chapter Fifteen

The next morning at breakfast, Jack told Beatrice that he would appreciate it if she would accompany him to the grocery store to buy supplies for the cookout.

"Oh that won't be necessary, sir, we have everything you could possibly need right here in Willow House."

"I'm sure you do have much of what I need, Beatrice, but there are certain spices that I use in my sauce that you couldn't possibly have; and besides, I need to stop at the local music store and pick up some CDs."

"Mr. Bloom, I really hate to spoil your party tonight, but I believe I am coming down with something and I'm afraid it may be contagious. Do you think you can postpone it for another time?"

"Well, certainly we can, Beatrice; in fact, I will take you to the doctor myself."

"Oh, no sir, that won't be necessary."

"Of course it is, Beatrice, especially if you are contagious."

"Well alright then sir, but first let me call my doctor and see what he says first."

After about fifteen minutes, Beatrice returned and said that she described her symptoms to her doctor and he said it was just side effects of a new medication she was taking for her allergies.

"I feel so silly, sir."

"Nonsense, Beatrice, it's perfectly understandable. This will be the perfect opportunity for you to take the evening off and rest and relax in your quarters."

If you recall, I gave the staff the evening off anyway."

"Yes sir, I do recall and I am so sorry that I cannot accompany you to the grocery."

"No problem, Beatrice. I'll just take Martha with me."

"I'm afraid that Martha is not here, sir. There was another call from her aunt and she had to go to her after all. Franklin drove her. In fact, I asked that he stay and rest today before heading back."

"I see, so you are the only one left at Willow House besides myself, Evan and Madison."

"I'm afraid so, sir."

"No problem, Beatrice. We will be outside most of the time so I'm sure we won't disturb you, but should you need anything, please let one of us know."

"Thank you, sir, and if it's okay with you, I will return to my quarters now."

"By all means Beatrice and I hope you feel better."

"I'm sure by tomorrow I will be feeling much better sir."

Jack couldn't help but notice a little sneer on Beatrice's face as she turned away from him, but he figured it was because her plan to spoil their cookout had failed, so he grabbed a pen and paper and headed for the front porch.

I'll just sit outside and make my grocery list, he thought. *Evan and Madison should be rolling out of bed soon, and I'll find out if there is anything special they want,* but the moment he walked through the front door, he saw Madison walking from the beach, back toward the house."

"Finally decided to roll out of bed big brother?"

Startled, Jack turned to see Evan sitting in the swing on the far end of the porch.

"Did you and Maddie even go to bed last night?"

"I haven't actually been up that long Jackie, though I can't say the same for Maddie. I think she is excited about the cookout tonight."

By this time, Madison was walking up the steps to the front

porch. Jack noticed a rosy glow in her cheeks, and this was a welcome sight.

Jack, Evan and Maddie were all very close to their parents, but Maddie seemed to be having a much harder time dealing with their death than he and Evan. Sometimes he felt that she didn't really believe they were actually dead. Maybe it was because they never found their bodies, but whatever the reason, he and Evan agreed to keep a close eye on her until she became better adjusted.

"Hey you two old fellas, I was wondering if you were ever going to get out of bed. We have lots to do before tonight."

"Got it all under control, sis, I'm making my grocery list, and if you and Evan want to come along, that would be great."

Chapter Sixteen

"I have had it with the two of you," said Beatrice, as she paced back and forth across the floor of the attic. "As far as I'm concerned, you can join the rest of the Bienvenue family."

Now, I'm going to take the tape off of your mouths, but don't even bother to yell for help because the three youngest Bienvenues have gone grocery shopping for their cookout tonight."

"I'm so sorry Miss Beatrice," said Martha "I was just so afraid that…"

"Don't apologize, Martha," said Franklin. "Beatrice has no compassion for anyone."

"Don't talk to me about compassion, Franklin, do you think Tempest Bienvenue had compassion for you? You were his illegitimate son after all and he had absolutely no compassion for you. True, he allowed you to live here because the head housekeeper was your mother, but he never acknowledged that you were his flesh and blood."

"My mother was terrified of him, you know that Beatrice, and I never knew he was my father until my mother told me on her deathbed."

"What are you going to do with us?" asked Martha.

"I haven't decided yet. You have already tried to leave Willow House, so I don't dare set you free."

"Look, Beatrice, we are no good to you in this attic, and our guests are going to get suspicious if we just disappear. They won't be here much longer and then everything will return to normal."

"Normal? You have lived in this house your entire life

Franklin, you grew up surrounded by insanity. You don't know what normal is."

"Perhaps you are right, Beatrice; however, I don't want to leave Willow House any more than you do, it's the only home I've ever known."

"So why did you threaten to tell those three intruders the truth?"

"I was just upset, Beatrice. They were getting far too comfortable here and you were nagging me to get rid of them. You know I would never tell them the truth and chance being thrown out of Willow House."

"Fine, then I will make a deal with the both of you. If I set you free and either one of you tries to leave this house or tell those intruders the truth about Willow House, I will make sure that all of you join the others."

"Oh please, Ms. Beatrice, I will do whatever you want. I will never try and leave again. Just don't send me to that place."

"What about you, Franklin?"

"I feel the same way, Beatrice. Let us go and we will do whatever you say."

"Fine, just remember what will happen to both you and your relatives if you try anything."

Now, those idiots will be back soon so we don't have much time."

"What are you planning to do?"

"I'm not quite ready to share that with the two of you Franklin. I told them that you drove Martha to Gulfport to stay with her aunt that was sick, so when they return, I will tell them that the daughter was able to come in after all and that the two of you returned and were resting in your quarters."

"How do you know they didn't check the garage and see that the cars were still there?" asked Franklin.

"Because I watched them this morning, and they didn't go near the garage. All you two need to worry about is keeping your mouths shut, and doing what I say, understood?"

Chapter Seventeen

"I just love this town," said Madison, as she and her brothers began unloading groceries. "Everyone is so friendly and accommodating."

"That's because they don't know that we are staying in the house of the living dead," said Evan, "or that we are the descendents of the terrible Tempest Bienvenue."

"Not listening Evan, I am really very excited about this place. Willow House has so much potential, and just look at the grounds. This is the most beautiful piece of property in Ocean Springs."

"God, now you're even talking like a native of Ocean Springs," said Evan. "Oh, this is the most beautiful property in the Ocean Springs."

"You won't believe this," said Jack. "We never checked to see if there was a grill here."

"Maddie, would you mind asking Beatrice if there is any kind of an outdoor cooker here? Evan and I can handle the groceries."

As Maddie ran up the front steps to the porch, Jack asked Evan to back off Maddie a little bit.

"Evan, you know that we have been trying to get her to loosen up a little and have some fun. She has been so withdrawn since…"

"I know, and you are right. She is pretty excited about the cookout tonight, and I'm sure it has nothing to do with a certain fella named Andy."

"You see, that's exactly what I mean, Evan. You are teasing her entirely too much about Andy. I know that the two of you have always tried to one-up each other, but this is the happiest I have seen her since the accident so if you could just ease up a little."

"I admit that I have probably teased her a little too much about Andy, but you know it's hard to break old habits. I have always teased her about her boyfriends, and she has always browbeat me about my choices in girlfriends, it's just who we are Jack. You have always been the mature one, and now you are asking me to be the mature one. I'm getting a headache just thinking about it."

"You are hopeless, Evan, but I know you have Maddie's best interest at heart so I will say no more."

"Hello, Beatrice, hello, is anybody home?"

"Yes, Miss Madison?" said Martha.

"Martha, I thought you were in Gulfport with your aunt."

"I was, Miss Madison, but her daughter arrived early this morning so Franklin and I thought it best we return as soon as possible in case you might need us."

"I think we have everything under control Martha; however, there is something I need to ask you."

"What is it, Miss Madison?"

"Do you know if there is an outdoor cooker here? You know, like a barbecue grill?"

"No, Miss Madison, there have never been any meals prepared on the grounds of Willow House, so I can assure you there is not an outdoor cooker here."

Just then, Jack and Evan walked in carrying the supplies for the cookout.

"Jack, I'm afraid you are going to have to go buy a grill. Martha said they don't prepare any meals outdoors."

"Why didn't I know that," thought Jack.

"Martha, what are you…." said Evan

"Franklin and Martha were not needed in Gulfport so they came home," said Madison.

"Look, Jack," said Evan, "no sense in both of us going back

out. You go ahead and get started on your so called secret marinade, I'm sure there's a Wal-Mart somewhere nearby."

"I'll get started on the potato salad and baked beans," said Madison.

"Are you sure there isn't something I can do to help?" asked Martha.

"Hey, I know what you can do Martha, you can go with Evan and show him the way to Wal-Mart so he won't get lost."

"Oh, no, Miss Madison, I cannot leave the house, I'm sorry, I need to go see if Beatrice needs me now."

"What was that all about?" asked Madison after she was sure that Martha was out of ear shot.

Jack just put his finger to his lips so that Madison wouldn't say another word, and nodding her head, Madison pointed toward the front porch.

After the three stepped outside, Jack said that Martha acted as if she were terrified of something.

"Or someone," said Evan. "Probably old eagle eye Beatrice. She never seems to miss a thing, and both Franklin and Martha seem very afraid of her."

"I don't understand though," said Madison. "She just returned from Gulfport, and yet she says she cannot leave the house."

"Maybe she meant that Beatrice won't let her go back out," said Jack.

"I never thought I would say this," said Evan, "but I can't wait to go to Wal-Mart."

Jack and Madison started laughing as Evan turned and headed down the stairs.

"Jack, there is something very wrong here."

"I agree with you Maddie, but there is nothing we can do about it until tomorrow. Maybe you can talk to Andy about helping us investigate what is going on here. He is a detective after all, and remember, he said that he has always been fascinated with Willow House."

"You're right, Jack. Maybe he can help with the treasure hunt also."

"Just make sure you don't discuss any of this inside the house. I just don't have a good feeling about the staff, especially Beatrice."

Chapter Eighteen

Later that afternoon, Franklin appeared in the kitchen and asked Jack if he could do anything to help him.

"As a matter of fact, Franklin, there is something you can do for me, you can show me where all the kitchen tools are."

He thought this might be a good time to speak with Franklin alone, and if he could get him to relax a little, well who knows what he might say so he opened the kitchen door that led to a back porch and motioned for Franklin to follow him outside. He pulled two cigars from his shirt pocket and offered one to Franklin. Franklin shook his head to decline the offer, but Jack lit up anyway because he needed an excuse to talk to him outside the house.

"Franklin, I did give you the night off, so I would really like it if you would join me for a cocktail while my ribs are marinating,"

"But I thought you wanted me to show you around the kitchen, sir."

"That can wait, Franklin, right now I am ready for an afternoon break. Now, what's your poison?"

"I beg your pardon, sir?"

"Your favorite cocktail, Franklin, I was just asking what type of alcohol you prefer."

Jack noticed Franklin seemed a little nervous and that could very well work to his benefit if he handled it right.

"You look like a scotch drinker to me, Franklin."

"No sir, in fact I rarely drink at all anymore. Oh not that I'm an alcoholic or anything, I just don't find many occasions to celebrate anymore."

"Franklin, you don't have to have an occasion to celebrate in order to enjoy an afternoon cocktail."

"To be honest, sir, Beatrice doesn't imbibe at all and prefers that I abstain as well."

"I'll make a deal with you, Franklin. You go and tell Beatrice that you will be working tonight after all, which is true because I do need you to assist me with a few things, and when you return, we will both have a nice relaxing cocktail before we get started. Scotch and soda sound okay to you?"

"Actually I prefer it neat, sir."

And as Franklin left the room, Jack couldn't help but chuckle to himself and wonder what kind of hold Beatrice had over the old boy."

As jack was leaving the kitchen, he almost collided with Madison.

"Slow down, Maddie, I have everything under control. In fact I am about to take a break and have a cocktail, can I get you something?"

"Oh, no thanks, I was actually looking for Martha because I decided that she could probably be a help to me after all, but then I ran into Franklin and he said he would see that she got my message."

"Jack, if I didn't know better, it looked like he was almost smiling; I mean he wasn't really smiling, but he wasn't frowning either like he usually does."

Jack motioned for her to step outside and he told her what he had planned for Franklin to loosen him up a bit.

"It probably wouldn't hurt to loosen Martha up a little also and see what you can get out of her."

"I don't think so, Bro." I don't think I need to plow her with alcohol to get information, I'll just stick to my usual style."

"And what would that be?" said Evan as he walked up the steps to the front porch "Do you plan to badger her or bore her to death?"

"I plan on locking her in a room with you for an hour. I figure that will be more than sufficient time to break her."

"Save it for later, you two, I need to fill Evan in on my plan."

"Good, talk while you are helping me unload the grill."

"Maddie, do me a favor and go inside and wait for Franklin to come down," said Jack. "Ask him to join me on the front porch, I 'm going to ask him to help me set up a bar in the gazebo."

"Good idea Jack, keep him near the liquor and away from Beatrice."

"Now who's sounding like Evan?"

"I must have missed something," said Evan.

"Never mind, let's go unload that grill."

Chapter Nineteen

"Before the two of you go back downstairs to baby sit those worthless Bienvenues, know that I can hear everything that goes on inside Willow House, and if you happen to be outside at anytime, I expect you to pay close attention to the conversations so that you can fill me in later. I need to know just when they are planning to start there treasure hunt, and also how much longer they intend to stay."

Franklin and Martha both agreed to report back to Beatrice later that evening but truth be known they probably both wished that Willow House would swallow her up like it did the others.

As Madison watched Franklin and Martha descend the stairs, she noticed how terribly sad they both looked. *I guess if I had to deal with Beatrice, I would be sad as well,"* She thought.

"Hi Martha, I'm so glad you are able to help me out this evening. I thought I could handle it alone, but for some reason I'm feeling a little apprehensive."

"Oh, Franklin, Jack asked me to have you meet him on the front porch, if you don't mind. Martha and I will be in the kitchen if anyone needs us."

"Just in time," said Jack as Franklin walked outside. "Evan is setting up the grill, and I was wondering if you could help me set up a bar down at the gazebo. In fact, that is a great place for the two of us to have our cocktail and have a little chat. It's near the water, very relaxing, and it will give us a chance to get to know each other a little better."

Madison noticed that Martha was very quiet as she helped her prepare the appetizers. She knew better than to say anything that Beatrice might overhear so she suggested that the two of them bring a tray of the appetizers out to the boys to sample. Once they were outside, she asked Martha point blank what she was so afraid of.

"My brother's say that I am a little too nosy, but they're men, after all so what do they know? I'm really just concerned Martha because you really are a nice lady."

"Miss Madison, I'm just concerned about my aunt in Gulfport. I guess I'm just preoccupied with that."

"Martha, were you here when my mother was a little girl? You look about the same age as my mother."

"Miss Madison, you are very sweet to say that but I am a bit older than your mother. I was raised in Willow House because my parents were members of the staff, but unfortunately they are deceased. I did know your mother and though it would have been frowned upon by your Grandfather, your mother and I became friends. We had to keep it a secret, of course. She always said that I was the older sister she never had and I did love her as if she were my little sister. At times she was the only sanity in Willow House, and when she left, everything became very dark, as far as I was concerned.

"Martha, please tell me more about my mother when she was a young girl. I can tell that you feel comfortable with me and that you trust me, at least a little. I'm going to go out on a limb here myself Martha and tell you that I feel that Beatrice is not such a nice person. I believe that there is a system in the house that allows her to hear everything that we say and that is the reason that I asked you to come with me to bring appetizers to the guys. I promise you that I will protect you no matter what."

"Miss Madison, I have no idea what you are talking about. What I do know is that you are the spitting image of your mother, and I know that she is very, very proud of you."

"What do you mean, Martha? How can she be proud of me when she is dead?"

"I'm sorry, Miss Madison, It's just that I don't really believe in death. I believe that souls leave their bodies but never cease to exist. I believe that your mother still has a connection to you and that no matter what you do with your life, she will always love you and always be proud of you."

"I'm the one who should apologize; it's just that I cannot accept that she has died. I feel her presence every day and my brothers don't seem to get it."

"Oh, I think they understand, Miss Madison. You know that the male species likes to think that they can control their emotions better than the female species. Deep down I'm sure they are grieving as deeply as you, they just don't show it."

"You know something Martha; that is something my mother would have said to me. Thank you for that. For some strange reason I actually feel like my mother is very near to me."

Martha smiled at Madison, but when she turned and saw Beatrice walking close behind her, the smile turned into a look of fear that was so noticeable that both Jack and Evan caught it immediately.

"Wow, those appetizers look amazing," said Jack. "Are we special or just guinea pigs?"

"They do look great," said Evan. "I guess Beatrice must have smelled them all the way from her room, cause she seems to be on a mission."

Hearing what Evan said, Madison turned to see Beatrice moving closer and closer and as she turned back around, she caught a glimpse of the expression on Martha's face and was convinced that Beatrice was truly an evil force residing in Willow House.

Chapter Twenty

"Well, Beatrice," said Jack "you certainly look spry for someone so ill."

"Oh I feel much better, sir. In fact I am going to relieve Martha of her duties tonight."

"I don't think so," said Madison with such authority that you would have already thought her to be the Lady of Willow House, "I am really not comfortable with you being around my guests, Beatrice. I know that you want to help, and I do appreciate it; however, I would feel better if you would just retire to your quarters and get some more rest. I really don't want to take any chances on my guests being infected. Martha and Franklin are handling things quite well."

"But Miss Madison, the doctor said that I was not contagious."

"Never the less we cannot take any chances can we?"

Beatrice had no choice but to retreat back to her room, but Martha and Franklin knew that she must be fuming over not being in control.

Madison leaned over and whispered something to Evan and then announced that she was going in to freshen up for the party.

"Okay what are you and Madison up to now?" asked Jack, as he watched his sister running toward the house.

"Hey, I'm not up to anything," said Evan. "Madison just asked me not to let Franklin or Martha out of my sight until she returned, and after what she said to Beatrice, I'm a little afraid not to do what she asks."

"She was pretty forceful wasn't she? You know I can't believe

I'm saying this but I agree with her, I think we should keep Franklin and Martha nearby for the rest of the evening, I saw the look on Martha's face when she realized that Beatrice was behind her and I have to tell you, it was a look of pure terror."

"See, I knew that Franklin and Martha were afraid of that troll, I say we burn her at the stake."

"Get serious, Evan. Beatrice is hiding something and I think we need to find out what it is, if only for Franklin and Martha. I have to say that I really didn't believe the buried treasure thing, but she is terribly anxious for us to leave Willow House which causes me to think that maybe the Blooms should just stick around awhile and solve the mystery that seems to have cursed the Bienvenue family."

Beatrice stood peering out her window, down at the descendents of Tempest Bienvenue and the look on her face was nothing less than pure evil.

Who does that little witch think she is, she thought, *why couldn't she be more like her mother. That one couldn't wait to get as far away from* Willow House *as possible.*

Well I can promise you this much, little missy, if you and your brothers are not out of here by the end of the week, I will have no choice but to see to it that you join your ancestors.

Madison returned to the gazebo just in time to greet her first guests.

"Andy, Andre, welcome to Willow House."

"Thank you for inviting us Madison" said Andre "This is my wife Danielle. Danielle, this is Madison Bloom and her brothers, Jack and Evan."

"It's so nice meeting you all," said Danielle. "I guess Andy told you that Willow House has always intrigued me and now after all these years, to finally have an opportunity to see the inside is so exciting to me."

"I guess you can tell that Danielle is expecting the grand tour," said Andre.

"And the grand tour, she shall have," said Madison, but first let's get you all something cold to drink, and by the way, it is wonderful meeting you Danielle."

"I'll just go inside and get some fresh hordeurves," said Martha.

"No, wait, Martha, Evan would you mind helping Martha?"

"Oh that is not necessary, Miss Madison, I can handle it by myself."

"But I insist on helping you, Martha," said Evan, "I'm in training, you know."

"Training for what, Sir?"

"For marriage, Martha, what else?"

"Oh, Mr. Evan, I thought you were serious."

"Your brother is quite charming, Madison," said Danielle as she watched him and Martha walking toward the house.

"Oh please don't tell him that, Danielle," said Jack. "He is hard enough to live with as it is."

Madison was thinking about how absolutely perfect this evening had started out when Andy walked up behind her, tapped her on the shoulder and asked her if she would like to dance.

Madison turned around and looked up into the most beautiful brown eyes she had ever seen in her life.

"Remind me to thank Evan later for bringing a CD player with him," said Madison "although I can't imagine what made him even think of it."

"Is that a yes?"

"That is definitely a yes, Andy, I would love to dance with you."

"As Jack watched his sister and Andy dancing beneath the stars, he couldn't help but wonder what their mother would think if she knew they were at Willow House, the house that she was so anxious to flee from, the house and family that she chose never to talk about, never to return to, that is until a year ago.

Chapter Twenty One

"Joe, Angie, I'm so glad you could make it," said Jack.

"Are you kidding?" said Joe "She is as bad as Danielle about Willow House. I think she would have made me close the restaurant rather than miss an invitation to get a peek of the inside of this place, and please tell me she is going to get to go inside, even if it's to use the restroom."

"Of course you will be allowed inside Willow House, in fact, Madison was waiting for you to arrive so she could give you and Danielle the grand tour."

"Somehow I believe Madison has other things on her mind besides taking Danielle on a tour of Willow House."

"Nonsense," said Evan as he and Martha arrived with fresh hors d'oeuvres; however if Madison doesn't take you ladies on the grand tour, then I will be honored to take her place, by the way, it's good to see you both, Joe, Angie."

"Thank you, Evan," said Joe as they shook hands, "we appreciate the invite."

"Jack, your brother is quite the charmer," said Angie.

"I don't believe I have ever heard the words, Evan and charmer, used in the same sentence," said Madison as she greeted Joe and Angie. "I am so happy you came tonight, in fact, why don't you and I and Danielle grab a glass of wine and get this tour started."

"You mean over with, don't you, Madison?" asked Joe.

"Of course not, Joe, you know it's not as if I have ever given a tour of Willow House before. To be honest, I'm not sure I have seen every little nook and cranny in the house myself."

"It just amazes me that you have never been to Willow House

before," said Angie as she, Madison and Danielle headed toward the house.

"Not me," said Danielle. "Until last year, I don't believe Camille ever came back to visit. I'm sorry, Madison. I didn't mean to be rude, it's just that …."

"I know, Danielle. Willow House is such a mystery to me and my brothers. Growing up, my mother never really shared much about her childhood with us, she would just say that she grew up in a small town in Mississippi and that she had no relatives left in the area. We had no idea that she grew up in a place like this until we received a letter from our great aunt telling us that we inherited Willow House."

"Actually there is much more to it, but I really don't want to bore you two with the details."

"Bore us, please," said Danielle. "Willow House has always been fascinating to me when I was growing up."

"Okay, after our parents died in the car wreck last April…"

"April?" said Angie "I'm sorry, I don't mean to interrupt, but you must mean May. Your mother and father were in the restaurant last May."

"Are you sure, Angie?"

"I'm positive, Madison, it was May 5th, Cinco De Mayo, which is also my birthday. Joe wanted to do something special for my birthday, but we were short of help and I knew we would be pretty busy that night even though we are not a Mexican restaurant, it's still a holiday celebration and everyone seems to be busy that night."

"Your mother and father came in earlier that afternoon and said they were heading back home and wanted to try some of Joe's Gumbo before they left. Camille said that she heard that Joe had become a pretty good Cajun cook over the years."

By this time, Madison, Danielle and Angie were on the front porch of Willow House and Madison asked Angie if she minded waiting a bit before they went inside the house.

"I'm not exactly sure how to say this, though; I really feel that

I can trust the two of you so I'm just going to say it. My brothers and I believe the house is bugged so I don't want to talk about any of this inside, and although this sounds so ridiculous, we believe that our mother was very terrified of something concerning this house. Why else would she not tell us about the house she grew up in and why would she never bring us here for a visit?"

"Madison, sweetheart," said Danielle, "there is definitely a mystery here and Andy is the perfect person to help you solve it."

"You know, my mother would love the two of you so much because you are so much like her. It's just too bad she never had the opportunity to develop any friendships while she was growing up."

"That does it," said Angie, "Danielle and I are going to help you find out what happened to your mother when she lived in his house. Neither one of us has a daughter, but if we did, I think I speak for Angie, we would want her to be just like you."

For the first time in many months, Madison felt a warmth like she had not felt since before her mother's death.

"Angie is right, " said Danielle, "I didn't know your mother very well because she would not allow anyone to get close to her, but I always felt that she had something that haunted her. "

"Face it, I was very jealous of her because Andre was so enamored of her and being a typical teenager, I reacted with jealousy."

"Well, from the way Andre looks at you, I would say that what he had for my mother was a crush on someone that seemed very mysterious and what he has for you is true love."

"Well, if you are anything like your mother was, I can see why he had a crush on her."

Chapter Twenty Two

"I only wish I could have made the tour of Willow House more exciting" said Madison, "I just don't know that much about the place"

"Very understandable." said Andy, as he walked up to greet the ladies as they returned from their tour of Willow House.

So was Willow House all that you imagined it to be?" he asked.

"It was indeed," said Angie and Danielle agreed.

"In fact it was more than we imagined," said Danielle. "Madison will fill you in later."

Andy told Madison that it sounded like her tour was much more impressive than she thought, but Madison just waved her hand in the air and said that it wasn't the tour that impressed them so much, it was the fact that she believes that Willow House may have some secrets and that the caretakers may be the only ones that know what they are.

"Andy, my mother obviously wanted nothing to do with Willow House and went to great lengths to make sure that we never came near this place."

"I mean, think about it, she left right after high school and never returned until last year. Why did she come back?"

"I don't know, maybe she wanted to make peace with her ghosts."

"I believe that she wanted to make sure that we never inherited her ghosts to tell you the truth."

"You see, our great aunt in South Carolina was the last to inherit Willow House, and if she passed, it would go to my mother. I believe she came back here to make sure that didn't happen. I don't know what took place when she was here, and I don't believe her death was accidental."

"You are serious, aren't you Madison?"

But before she had a chance to answer, Jack announced that his world famous barbecue was ready.

Madison told Andy that she would fill him in later on this evening.

"You know your Mother volunteered your services to me, in fact, she said you would be perfect for the job."

"She said that? Well then how can I refuse?"

"But not sure I can afford your services, Mr. Bergeron."

"Oh I don't think that will be a problem, Miss Bloom" and as Madison looked up and saw that smile, she felt as if she had finally come home.

After filling up on what Andy called the *best barbecue ribs he had ever eaten*, he and Madison decided to take a walk along the beachfront for what they called digestion purposes; however, everyone knew that those two had really hit it off and just wanted to get away from the watchful eyes of mothers, fathers and brothers.

The two walked without saying a word until they reached the shoreline, then Madison broke the silence.

She told Andy about everything that had transpired in the last few weeks and how she and her brothers believe that there is no treasure, just a story that Beatrice may have concocted in order to remain in Willow House.

"But what about your great aunt's will?

"Well maybe Beatrice tricked her too."

"One way to find out, I'll check the authenticity of the will."

"I guess that means you're on the case huh?"

"Yeah, as long as you don't call me Sherlock."

"Clouseau, maybe, but never Sherlock."

Madison couldn't believe how comfortable she felt with Andy.

There was no tension between the two of them like there was on a first date in fact it felt as if she had known him a lifetime.

The rest of the evening seemed to just fly by for Madison and as she and Andy headed back toward the party, they were both surprised to find that everyone had gone home. Madison noticed that Jack and Evan were helping Franklin and Martha with the cleanup so she asked them why everyone left so early.

"Sweetheart, it's not all that early" said Evan, "unless you consider midnight to be early."

"Midnight, I had no idea. I guess the time just got away from us."

"Indeed little sis, time does fly when you're having fun."

Andy seemed a little embarrassed and offered to help with the clean-up but Jack assured him that they had it all under control.

"Then I guess I should get going myself. I have a new job that I'm starting in the morning and I certainly don't want to be late."

"Jack, Evan, Madison, thank you so much for inviting me. I had a great time."

Both Jack and Evan thanked Andy for coming and Madison offered to walk him to his car.

The two walked in silence and as they reached Andy's car, he turned to Madison and said that he could not remember when he had had such a wonderful evening.

"Madison, I know we just met, but I feel such a connection to you. It's as if I have known you forever. I do hope you plan on staying awhile so that I can get to know you better."

"Well you know I have a treasure to find and if I leave without finding it, I forfeit all rights to Willow House and I am not about to do that, besides, we have a mystery to solve, don't we?"

"We do indeed and I can't remember a case I have ever been as eager to start on as I am this one."

"Then I will see you tomorrow morning?"

"Yes, but why don't you meet me the *View* for breakfast.

Bring Jack and Evan too so that we can put a game plan together without the staff at Willow House becoming suspicious."

"How's nine sound?"

"Perfect" said Andy as he leaned in and kissed Madison gently on the cheek. "See you at nine.

Chapter Twenty Three

The next morning Jack told Martha they would be having breakfast in town. He said they wanted to see a little more of the town before they went back to Louisiana. He felt it best to act as if they didn't believe the nonsense about a treasure on the grounds.

"You know, Martha, I think old man Bienvenue made this treasure thing up so that no one in the family ever got their hands on Willow House, because he was afraid if a family member actually inherited it, they might just sell it and I don't think he could stand the thought that."

"I suppose you could be right sir, it does make sense under the circumstances."

"What circumstances?"

"Martha," yelled Beatrice, in a voice so shrill that Jack thought he actually saw the chandelier in the dining room shake.

"I'm sorry sir I really must go see what Miss Beatrice needs."

"Well she certainly doesn't sound like someone that feels as well as she said she did yesterday. Please tell her that if she feels the need to scream out like that again, I will come to her myself and see what is so dammed important."

"Yes sir, thank you sir, I mean I will see you later today sir."

Jack couldn't help but smile and wink at Martha as he turned and walked away. He had an idea that Beatrice overheard his conversation with Martha and was afraid that she may slip up and reveal something she shouldn't. Well if she was listening in, he made sure that she heard him imply that he didn't appreciate her yelling out the way she did.

"You know Evan" said Jack as the two waited on the front

porch for Madison "I don't know if there really is a treasure to be found here, but I do know that Beatrice wants us out of here as soon as possible and that makes me feel that there is something going on that she doesn't want us to know about."

"I do think that we can stay one step ahead of her, though, if we act as if we don't intend to waste our time looking for a phantom treasure and that we just want to enjoy a much needed vacation."

"I agree," said Madison as she walked in on the conversation. "Something is very off here. I don't know about the two of you but I want to know why our mother hated it here so much and I want to know why she came back here after so many years."

"Hey, I just want to get the deed to the place so I can remodel it," said Evan. "It looks like *Tara* in "Gone with the Wind." I halfway expect to see Scarlett come down the stairs wearing the living room drapes."

"Hey, for once I do agree with you," said Madison, "that place could use an overhaul."

Beatrice stared out the window at the Blooms as they got into the old 1936 Rolls Royce Phantom and she cringed because she felt that they had no rights to any property involving Willow House. Her only consolation was that they didn't seem to believe that there was a treasure and that it was only a matter of time before they would grow tired of Willow House and leave and of course if they left without finding the treasure, they could never return.

I'll just bide my time a little longer she thought, *after all, I have too much to lose and I'll be damned if I let those blooming idiot Blooms take what I've worked so long and hard for.*

As Jack, Evan and Madison entered the *View*, Joe and Angie's restaurant, they all looked at each other and smiled as if to say *this really smells like home.*

Julie, the waitress that served them before, approached them, said good morning and let them know that Mr. Bergeron was waiting for them on the deck.

"Thank you, Julie" said Evan "I do hope you will be our server."

"I will, in fact when Mr. Bergeron said that you would be joining him, I asked if I could be your server."

Really, did my brother tip you that well or was it because I impressed you so much?"

"No sir, it was neither, although that really didn't sound right either. What I meant was that I am going to live with my cousin in Shreveport soon and I heard Joe and Angie say that you were from Shreveport so I thought you might fill me in on what there is to do for fun there."

Madison chimed in and said that she would be glad to give her some info on what to do in Shreveport since she was much closer to her age than Jack or Evan.

"When is your break, Julie?"

"Actually it's after the breakfast shift, about ten thirty."

"That's perfect, we can meet on the beach in front of the restaurant."

"That is so kind of you, Miss…"

"Just call me Madison, please."

"Alright Madison Anyway, it really is so nice of you to take the time to speak with me, not many people would do that. I only have about half hour break so I won't take too much of your time."

"No problem, Julie, I don't mind at all."

Chapter Twenty Four

During breakfast, Jack, Evan. Madison and Andy discussed how they would have to conduct an investigation, yet keep Beatrice from finding out.

"I'm pretty sure that Beatrice doesn't know that I am a private investigator so let's just tell her that I'm an off-shore worker, should she ask, and that would account for my hanging around so much. We'll say I work a month and that I'm off for a month."

"But how are we going to keep her from knowing that we are snooping around the property?" asked Madison.

"Well the first thing the three of you have to do is take turns keeping Franklin, Martha and Beatrice occupied while the rest of us do the actual snooping."

"I think we should include Franklin and Martha in on our plan," said Jack. "They are so terrified of her that I don't believe they will dare tell her anything for fear she will assume they are involved."

Madison asked Jack if he thought that was a good idea, considering the fact that they already know more than they are letting on.

"I do think it's a good idea, Maddie. I won't actually tell them that we are conducting an investigation, I'll just tell them that we just want to go on our treasure hunt without Beatrice following us around then they may be willing to help keep her distracted."

"Especially if there really is no treasure," said Evan, "face it, none of them seem too concerned that anyone will find a hidden treasure anyway so they will probably count on us getting bored and leaving Willow House once and for all."

"They don't know me, do they, Jack, I don't give up that easily?"

"Nope, Maddie, you're like a dog with a bone" said Evan.

"When did you change your name to Jack?" asked Maddie.

"Enough you two," said Jack. "I'm sure Andy is not amused."

"Actually I am amused, Jack. You see I'm an only child so…"

"I'm sorry to interrupt your conversation," said Julie, "but I'm about to go on my break now, so if you are done with breakfast, I will clear the table and get you all some more coffee, if you like."

Andy told Julie they were done with breakfast and that fresh coffee sounded wonderful.

Madison said she would meet her downstairs on the beach in front of the restaurant.

"I know the last thing you want to do is walk, Julie, so why don't we sit down on this log and talk. It's such a beautiful day and the water is so relaxing."

"That sounds perfect, I'm working the lunch and dinner shift today so I guess I should sit while I can. I do appreciate whatever you can tell me about Shreveport Ms…I mean Madison."

"Now, what would you like to know about Shreveport? I've been there my entire life; in fact, when we go home I'll be glad to take you on a grand tour.

Just give me your cousin's name, address and phone number and I will give you a call when we get back."

"I don't have her address with me, but I can call you on your cell tomorrow if that's okay."

"That's perfect, I'll write my number down before we go and leave it for you.

Now, I know your break isn't very long but trust me it won't take that long for me to fill you in on all the fun stuff to do for someone your age. You see, I'm not that many years older than you and when I was your age, my middle name was party."

"Really? You just don't seem to be the type."

"Well I wasn't into drugs and alcohol if that's what you thought I meant, I just had lots of friends and I stayed on the go."

"Oh, no, Madison, I didn't mean that I thought you were wild or anything, it's just that I never was very popular in school, you see my father passed away when I was very young and my mother had to work pretty long hours so I wasn't allowed to go anywhere after school and I wasn't allowed to have company over when she wasn't at home so…"

"I'm sorry Julie, I didn't know."

"Well how could you know, besides, I really am quite happy, Madison. I might not have had much of a childhood, but no one abused me, and I never had to go hungry and cold like many other children in this world."

"You know they say "that which does not kill us makes us stronger.""

"You are quite a young lady, Julie and I'm looking forward to spending more time together, if that's okay with you?"

Julie smiled and said she looked forward to it.

After Madison filled her in on what she considered the best places to go in Shreveport, she told Julie they could get together again sometime soon if she would like to continue Shreveport 101.

"I would love that, Madison, and thank you again for your time, but I guess I'd better get back to work now, don't forget to leave you number."

Chapter Twenty Five

"Now then, you two, I need a word with you before those pests return. I want to know what they are up to and don't tell me you don't know. It's awfully strange to me that they never have any private conversations inside this house. It's almost as if they know that someone is listening."

"I suppose that's possible Beatrice," said Franklin, "however, Martha and I would have nothing to gain by alerting them to that possibility."

"No you do not have anything to gain, but you do have much to lose if you cross me, so keep your eyes and ears open and find out just how much longer these trespassers intend on staying here."

Franklin didn't really care anymore about what Beatrice would do to him, but he knew that he could not allow Martha to live the rest of her life in fear of this demonic old shrew.

He was ashamed that he had allowed this to go on as long as it had. In the beginning he believed that one of Bienvenue descendents would inherit Willow House and the curse would end and everyone would be free, but as the years passed, he lost hope that he would ever see his loved ones again, but there was still time for Martha.

I know what I must do now, thought Franklin, as he motioned to Martha to meet him on the front porch.

As Madison, Jack, Evan and Andy were leaving the restaurant, Madison reminded Jack that he told Martha that he didn't believe there was a treasure.

"I know, Maddie, I thought about that too."

"Not to worry big brother, I have come up with the perfect

solution. Halloween is coming up so I'll tell Beatrice that we want to have a Halloween party and that though we don't believe there is a hidden treasure, we decided to hide our own booty all over the property and on all Hallow's Eve, we will have the last Bienvenue treasure hunt.

That should keep her out of our hair for awhile and by the time any of us have children old enough to inherit Willow House, Beatrice will be dead."

"One can only hope," said Evan. "But hey, I like it. It sounds devious, like something I would come up with."

"I learned at the foot of the master."

"Yes you did and I am so proud of my little sis."

"See what I mean, Jack," said Andy as the walked across the parking lot to their cars, "I missed out on all this by being an only child."

Jack laughed and said that having siblings did have its moments.

"Oh, by the way, Madison, I was wondering if you were available for dinner tonight. This new little supper club just opened and Mom and Dad gave it rave reviews. Sorry Jack, Evan, I would invite you but it's the kind of place you take a date, not a date and her brothers."

"Oh I am crushed," said Evan. "In fact, I'm not sure I can allow you to take my little sister out on a date."

"Allow? Did you say allow? Why, I would love to have dinner with you tonight, Andy, and thank you for not inviting Lenny and Squiggy."

Andy laughed and said he would pick her up at seven if that was okay with her.

"Why don't you come around six for cocktails," said Jack. "I'm going to speak with Franklin this afternoon about our treasure hunt and hopefully I'll have something to report to you tonight."

"Six it is then, Lenny, or is it Squiggy? By the way, I love the wheels, got anymore like it back at the homestead?"

"Good save," said Evan, "you must have known that Jack was a car freak. Come early and we'll bring all the show cars out of the garage. Jack will love showing them, I'll just enjoy seeing Beatrice squirm. I could almost feel her glaring at us out of her bedroom window as we drove off in the family Rolls. You know I really believe she thinks that she is part of the family and that we are the outsiders."

Andy said he hoped to find out very soon just what Beatrice was up to. He really liked this Bloom family, and he wanted to make sure they inherited Willow House, besides, if Willow House became their property, there was a chance he would see much more of Madison.

Chapter Twenty Six

Jack decided to drive around town for awhile since they said they were going to have breakfast out and do a little scenic tour.

This really is a beautiful little town, he thought, *I could like it here myself.*

Madison made a comment about how much she loved this little town and Evan even said that he wouldn't mind coming back for a visit.

"There's just something about this place," he said, "I can't quite put my finger on it but it almost feels like home."

Jack said he got the same feeling. "It almost feels like we are supposed to be here."

Madison said she couldn't believe the two of them felt that way. She said she was afraid to tell them just how much she really loved it here because she was afraid they would tease her and say it was because of Andy.

"Well, sis," said Evan, "a few days ago I probably would have done just that, but I seriously feel a connection to this town and you might laugh, but I feel very close to Mom here."

Jack looked at Madison and saw big tears running down her face. "You feel close to Mom here too, don't you, Maddie? Guess that makes three because so do I."

After riding around town for awhile Jack decided that it was time to return to Willow House and after this afternoon he was more determined than ever to find out exactly what Beatrice was up to. After all, this was the Bienvenue family's home and he intended to find out number one, why his mother ran away from it, two, why she came back and three, what really happened to his parents after they left Willow House.

"Franklin, we're home," yelled Jack as they entered the foyer.

"Yes sir, right here, sir. I didn't expect you back so soon."

Jack made some excuse about not sleeping very well the night before and that he thought he might take a little nap.

"What about dinner tonight sir?"

Madison spoke up and said that she would be dinning out tonight.

"Evan and I will be here, though, In fact, if you will wake me in about an hour, I would very much appreciate it."

"Certainly sir, by the way, does roast chicken sound okay for dinner?"

"Sounds wonderful, Franklin, see you in an hour."

Madison asked Franklin where Martha was. "I wanted to ask her about her recipe for the crab dip she served last night. Everyone raved about it."

Franklin said she was around somewhere and he hurried off to find her.

Knowing that Beatrice was listening, Jack made a comment about getting a little bored with Ocean Springs and Evan chimed in and said they all should be getting back home pretty soon.

"I agree," said Madison, "but I do not want to leave until after Halloween. I think it would be fun to have one last party here, especially on Halloween since it looks like a haunted house anyway. In fact, I have some ideas about hiding prizes as if they were the hidden treasure that doesn't really exist."

Evan asked who she thought she was going to invite since she hardly knew anyone in Ocean Springs.

"Well, there's Andy and his mother and father, Joe and Danielle, and of course Julie. Hey, I'm sure we can scare up a few more people before Halloween."

"Very funny," said Evan. "All I know is that the sooner we leave this old dungeon, the better."

Jack said that he would agree to the Halloween party if Madison agreed to leave the following day.

Of course Beatrice was indeed listening to every word the Blooms said and though she was a little disturbed that they were planning a party on Halloween, the fact that they would be leaving the day after the party made her feel a little more relieved.

I can make it for one more week she thought, *in fact, I will even offer to help with the party so they won't think I am too anxious to get rid of them.*

I'll bet old Tempest would roll over in his grave if he knew there was to be any kind of a party in Willow House, *much less a Halloween party.*

Then again, maybe he'll make an appearance, that is, if they let him out of hell.

Chapter Twenty Seven

Later that afternoon, Jack told Franklin about their plans for a Halloween party and that they planned on leaving the day after to return home. He said that he would like for Martha to help Madison decorate if that was okay and that he didn't want to be rude, but he would prefer it if Beatrice stayed in her room that night.

"I know that she wants us gone, but until we do leave, I will not tolerate her attitude anymore."

"It won't be necessary for me to stay in my room, Mr. Bloom" said Beatrice as she entered the room "I know I have been behaving very badly and I am terribly sorry. I guess I have been here so long that I started thinking of Willow House as mine and I know that it belongs to you for as long as you chose to stay, in fact I would like to make it up to you all by helping with the party if I may."

"Thank you, Beatrice, for your apology and for offering to help Madison with the party. I'm sure she will appreciate it and by the way, we have decided to leave the day after Halloween, so you won't have to put up with us much longer."

Beatrice said something about them being no trouble at all but Jack noticed that there was no look of surprise when he said they were leaving. He was more convinced than ever that she could hear from every room in the house, but at least she would drop her guard a little since she knew they would be leaving soon."

"Please come in, Mr. Bergeron," said Franklin as he opened

the front door, "Mr. Jack is waiting for you in the library and I will let Miss Madison know you are here."

"I'm glad you came a little early, Andy," whispered Jack, as he put his finger to his lips, as if to say, *don't forget that the walls have ears.*

"Hi Andy," said Evan as he walked into the library. "I guess Jack told you about the Halloween party."

"No, I didn't, Evan, in fact I was going to let Madison tell him."

"Hey, no problem, I'll pretend to know nothing about it. I wouldn't want to ruin her surprise."

"Good, now who's up for a cocktail?"

"I'll be happy to make them," said Franklin, as he entered the room. "I didn't mean to interrupt but I wanted to let you know that Miss Madison would be down soon."

Andy reminded Jack that he promised to show him the cars and asked Franklin to tell Maddie not to rush.

"I did not forget Andy, that is why I'm glad you came early, in fact I just made a pitcher of Martinis, Franklin, so you are off the hook."

Madison could see the men walking toward the garage from her bedroom window so she took this opportunity to snoop around by herself.

My brothers are just not nearly as curious as I am about this house she thought, *I'm glad to have a little time to explore on my own.*

"May I help you find something, Miss Bloom?"

Startled, Madison turned around to see Beatrice standing in the doorway of the library with a look on her face that Madison could only describe later to Andy as sinister.

"I don't think so, Beatrice. I was just waiting for Andy and my brothers to return from looking at the car collection so I thought I would kill some time looking through some of the old books in my grandfather's library."

Madison cringed at the thought of claiming Tempest

Bienvenue as her grandfather, but she thought it would be in her best interest to remind Beatrice that she was not just a guest in Willow House, but indeed a member of the Bienvenue family.

"By the way, where is Martha? I wanted to ask for her help with a Halloween party my brothers and I are having. You don't have a problem with that, do you?"

"Of course not, Miss Bloom, in fact I apologized to your brothers earlier this afternoon about my attitude and I was actually looking for you so that I could offer my apologies to you as well."

"I do hope you will forgive me and allow me to help with the party. I am just an old woman that has lived here so long that I guess I was afraid that you and your brothers might not allow me to stay should you find the treasure and claim Willow House for your own."

"I do realize that I was being paranoid and that you would never throw, Franklin and me out of the only place we have ever called home."

"Apology accepted, Beatrice and I would love for you to help with my party, but I would also like Martha's help so if you tell me where I can find her…"

"I'm right here, Miss Madison."

"Oh, hi Martha, I've been looking for you all afternoon but unfortunately I am about to go out for the evening so we'll talk in the morning, okay?

Beatrice will fill you in on what it's all about."

After Madison left the house, Beatrice went to the window and watched her walking toward the three men that were heading toward Willow House.

"The little twit wants to throw a Halloween party here and I swear if they were not leaving the day after, I would turn the three of them into ghosts permanently."

Chapter Twenty Eight

After the hostess seated Andy and Madison at their table in the new, supper club, Andy asked what she thought about the place.

"I think it's perfect. You rarely see supper clubs anymore, especially with piano bars."

"I'm glad you approve, Madison, because *La Petit Bistro* belongs to me."

"What did you say?"

"I said I'm glad you like…."

"No, after that."

"I said I own *La Petit Bistro* which is what I named the place because it's not very big and it looks like a French bistro, don't you agree?"

"Andy Bergeron, I can't believe you didn't tell me, in fact I can't believe your mother or Danielle didn't mention it."

"Oh I gave them all strict orders not to. I was planning on asking you out on a date and I wanted to get your honest opinion about the place. It's only been open for a few weeks and it still needs some finishing touches, but it seems to be catching on, in fact, I had to make reservations myself."

Madison said that she was very impressed with *La Petit Bistro*.

"In fact I love this place so much that I am going to bring my brothers here before we go back to Shreveport."

Before Jack could reply, a waiter approached and introduced himself.

"Good evening Sir, Madame, my name is Blaine and I will be your server tonight."

"Would you like to start with a cocktail?"

"You can relax, Blaine, I know that Mr. Bergeron owns this place, so you don't have to pretend not to know him."

"Excuse me, Miss, I don't understand. Who is Mr. Bergeron?"

"Andy, tell him it's okay to stop acting like he doesn't know you."

"I'm afraid I can't do that Madison because he doesn't know me. I've never seen him before either. My chef who is also my manager said that we needed more help so I suppose Blaine is our new addition."

"I'm so embarrassed," said Madison.

"I'm the one that should be embarrassed," said Blaine, "I didn't even know the owner."

"Well, I'm not embarrassed," said Andy, "however; I am pretty thirsty so if you would be so kind as to bring the lady and me a drink, we'll pretend this never happened."

Later that night as Andy was driving Madison home, he made a comment that he couldn't remember when he had laughed so much in his entire life. Poor Blaine, did you see his face when I told him you were my third ex wife and that I would be bringing my future fourth wife in tomorrow night for dinner and wanted him to be our server?"

"That was pretty funny, but I'm glad you told him later that you were kidding. Poor kid will never know if you are telling him the truth or not."

"Just so you always know when I'm telling the truth." said Andy, as he pulled into the driveway of Willow House.

"What do you mean, Andy?"

"Let's take a walk on the beach and I'll tell you."

As the two reached the beach, Maddie took her shoes off and said that she loved to feel the cool sand on her feet.

Andy smiled and as he took her hand in his, he said something that caused Madison's heart to feel as if it would leap from her chest.

"I don't want you to leave, Madison. I know we just met and we don't know each other very well, but tonight when we danced and I held you in my arms, I never wanted to let you go."

"I have always felt as if something was missing in my life and tonight I felt as if I had finally found it."

"I don't know what to say Andy, except that I really don't want to go back home right now either. I feel like there could be something very special between us also, but on the other hand it feels as if it's happening much too quickly."

Andy stopped and pulled Madison gently into his arms and as his lips met hers, Madison felt as if the world had dissolved around her.

Chapter Twenty Nine

"Well you certainly look like you just got off a merry-go-round," said Evan as Madison walked through the front door.

"Jack and I were about to sit outside for awhile; want to join us?"

"No, I don't want to spoil this glorious feeling I'm experiencing so I will see the two of you in the morning."

"Well, you wanted her to find someone to cheer her up, Jack."

"I know, and I really like Andy but he lives here and she lives in Shreveport. I was kind of hoping she would find someone a little closer to home."

"Shreveport is not that far, Jack, and having Andy come visit will give her something to look forward to."

"Yes, but what if she decided to move to Ocean Springs?"

"Well, our little girl has to grow up sometime, doesn't she?"

Jack just shot Evan a disgusted look and said he felt as if she were his responsibility since their parents died.

"I just feel that Mom would have expected me to make sure Maddie was safe and happy and I can't look after her if she isn't close by."

"Stop acting like an old man, Jackie. We will only be here another week, and what could possibly happen in that short period of time?"

Chapter Thirty

Beatrice had been looking out her bedroom window when Madison came home and when she saw her and Andy walking toward the beach she couldn't help but think back to a time when she too walked on that very beach with the man that she once loved.

That was very long ago, she thought, *but not so long ago that I forgot what he did to me and even though I made him pay, it just wasn't enough. I will go on making him pay, through his descendents.*

No Bienvenue will ever own Willow House, *not until one of them finds the hidden treasure and I have made sure that never happens.*

As Beatrice turned away from the window, she caught a glimpse of herself in the mirror and wondered where all the years went. She thought how differently her life might have been if her youth had not been stolen from her and as she opened the door to her closet and stepped inside she knew what she must do now.

As she reached behind an overcoat in the far corner and pushed her fingers gently against one of the panels, the back wall of the closet opened up to reveal a dark hallway, and as Beatrice walked softly down the hallway, little did she know that someone was watching her.

Martha was passing by Beatrice's room on her way to her own room when she thought she heard voices. She stopped and listened quietly at the door but all she could hear was what sounded like thunder. She opened the door gently and entered the room, just in time to see Beatrice walk into what looked like a secret passage.

"Martha," whispered Franklin, "where is Beatrice, and what are you doing in her room?"

"Franklin, you startled me. Let's go outside and we'll talk."

As soon as Franklin and Martha stepped out onto the front porch, Martha began telling him what just taken place in Beatrice's room.

Neither one of the two noticed that Jack and Evan were sitting on the far end of the porch having a nightcap until Martha had already told Franklin what she saw.

"Good evening, Sirs," said Franklin, "I guess we didn't see the two of you sitting there."

"Well now that you know we are here, would the two of you like to join us for a nightcap and fill us in on what Beatrice is up to?"

Martha looked like she wanted to bolt right back into the house, but she knew that she had no choice but to stay calm and hope that Jack and Evan didn't hear the things she had said to Franklin.

As if he had read her mind, Jack told Martha he heard everything she told Franklin about Beatrice and the secret passageway and he felt it was time they shared everything they knew about Beatrice and what had happened at Willow House.

Franklin told Jack that he would really rather keep Martha out of this for now, so Jack dismissed her and promised her that he would take care of everything.

"I think you know, by now, that you can trust us, Franklin, and I promise you that none of what you tell us will get back to Beatrice, in fact, we just might be able to free you from whatever it is she has over you."

"You know, Mr. Jack, I am tired of living in fear of what Beatrice will do if I cross her. Personally I would rather die than go on like this, besides this family deserves to know as much about their family as we can tell them."

There are a couple of things I need to ask you before I tell you what I know."

"What's that, Franklin?"

"First, I want you to see that Martha is kept safe."

"And what's the second thing?"

"I would really like to have that night-cap you offered me."

Chapter Thirty One

Early the next morning, Madison came flying down the stairs babbling about what a beautiful day it was and how hungry she was and how she couldn't wait to start shopping and decorating for Halloween.

Jack had just poured himself a cup of coffee and when he saw how hyped up Madison was, he suggested she have decaf.

"Oh, Jack, I'm just excited. I haven't relaxed and enjoyed myself in forever."

"Alright, Maddie, let's take a walk outside in the fresh air and you can tell me all about your date last night."

By this time Evan was coming down the staircase and when he saw Jack and Madison going out the front door, he called to them to wait for him.

By the time the three had reached the gazebo near the beach, Maddie had given her brothers a play by play of her date with Andy; all but the part where he kissed her and told her that he didn't want her to leave.

"Sweetheart, I really hate to burst your bubble," said Jack, "but Evan and I need to speak with you about some pretty disturbing things that Franklin and Martha shared with us last night."

"About Andy?"

"Of course not Maddie, it was about Beatrice and our family and about Willow House.

It seems that Beatrice was madly in love with our grandfather, Rene`, before he met our grandmother, Juliette.

Of course when our great grandfather, Tempest found out that Rene` and Beatrice were sneaking behind his back to see each other, he flew into a rage. Beatrice was the hired help and he would never stand for the hired help to ever become a member of the family, so he sent Rene` away to boarding school in New Orleans and told Beatrice that if she ever went near him again, he would throw her out into the streets and see that no one ever hired her.

Franklin said that Tempest liked having people in his service that he could control, so he told Beatrice that he would employ her for as long as she wanted to stay; however she was never to mention her fling with his son to anyone lest she be severely punished.

"Hey it gets much better," said Evan, as he saw the shocked look on his sister's face. "Guess who was a big ole' hypocrite? That's right, old grandpa Tempest himself."

"It seems that grandpa Tempest was at one time fooling around with the hired help himself and when she told him she was with child, he told her that she could stay on at Willow House and raise her son as long as she never revealed that the child was his."

"Of course she had no choice but to do as he said because she could not support the child on her own or bear the shame that she and her son would suffer. You know back then they didn't have DNA tests and women were shunned if they were unwed mothers."

"What happened to the child?" "Well, sis, after he grew up, he stayed on at Willow House as an employee of our not so great grandfather."

"You mean, Franklin?

"Yes, indeed."

Did he ever know that Tempest was his Father?"

"Not until his mother died. She told him on her deathbed because she wanted him to know that he was not a bastard child without a name. She asked that he not reveal this to anyone until the day came that he would be able to claim his birthright.

I suppose she felt that one day he could actually become the master of Willow House."

"I'm beginning to see why our mother left Willow House. What happened next?"

"Jack, you tell her the rest," said Evan.

"Okay, well it seems that Beatrice overheard Tempest's mistress tell her son that he was indeed a Bienvenue so she decided that if she couldn't have Renee, she would have the other son. She then blackmailed him into marrying her so that she would someday inherit Willow House and become Lady of the Manor, once and for all. Unfortunately for her, she was barren so she never had children that could rightfully inherit Willow House."

"But if Franklin is really a Bienvenue, why hasn't he come forward to claim his birthright?"

"Remember the account that Tempest left to take care of Willow House? Well, that account is in Franklin's name only. He writes the checks, not Beatrice, and if they make it known that he is a Bienvenue, the bank takes over the account and Franklin and Beatrice are thrown out because the will states that Franklin, the bastard son of Tempest Bienvenue would be allowed to reside in Willow House as long as he never reveals who he is."

"No wonder Beatrice hates us so much. She has been waiting her whole life to have Willow House all for herself. So what are we going to do now?"

Jack then told Madison about the secret passageway in Beatrice's closet and that Franklin and Martha were going to help them find out what Beatrice is up to."

"But how does Martha figure into all of this?"

"Well, it seems Martha was the cook and Franklin was pretty smitten with her. She was a good deal younger than him at the time so he never pursued her.

Of course after Beatrice put the whammy on him, he had to forget all about Martha."

"So I'm assuming you two have a plan as to how we are going to get rid of the wicked witch of the South?"

"Yes, but we need to meet with Andy also because we really need his help."

Madison then told them about Andy's restaurant and that she could arrange for them all to have dinner there tonight.

"Jack, I'm beginning to be a little concerned about Beatrice. What do Franklin and Martha think is in this secret passageway?"

"They never knew it existed Maddie but they did tell us that Beatrice tied them up once in the attic and they knew then that she was capable of anything.

Franklin has an idea that there really is a hidden treasure and that Beatrice found it. He said that right after we arrived he told her that he hoped that we didn't stay long because if we found the treasure, we would claim Willow House as our own. He said she never flinched or changed her expression when he mentioned the treasure which convinced him even more that she could have the treasure in her possession."

"So why doesn't she just take it and run?"

"Because she wants the whole enchilada, the house, the treasure and her connection to Rene`

"But we beat her at her own game, Maddie, I only wish Mom was here with us."

Chapter Thirty Two

"Welcome to La Petit Bistro," said Andy, as he greeted the Blooms at the entrance of his restaurant.

"Thank you for agreeing to meet us tonight," said Jack, "and by the way, I'm very impressed."

"As am I," said Evan. "Maddie said it was a cross between a bistro and supper club and I agree. You just don't find many places like this anymore."

Andy thanked them both and said that he was pretty proud of the place himself.

"You know Maddie agreed to help me with a few finishing touches, so I was hoping you would be able to extend your stay a little longer."

"I know you have a business to run, but I'm not sure if a week will be long enough for my investigation. I can't very well go prowling around Willow House if you three leave."

Jack told him that after they filled him in on what they learned last night, he may not be so eager to prowl around Willow House and as they were seated and the waiter came and took their drink order, Jack shared the information with him that Franklin had shared with him and Evan the night before.

"That's incredible," said Andy, "but why did Franklin suddenly decide to spill his guts to the two of you?"

Jack said he thought that it was because he felt that Beatrice was losing what little sanity she had and he was afraid of what she might do to us, if we stayed too long.

"You see, we told her we would be leaving the day after

Halloween and that seemed to settle her down quite a bit. She even offered to help with the Halloween party."

"Yes, and you know how hard it is to get an authentic witch these days," said Evan.

Madison asked Evan if he could maybe try and control himself in public, but Andy said that he did tend to agree with Evan.

"Authentic witches are pretty rare these days."

Jack looked at Madison, shook his head and said, "And then there were two."

"Oh please don't tell me my brother's personality is wearing off on you, Andy," "Come on, sis, you know that I'm your favorite. Remember, I promised I wouldn't tell Jack?"

Jack asked Andy if he was sure he wanted them to extend their stay.

"It's like dealing with Curly and Larry every day."

"Well I guess if I join the group," said Andy, "you'll finally have your Moe."

Jack couldn't help but burst out laughing and the next thing you know, Andy Evan and Madison were laughing hysterically, as well.

"Excuse me, people, I have had some complaints from the customers," said Blaine, as he returned to the table with the drink orders "They are saying that you are having much too much fun at this table."

"Oh yeah?" said Andy. "Well just wait until after dinner and we all start singing backup for the piano player."

Madison, playing along said that while the guys sang backup, she would be dancing on the piano.

Evan made a comment that this was the most fun he had had since they arrived and Jack said he had to admit that he was having a pretty good time himself.

"But we do need to discuss our game plan"

Andy agreed and said the ideal situation would be for Beatrice to go away for a few days, but because that was not likely to happen, someone was going to have to be in charge of knowing where she is at all times.

Evan said that it made more sense for Franklin and Martha to keep an eye on her, but he also said they could not follow her when she slips into the bat cave.

"You know Evan is right," said Andy, "I know that you both think he is a lunatic and he drives you both crazy, but he does have a point."

"I think there's a compliment in there somewhere,"

"Seriously Evan, you said that it made more sense for Franklin and Martha to keep an eye on Beatrice and that does makes sense under normal circumstances; however, since Beatrice is not what you would call normal, then perhaps it would make more sense if someone else kept an eye on Beatrice."

"I can hardly wait to find out who that *someone else* is."

Andy laughed and told Evan to relax because he was not the one he had in mind.

"Really, then who?"

Chapter Thirty Three

"Looks like a storms moving in this evening," said Martha as she stood at the window, staring up at the sky.

"Yes and I'm glad that Beatrice said she was retiring early because I just don't think I could have handled her and a storm this evening," said Franklin.

Martha told Franklin that she knew that he was tired of having to deal with Beatrice for all these years and she also said that truth be known, she only stayed on because of him.

Franklin seemed completely shocked at her statement.

"Martha, what are you talking about? Why would you have stayed here because of me?"

Martha then told him that she knew he cared for her and because she felt the same way about him, she was afraid to leave him alone with Beatrice.

"I overheard the two of you arguing one evening about your promise to your mother on her deathbed. I heard you say that if she had not blackmailed you, you would never have married her."

"I wanted to tell you then how I felt about you but I knew that Beatrice would never set you free so I just decided then and there that I would never leave you alone with that horrid old hag."

"But you did try to leave one night not very long ago remember?"

"I do remember. I was on my way to my room when I passed her room and overheard her talking to herself as she so often does. I really didn't think anything of it until I heard her say that she might have to arrange for Miss Madison to have the same kind of accident that killed Miss Juliette if she didn't take her brothers and leave Willow House soon."

"I just panicked and flew into my room and packed as fast as I could but she caught me going down the stairs and you know the rest."

"Actually you don't know the rest. She more or less implied that Mr. Tempest might still be alive and would arrange for something bad to happen to me, but the real reason I finally agreed to stay was because she implied that something terrible would happen to you if I left." I do believe she knows how much I care for you, Franklin, and that scares me more than anything."

"Martha, I told Mr. Jack and Mr. Evan everything, at least everything I know. I didn't tell them that I suspect Beatrice could have had something to do with their parents accident because I can't prove it and I'm afraid of what they might do and after what she said to you about Juliette, I'm even more convinced that she had a hand in Miss Camille's accident."

"Franklin, please promise me something. If the Blooms don't find the treasure and they have to leave Willow House, promise me that we will leave with them.

"I know that Willow House is your birthright but what good will it be to you if you are dead?

I'm sure that the Blooms will give us a job at their business in Shreveport and help us find a place to live."

"Why, Miss Martha Collins, are you asking me to move in with you."

"Well yes, as a matter of fact I am, Mr. Franklin Bienvenue, and judging by the big ole smile on your face, I would say it's the best offer you have had in years."

Franklin burst out in laughter at what Martha had said and for the first time in many, many years, he felt as if he might just have a chance at happiness after all.

Chapter Thirty Four

After Jack thanked Andy for dinner, he said they should be getting back to Willow House before Beatrice decided to change the locks.

Evan was just coming off the dance floor when he heard Jack say they were leaving.

"Hey, it's still early, bro. What's your hurry; scared you might miss Beatrice doing her Halloween practice flight on her broom?"

"Nothing says you have to leave, it's just that I told Franklin I would fill him in on our plans when we got home tonight."

I would love nothing more than to stay a while longer but I can't meet with Franklin during the day because Beatrice keeps a pretty close watch on him and I hate making the old fella wait up too late."

"Hey, Uncle Franks not that old and besides, he's probably having a rendezvous with Martha."

"Well in that case I'd better hurry before they take this relationship to the next level," said Jack.

"Stop, you two," said Madison, "I think it's very romantic that the two of them may have a chance at happiness after being in love for so many years and never being able to express it to one another."

"Oh yeah?" said Evan. "Well, I'll bet it won't be so romantical if old Hagatha hears about it. That said, I suppose I should go along to make sure she doesn't decide to cast a spell on Jack and turn him into a party animal."

"Hey, you guys wouldn't mind if Maddie stayed and had a

nightcap with me, would you? That is if she wants to. I mean I will be happy to drive her home."

"Hey, I'm right here and you really don't have to ask my brothers for permission to keep me out after midnight."

"I'm just kidding, Andy, I think it's very sweet that you consulted them, but just an FYI, I never do what they want me to do. Never have, never will."

As soon as Jack and Evan drove away, Andy pulled Madison into his arms and whispered, "I thought they would never leave."

Madison laughed and said "Why Mr. Bergeron, it sounds like you want to be alone with…."

But before she could finish her sentence, Andy pressed his lips to hers and her heart began to beat so hard that she was afraid that he could hear it.

"Wow that was unexpected, very nice but unexpected."

"Well should I warn you the next time or should I just start kissing you and never stop?"

"Right now the *never stop* part sounds a little too dangerous to me so I think we should go back inside and have that nightcap."

On the drive back home Jack asked Evan if he thought that Madison was getting serious about Andy.

"You know Maddie. She is interested until they become too serious and then she finds a way to end it."

"I don't know about this one, Evan. I've never seen stars in her eyes before."

"Well, ya know, we have been on vacation and we have all had more to drink than usual so maybe it's just a wine glow."

"I'm serious, Evan. I think she is falling for this guy."

"Well if that's true then I guess we'll just have to have him snuffed out."

"It's a good thing we are pulling into the driveway, Evan, cause I would hate to be driving a long distance with no one else in the car but you."

"Look, Opie, there's Aint Bea waiting on the front porch for us. I wonder where Uncle Frankenstein is."

Jack told Evan that he was glad he was amused by all this but that he better make damn sure he didn't slip up in front of Beatrice.

"Are you kidding, Jack? I'm afraid of her and even more so now that Halloween is near."

Chapter Thirty Five

"Good evening, Beatrice, how are you this evening?"

"I'm very well, Mr. Jack, and you?"

"Oh, I'm okay, Beatrice, just feeling a little homesick though.

Not that we haven't had a wonderful time, it's just that we've been gone longer than we should have and we do have a business to run."

"Yes Sir, I understand, sir, there's just no place like home."

Jack could see that Beatrice was very pleased that he was anxious to leave and that's exactly the reaction he was going for.

"By the way, Beatrice, can you get Franklin for me? I need his help with some things in the morning and I just wanted to make sure that he's available."

"Oh I think he has turned in for the night, Mr. Jack."

"No, No, I'm still awake, Beatrice. In fact I was in the library getting a book to read."

"Very well, then, May I get you all a nightcap before bed?"

"Jack, you and Franklin discuss what you need him to help you with tomorrow and I'll help Beatrice with the drinks."

"That won't be necessary, sir, I can handle it."

"Nonsense, Beatrice, Madison has given Jack some silly instructions about where she wants the tables and decorations for her Halloween party and I have to tell you, I am just not interested in Halloween. What about you, Beatrice, do you like Halloween?"

As Evan and Beatrice walked into the house, Franklin

muttered something under his breath and Jack could have sworn he heard him say *all witches like Halloween.*

"Did you say something, Franklin?"

"No Sir, I was just clearing my throat, but he could see a slight smile on his face and he thought to himself *I'll have to remember to tell Evan that I know where he gets his sense of humor from.*"

"Sir, What did Miss Madison say when you told her who I was?"

"She was shocked, just like I was, Franklin but you are family and when we find out what Beatrice is up to and if there really is a treasure, we are going to make sure that you are finally given the respect that you should have been given a long time ago."

"You have to keep saying sir to me while Beatrice is around because of the circumstances but when this is over, I will be calling you sir, is that clear?"

Franklin smiled and said that though it would make him very happy if we could find out what Beatrice is up to, he was already happier than he had been in years.

"I found out tonight that Martha cares very deeply for me and the fact that you and Mr. Evan and Miss Madison accept me as family, well that is more than I could ever hope for."

"Hey I ditched Aunt Bea if that's okay with you all," said Evan, as he headed toward the gazebo with a tray of drinks

"Evan, please"

"No that is quite alright. I have felt like ditching her for many, many years myself."

"Okay fellas, enough Bea bashing, let's get down to business."

"I don't believe you said Bea bashing Jack. That is so not you. Maybe I'm rubbing off on you."

"God I hope not, anyway, yes we do need to get down to business."

"If Beatrice asks you what we needed you for tonight, tell her that we needed to get your expertise on where we should hide our fake treasure on the grounds and that sort of thing."

"The problem will be devising a plan to keep Beatrice outside as much as possible on Halloween so that we will have enough time to figure out where the hidden hallway goes."

"That may not be a problem at all, sir, I mean Jack. You see Beatrice uses the old servant's quarters as a storage facility and if I tell her that people will be snooping around it then I'm sure she will be more than happy to be the outside tour guide."

"I'll tell her that she might want to keep her eye on everyone as they search for the Halloween treasure because they might just decide to break into her storage facility."

"She is very protective of that old house in fact she won't even allow Martha or me to go in it."

"Well, now that in itself is pretty interesting, Franklin; so why do you think she is so protective of a bunch of junk?"

"You know, Jack, over the years I have come to ignore most of what Beatrice does. I just assumed that she was sneaking heirlooms out of the main house and storing them there."

"But why would she do that?"

"Probably so that she could have her own stash to sell when she finally got kicked out of Willow House," said Evan.

"Jack said it just sounded very fishy to him and that after they checked out the secret passageway, they might just need to check out the old servant's quarters."

Chapter Thirty Six

Andy and Madison were the only couple left on the dance floor when the bistro closed.

"And just how is this going to look to your future fourth wife, Mr. Bergeron?"

"Well I'm not going to tell her, are you?"

"I might, unless you can convince me otherwise."

"Oh I think I can manage that."

"Is that so? Well you don't have much time to convince me, you know. I will be leaving in a few days."

"You could have gone all night without saying that. I think you should extend your visit indefinitely."

"Well I will give it some serious thought; however if I don't get in at a decent hour tonight, my brothers will probably cuff me and drag me back to Shreveport tomorrow."

"Okay, I'll take you home on one condition. You must swear to me that you will stay at least one more night after your brothers' leave. I promise that I will drive you back to Shreveport myself."

"That sounds reasonable, but let's just cross that bridge when we come to it. Right now we need to find out what Beatrice is up to and if there really is a hidden treasure."

I feel that I owe this to my mother. She didn't have a very happy childhood at Willow House and call it women's intuition, but I feel as if Beatrice has a lot to do with it."

As Andy and Madison pulled into the driveway, they noticed that no one was outside waiting for them.

"I guess that's a good sign," said Madison.

"It's a good sign for me," said Andy as he leaned over and kissed Madison gently on the lips.

"I don't want this evening to end either, Andy," said Madison, as she gazed into his deep brown eyes.

"I do promise you one thing, though. When the Halloween party is over, the rest of the night belongs to you and me."

After awhile, Andy walked Madison to the front door of Willow House and as she opened the front door, she reached inside and switched off the porch light.

"Now, Mr. Bergeron, how about a real goodnight kiss?"

The next morning Madison heard someone gently knocking on her door and just as she started to get out of her bed to see who it was, she noticed a piece of paper slide under her door.

Madison, it read, *meet Evan and me down at the gazebo for coffee, ASAP.*

Madison threw on a pair of jeans and a T shirt and hurried down to the gazebo.

"This had better be important boys, cause I sure could have used another couple of hours sleep."

As Jack poured Madison a cup of coffee, he immediately began filling her in on what Franklin told them last night about the old servant's quarters. He said that Franklin didn't seem to be very concerned, but that he and Evan felt like something was really off.

"Of course it's off," said Madison, "I cannot believe that Franklin and Martha never suspected that Beatrice might be hiding something from them."

"Sis, you have to understand that Franklin has lived with this troll for many years and has probably become oblivious to what she does," said Evan.

"For once I agree with Evan" said Madison "Franklin has probably ignored what she does as long as she stays away from him."

"Well whatever Beatrice has been up to for all these years is about to come to an end," said Jack. "I have no idea why she left

Willow House, but the three of us are about to find out, we owe this to our mother."

Madison felt empowered by Jack's statement and as she took another big gulp of coffee she told him that she was very surprised that he was so determined to pursue this.

"Maddie, I may seem like a stuffed shirt to you because I'm the oldest, but Mom and Dad's death hit me pretty hard also."

"I just wanted to be brave for you and Evan and the only way I knew how was to try and not show so much emotion."

Madison walked over to Jack and as she reached out for his hand she said that she always knew he was trying to be brave for her and Evan and that she loved him so much for that but she also said it was time for him to allow her and Evan to be strong for him also.

"Jackie, you have been my life line and I love you so much for it but I am a lot stronger than you think I am and it's time that you, Evan, and I become a team."

"You know that Dad and Mom raised us to become a force to be reckoned with and I think the time has come for us to bond together and finally be that force."

"I have no doubt that Dad and Mom are proud of us, but I also feel that if they were standing here right now they would say, especially Mom. *Jackie, your sister is always right.*"

Evan told Madison that he couldn't believe she used their mother's voice for her own betterment.

"What can I say, Evan? I just felt like Mom would get a kick out of it."

"You know what, you two?" said Jack, "I just want to go home. I want to go back to the day to day routine that kept me from going insane so let's just find out what caused our mother so much grief in her childhood and maybe she can finally have some peace."

Chapter Thirty Seven

For the next few days the Blooms, along with Andy, decorated the entire outside of the house for Halloween. And by the time Halloween arrived, Willow House looked like something out of a horror movie.

That afternoon as Madison was getting dressed for the party, Martha stopped by to see if she needed any help.

"Miss Madison I brought you a light snack and some juice and I wanted to see if you needed any help getting dressed."

"Thank you, Martha, I do appreciate the snack and as far as needing help getting dressed, well you stopped by just in time because I do need someone to lace up my corset."

Madison noticed that Martha had a sort of blank look on her face.

"Martha I know you probably never saw the movie, "Pirates of the Caribbean," so I'm sure my costume makes no sense to you at all, so to keep it simple, I will just say that Andy is dressing as the character Captain Jack Sparrow and I am dressing as Elizabeth Swan. Not very original, I know, but we really didn't have very long to plan for this."

"Miss Madison I think you will look beautiful no matter what you dress up as."

"Thank you, Martha, and now if you can just give me a hand here."

After Martha left, Madison finished her makeup and took one last look in the mirror before heading downstairs to make sure everything was ready for their guests.

Evan and Jack had just finished setting up the outside bar down by the gazebo when Madison arrived.

"Well if it isn't the winch, Elizabeth Swan," said Evan.

"Martha told you who I was, didn't she?"

"Yes, she did, sis. Nothing gets past you, does it?"

"Not much, Evan, besides, you never remember the characters names in movies."

"You got me there, sis, and by the way, who all is coming to this shindig? The only people we know are the ones that came to our cook-out when we first arrived."

"Well, they are all coming tonight as well as Julie from Joe's restaurant, Blaine from the Bistro, and several single young ladies that Andy grew up with."

"Really, he's bringing several single girls to the party? Gosh, I thought he was your date."

Jack said that he hoped that Andy wasn't trying to fix him up with anyone because he didn't plan on being in Ocean Springs much longer.

"I know, Jack but if we find out what Beatrice is up to, we may just be able to get rid of her."

"I know it was in the will that she could stay on until the treasure was found and ownership of Willow House changed, and that could just happen you know."

As long as one of you stays with Beatrice throughout the evening, Andy and I can find out where the secret passage leads then later, after she goes to bed, we can search the old servant's quarters."

"I realize that we could just tell her that we wanted to see inside the old house, but if she really is up to something, we stand a better chance of catching her if she thinks we're clueless and I don't want to hear any smart remarks from you, Evan."

"What are you talking about? I didn't say a word."

"No, but you were about to."

"Wow, I thought that old *eyes in the back of your head* thing was just something that mothers had, but I guess all females have it; and by the way, sis, you really do look beautiful and I'm being serious about that."

"Yes, you do look beautiful, Maddie," said Jack. "More and more like Mother every day."

"Thank you, Jack, and thank you, Evan, now, I think the two of you need to go get your costumes on so I can get some pictures before the guests arrive and speaking of guests, Andy just pulled into the drive. I asked him to come early so that the four of us could go over our plan again and make sure we haven't forgotten anything."

"Hey, what's to forget, sis" said Evan as he and Jack started walking toward the house, "all we have to do is keep an eye on old mullet face while you and Andy hide out in her closet and make out."

By this time Evan had begun to run and Madison was right behind him.

"Slow down, Miss Swan," said Andy as he watched her run past him.

Madison stopped and looked back at Andy in his costume and everything left her mind except how very, very handsome he looked for a pirate.

"Why, Captain Jack Sparrow, I do believe you are the most gorgeous pirate that ever landed in Ocean Springs."

"Well I'll be sure and tell Jean Lafitte you said that when I see him again. And may I also say how radiant you look this evening, Miss Swan?"

"You may indeed, Captain, and do remind me to thank you properly after the party is over."

"I can hardly wait."

Chapter Thirty Eight

"It's a good thing there's a cold front moving in tonight," said Evan as he and Jack arrived at the gazebo and started making themselves a drink, "this costume is a little warm."

"Well, you chose them."

"I just thought it would be appropriate for us to be Hernando De Soto and Pierre Le Moyne d'iberville since they were a big part of the history of the Mississippi Gulf coast.

Andy overheard the conversation and said that he was very impressed that Evan knew the history of Ocean Springs.

Andy said that he really couldn't take credit because it was Franklin that actually filled him in on some of the History of the Mississippi Gulf Coast."

"Well Franklin, I guess you are the expert on the history of the Mississippi Coast. By the way, would you and Martha mind keeping an eye out while Madison and I are upstairs, I just want to make sure that the guests stay on the first floor of the house? We certainly can't have them wandering around the upper floors."

"Certainly sir."

"Please, Franklin, its Andy.

Now, since Jack will be in charge of Beatrice, Evan, you will be in charge of warning us if anything goes wrong."

"And just how am I supposed to do that?"

"Franklin will give you a flashlight and if you see Beatrice heading toward the house, you simply turn the flashlight on and point it towards the front door of Willow House."

"Franklin, just make sure that one of you is always out on the front porch."

"Now, Madison will have Beatrice tell the guests when it is time to start the treasure hunt and that Madison, Evan and I will be taking care of the trick-or-treaters as they arrive at the gates of the property. She thinks we put the word out around town that Willow House would be giving out candy for Halloween this year. You could tell that she hated the idea but I think that she felt like she could handle it for one more day."

"I take it there really won't be any trick-or-treaters at the gate?" said Evan.

"That's right. Franklin will lock the gate as soon as the last guest arrives and Beatrice won't know the difference."

"So if Franklin and Martha are on the front porch, Madison and Andy are upstairs and Jack will be with Beatrice and the guests on the treasure hunt, I guess that means that I will be all by myself."

"No indeed Evan, I have that covered also. Remember the cute little blonde that you were dancing with last night? Well she just happens to be my cousin, as well as my secretary, and I invited her here tonight to keep you company."

"But she said she was married and was just out with friends."

"I know, I told her to tell you that because I wanted to make sure the two of you hit it off before I invited her and when Jack said that you were pretty disappointed when she said she was married, I ask her what she thought about you, and she said she thought you were a lot of fun so I told her I was working on a case for your family and that you could use a sidekick."

"Don't worry though because she won't ask any questions, but she can help you keep a watch out if Beatrice gets too close."

"Wow, Andy, now I'm impressed. It seems that you've thought of everything.

Chapter Thirty Nine

Beatrice was standing at her bedroom window watching as the guests began to arrive. She couldn't believe that she would have to endure another night of outsiders nosing around *and of all nights,* she thought, *Halloween. Well at least they would all stay outside where I can control them and tomorrow when the last of the descendents of Tempest Bienvenue leaves, all their rights to* Willow House *will be relinquished and* Willow House *will finally be mine.*

I can't wait to see the look on Franklin and Martha's faces when I tell them my little secret and then throw them out in the streets.

No, after tomorrow I will not need Franklin here to write checks for me because I will finally be the Mistress of Willow House *and Tempest Bienvenue will rue the day he kept me from marrying my true love.*

After about an hour after the last guest arrived, Madison went up to the house to tell Beatrice it was time to start the treasure hunt and that it should only take about an hour from start to finish.

"Just be sure and keep them away from that junky old storage house, Beatrice, I don't want anyone getting hurt."

"Oh, you don't have to worry about that, Miss Madison, I won't let anyone near that place."

I'll just bet you won't, thought Madison.

"Well, okay then, Beatrice let's get this treasure hunt started."

As Andy and Madison started down the hall that lead to the

servant's quarters, Madison began having second thoughts about bringing Andy into her family's problems.

"Andy, you know you can still back out if you want to."

"And why would I want to?"

"Well this could turn out to be dangerous and it really isn't your problem."

"Listen, I am a private investigator and you did give me half my fee up front so it really is my problem now,"

"What are you talking about? I didn't pay you a dime."

"Oh yes you did. Remember that kiss you gave me last night on the front porch?"

"I do."

"Well that was half the fee."

"Okay, well what am I supposed to do about the rest of your fee?"

"Well, you said you were going to thank me properly when the party was over, so I'll consider that payment in full."

"That's a deal, Mr. Bergeron, and if you do a really good job, they'll be a bonus in it for you."

"Oh, I always do a really good job, Miss Bloom."

By this time the two had reached Beatrice's room and as Andy expected, it was locked.

"I didn't even think about the door being locked, Andy."

"Well that's what you have me for."

"What? To think for me?"

"No, silly, to pick the lock. You know when you graduate from the School of Clouseau, they give you a whole kit full of gadgets."

Madison just smiled and shook her head as Andy opened the door to Beatrice's room, in about five seconds, and as soon as he opened the door to her closet, a feeling of dread came over Madison and she began to wonder if she was getting in over her head.

Andy, seeing the look on Madison's face said that she could stay behind if she wanted to and he would go on by himself.

"No, I'll be okay. I need to do this for my mother and my grandmother. It seems that she didn't have a very happy life here either."

Madison stepped into the closet, moved the clothes aside, pulled the lever in the corner and the wall slid open just exactly as Martha said it would.

This is just too easy, thought Andy, and as he stepped into what seemed to be hallway, he looked to make sure there was a way out before he motioned for Madison to enter, then as he let go of the panel, it automatically closed.

Chapter Forty

Evan and Aimee were sitting in the gazebo talking and getting to know each other a little better when suddenly Evan noticed a shadow emerging from the back of the old servant's quarters.

"Wait here, Aimee, I'll be right back and if you see anyone at all go near Willow House, turn this flashlight on and point it straight toward the house."

"Where are you going?"

"I just thought I saw someone over by the old house and I just want to make sure that none of the guests are snooping around there. There seems to be a lot of junk stored inside and I'm not sure how safe it is."

Though it had only been about fifteen minutes since the treasure hunt started, Beatrice felt as if it had been fifteen hours.

"Are you okay, Beatrice?" asked Jack "You seem a little tired. I can handle this by myself if you like. There have only been a few nosy guests so far to try and sneak away from the group and check out the old house. Hopefully no one else will try and go off on their own."

"I'm perfectly fine, sir, and I certainly wouldn't want anyone to get hurt just because they were curious."

The old house has so much junk stored inside and we cannot risk anyone being hurt, now can we, sir?"

"We certainly cannot Beatrice and besides, we do make a pretty good team."

You are so like your grandfather Rene`,* thought Beatrice, *at least in looks. Rene` was a coward and somehow I think you would fight for the woman you loved.

"Did you hear me, Beatrice?"

"Oh I'm sorry sir, what did you say?"

"I just said that we make a pretty good team and I don't want you to overdo."

"Yes, Rene` I did hear you and I am quite fine."

Jack did not react to Beatrice calling him Rene` because he realized that she was oblivious to the fact that she had even called him by his grandfather's name, he simply smiled at her and offered her his arm as they continued to lead the guests on the treasure hunt.

"Stay behind me, Madison," whispered Andy as the two walked gently along the passageway.

"Count on it, I'm not about to bolt in front of you."

As Andy and Madison walked slowly through the hallway, it felt as if they were walking downward.

"Does it feel as if we are going lower?" asked Madison.

"It did for a few minutes but now it seems to have leveled out.

I think we need to be very quiet for the rest of the way, though, just in case."

Madison looked at him, nodded and stayed as close to him as she possibility could.

Andy was thinking about how much more he would enjoy her nearness under different circumstances when suddenly the hallway ended. He put his fingers to his lips as if to say be very quiet and as he gently touched the wall at the end of the hallway, it began to slide open and as it opened, Madison began to tremble and her heart began to pound so hard that she was afraid it might explode.

Before them was a rather large room, nicely decorated and it seemed to have all the comforts of home.

"Oh my God in Heaven, who are you?" said Madison as she saw someone immerge from the shadows and he seemed to be chained to the bed.

"My name is Renee` Bienvenue. Who are you and how did you get in here?"

"Never mind that," said Andy. "Is this as far as the passageway goes?"

"I don't think so. Beatrice comes in here every day, blindfolds me and takes me somewhere so that I can exercise. I can smell fresh air and sometimes I can even feel the sun."

"She says that she will take me out of here soon but I have been down here so long that I doubt she will ever let me go."

"Look, we don't have much time and I promise we will get you out of her but you must trust us," said Andy.

"And why should I?"

"Because I am your granddaughter," said Madison.

Chapter Forty One

The treasure hunt was going pretty well, as far as Evan could tell, at least he had not seen Beatrice so far and that was good news, but he kept thinking that he would feel a lot better if he saw Andy and Madison immerge from Willow House before the treasure hunt was over.

Meanwhile Jack was becoming a little nervous because he felt that Beatrice was growing tired and he was afraid she might just decide to leave the guests to him so he decided he had better think of something just in case.

"Beatrice, do you need to take a break? We can sit and rest awhile if you like."

"No, sir, I am fine. There are only a few more places that the guests will be allowed to search."

Realizing what she said, Beatrice said that she meant to say that there were only a few more places left that had hidden treasure because Franklin told her where he had hidden everything."

"Oh, I knew what you meant, Beatrice, and I am glad that you are able to hang in there with me because I overheard a few of the guests say that they were going to search the old servant's quarters, so I really do need you to help me keep them in line."

"Mr. Bienvenue, look, I found one of the treasures," said Julie, as she came running up to where Jack and Beatrice were standing. "I'm sorry, I didn't mean to be rude, my name is Julie, Julie Babineaux."

"Did you say Babineaux?"

"Yes Ma'am, my mother's name is Rene`, do you know her or maybe you knew my grandmother, Bernice."

Jack could see Beatrice's face by the light from the lantern he was carrying and she looked as white as a sheet and he was sure she had gone into shock because she seemed unable to move.

"Beatrice, are you alright? Beatrice answer me, are you alright, do I need to call a doctor?"

Suddenly Beatrice seemed to regain her composure.

"No, please, don't call a doctor, Mr. Bloom, I'm perfectly fine. Maybe I do need to sit down and rest for a few moments."

"Why don't you go ahead and make sure that the rest of the treasure hunters stay away from the old house, you know, so they won't get hurt."

"I hate to leave you alone, Beatrice."

"Go ahead, Mr. Bloom, she won't be alone, I'll stay with her until you return, that is if that's alright with you, Miss Beatrice, I've already found my treasure anyway."

"Okay then, I won't be long, but are you sure you will be okay, Beatrice?"

"Oh, I'll be better than okay. I'll just have a nice little chat with Julie while you're gone."

As Jack walk away, he made a mental note to question Julie later to find what she and Beatrice talked about. Beatrice was obviously shaken when the name Babineaux was mentioned and then when she said that her Mother's name was Rene`.

This is way too bazaar, he thought, *Franklin's half brother's name was Rene` and his wife's name was Juliette. Could this just be a coincidence or could Julie be another descendent of Tempest Bienvenue.*

Chapter Forty Two

After Rene` and Madison got over the initial shock of finding out that they were in fact grandfather and granddaughter, Andy suggested they try and find out if anyone else was being held prisoner by Beatrice.

"There's just one little problem here," said Rene`, "I'm chained to the bed."

As Andy began working to free him, Madison asked him how long he had been down here.

"I'm not sure because my memory is pretty fuzzy. I remember the day your mother left Willow House and when she said she would never return I was heartbroken. I just didn't think I could stand to lose her too. You see her mother, my Juliette, passed away not long before and Camille thought Willow House was cursed. She begged me to come with her, but I knew if I left, I would never be allowed to return and I honestly believed your mother would come back home some day."

"She did keep in touch for several years but she refused to come back here to visit and each time I thought about visiting her, I would become terribly ill, eventually I stopped getting letters from her and I just don't remember anything after that except being in here."

Andy made the comment that Rene` looked remarkably well for being locked away for God knows how long.

"I know," said Madison. "It just doesn't make sense, but then nothing has made sense from the day we arrived at Willow House."

Rene` asked Madison how long she had been at Willow House and if her mother was with her.

She didn't have the heart to tell him that his daughter had passed, so she just said that she would fill him in on everything later.

"Okay now, I managed to free you, but until we get out of here, you might have to drag a few chains around with you."

"I don't care what I have to drag around, I just want to get out of here and see my Camille, again."

Andy looked at Madison and he knew her heart was breaking at the reminder of her mother and the fact that she had to tell her grandfather that his only child had passed when it was still so painful for her to speak about.

"Hey, Maddie, are you okay?"

"Of course I'm okay, I just met my grandfather for the first time in my life, why wouldn't I be okay?"

Andy knew right then and there that Madison Bloom was truly the lady that he wanted to be his wife, the mother of his children and the love of his life for eternity.

Here she is being strong for her grandfather, a man she never met before, when her heart must be breaking.

Rene`s voice interrupted his thoughts.

"Beatrice always turns me to the left when she takes me from this room."

Andy knew right then that there had to be another exit because she would have had to turn him to the right in order to take him out the way they came in.

As he began to tap his fingers along the wall, he noticed that the wall began to move.

"I guess I touched the right spot" he said as the wall slid completely open "let's go, I know that Jack said he would try and keep Beatrice as long as possible, but face it, there is only so much that he can do to keep her attention."

Neither Andy nor Madison knew that Beatrice was becoming very fascinated with Jack, because she had begun to noticed just how much he was like her Rene` at his age; however, Jack had noticed and was using it to keep her occupied.

Madison made a comment about how dark and cold it was in the passageway they had entered and Rene` said that it always felt cold in that area but after awhile it did began to warm up.

As the three walked slowly through the passageway, Andy leading the way with his flashlight, Rene` made a comment about it not being much farther until they would begin to reach the warm place and sure enough, Madison did began to feel heat coming from somewhere and strangely enough, she began to feel calm and peaceful, very, very peaceful.

Chapter Forty Three

Beatrice and Julie sat down on a bench that was sitting under one of the large 0ak trees and as soon as they were settled, Beatrice asked Julie to tell her all about her family.

"I don't mean to be nosy, dear, I guess it's just because I never had a family of my own."

"Oh I understand, Ms. Beatrice. I never had much of a family myself."

"My grandfather and my father died when I was very small so my mother and grandmother had to raise me on their own. I'm not complaining though. I had a wonderful grandmother and a mother, just as wonderful."

It was a good thing that it was dark and Julie couldn't see Beatrice's face because when she said that her grandmother and mother had passed, Beatrice's eyes filled with tears.

"Forgive me dear, I'm afraid I'm beginning to get a bit of a cold."

"You do sound a little sniffley. Maybe I should take you inside the house."

"That would be lovely my dear."

I am not about to lose Rene` and Willow House, thought Beatrice, *I had no idea that my twin sister had passed and now I find out that the child has passed as well.*

Don't you worry one little bit my darling, Rene` we still have our granddaughter and a beauty she is, why she looks just like you.

As Beatrice walked alongside Julie toward Willow House, she began thinking of how happy she would be once everyone was gone from Willow House once and for all. Everyone that is, except she and Rene`, oh and of course their beautiful granddaughter,

Julie, although she was going to have to do something about her name, Julie, Juliette, what was my sister thinking?

Evan noticed that Beatrice and Julie were walking toward Willow House and quickly started flashing his light so that Franklin could alert Andy and Madison.

It seemed strange to him that Julie would be with her. It would seem that if she slipped away from Jack, she certainly wouldn't bring someone with her.

Well I guess it doesn't matter, he thought, *she is still headed for* Willow House.

Evan flashed his light again, just to make sure that Franklin and Martha saw him.

Franklin, seeing the lights flash told Martha not to panic but to do whatever it took to keep them on the first floor.

"I'll be back as soon as I can."

Franklin ascended the stairs as fast as he could and headed straight for Beatrice's room. When he arrived, he found the door open and when he entered the room, he proceeded right to the closet and pulled the lever just as he had been instructed.

As the wall began to open, Franklin slid through, turned on his flashlight and practically ran through the passageway yelling out to Andy and Madison without a thought of what could be lying ahead for him.

"Do you hear that?" asked Madison. "It sounds like Franklin, which means that Beatrice is on her way to the house."

"Don't panic, let's just go back the way we came and when we reach Beatrice's room, we can make another decision."

"I'm sure that everyone is doing their best to delay Beatrice as long as possible."

As soon as Beatrice and Julie reached Willow House, Martha asked if they would like a cup of tea.

"Yes, Martha, that would be very nice and if you wouldn't mind, please bring it up to my room."

"Julie, my dear, would you mind terribly, having tea with me in my quarters? I would just be much more comfortable there."

As Andy, Madison and Rene` made their way back through the passageway they heard Franklin calling their names.

"Franklin, we're right ahead of you," said Andy, "stay there and we will come to you."

Rene` said that perhaps he should stay behind until they broke it to Franklin that he was alive.

"I wouldn't want to give the old boy a heart attack."

"I don't think we have that much time," said Andy. "Just stay behind Madison and she can try and soften the shock before he gets a good look at you."

"Too late, son, He got to us first and from the look on his face I believe he has already seen me."

Madison quickly ran up to Franklin to try and keep him calm.

"Franklin, please don't panic, he's not a ghost, Renee` is alive. Did you hear me? My grandfather is alive."

Martha knew she would have to be quick on her feet to keep Beatrice from going up to her room.

"Oh Ms. Beatrice, I'm so sorry but there is a terrible mess in the hallway upstairs, in fact I was just on my way down to get some cleaning supplies when I saw you headed toward the house."

"What sort of mess, and by the way, I thought you and Franklin were helping Mr. Evan with those little…um… trick-or- treaters."

"Yes, we were, that is Franklin still is. You see I was a little chilly so I ran up to my room to get a sweater and I guess I was in too much of a hurry because I knocked over the vase of fresh flowers in the hallway."

"I'm so sorry, Ma'am, should I get the tea first or clean up the mess?"

Julie noticed how tense Martha seemed to be so she said she would not mind making the tea so Martha could take care of the problem upstairs.

"In fact, it would be my pleasure, Ms. Beatrice. My mother, my grandmother and I used to have tea parties all the time and I would always help make the tea, so you see it would bring back some lovely memories for me."

"That does sound lovely, my dear. I will show you to the kitchen and we shall have our own tea party in the parlor."

Martha felt as if she had dodged more than a bullet, in fact she felt like she dodged a missile. So as soon as Beatrice and Julie left the foyer` she set out to find Franklin and warn him that the wicked witch of the South had landed.

I have had more excitement tonight than I have had in my entire life, thought Martha, *under different circumstances I believe I would just love Halloween.*

Chapter Forty Four

As the treasure hunt was coming to an end, Jack noticed Evan running toward him.

I have never seen Evan move that fast, so I know something must be wrong, he thought, so he ran to meet him.

"Jack, Jack, they're in the house, Beatrice and Julie are in the house."

"Oh, no, listen, Evan, go gather up all the guests and bring them back to the gazebo. Get the music going and make sure they all have drinks."

"What the hell am I thinking? I'm preaching to the choir, if anyone knows how to keep a party going it's you."

"You're right, Jack, so just go, and be careful."

Franklin knew that he had to pull it together very quickly because Beatrice could show up at any moment.

It's Halloween, thought Franklin, *how appropriate.*

Martha entered Beatrice's bedroom as Franklin and the others were immerging from the closet.

"Thank God you are all okay, but you must hurry because Beatrice is on the…..Oh my God it's"

"Yes, Martha, it is Renee`," said Franklin. "He is alive and Beatrice has been holding him prisoner."

"Now I know that this is a lot to take in but you must focus, for all our sakes."

Madison noticed how white Martha's face had become and she suddenly felt as if she were possessed by Evan.

I will never look at Martha White flour quite the same again, she thought. *I will also never tell Evan about this, or Jack, or Andy, or anyone for that matter.*

"Let's get out of here," whispered Andy, as the group immerged into the hallway. "Martha you need to go back downstairs and make sure Beatrice and Julie stay in the parlor long enough for us to get down the stairs and out the front door."

"That would be no problem if Beatrice and Julie were not coming up the stairs as we speak," said Martha.

Franklin then motioned for everyone to follow him, so Martha grabbed the vase of flowers that she had lied to Beatrice about knocking over earlier, handed it to Franklin and headed toward the staircase to try and slow Beatrice down.

"I've got the perfect place for us to hide" said Franklin as he led them to his bed- room "Beatrice would never dream of coming into my room."

If I were not so frightened right now, thought Madison, *that would be pretty funny*

"Boy, that was close," whispered Franklin, as he quietly closed the door to his room. "One more minute and Halloween would have taken on a whole new meaning."

"Franklin, I can't believe you have such an *Evan* sense of humor," whispered Madison.

Franklin just winked at her and smiled. It really hit Madison that so many people suffered because of one evil man, Tempest Bienvenue.

Just looking at Franklin right now, she thought, *and seeing how much more relaxed and different he is compared to when we arrived makes me realize why our mother ran away from* Willow House *as soon as she could, and why she never wanted us to know about her childhood.*

As soon as Martha saw Beatrice close the door to her room, she went to Franklin's room and let everyone know that it was safe to make a run for it. By the time they all reached the bottom of the stairs, Jack was opening the front door.

Andy pointed to the front door so that Jack would turn around and go back outside and he and the others followed.

Once they were far enough away from the house Jack asked where Beatrice was.

"And by the way, who is this man you have with you?"

"It's a long story, Jack," said Madison. "Right now all you need to know is that we just found another long lost uncle and if Beatrice finds out he's gone, well, she won't be very happy."

Chapter Forty Five

After Madison filled Jack in on what had transpired since they saw him last, he said that as far as he was concerned, they should all just get in the car and head out of there as fast as they could.

"We are dealing with a lunatic and I don't think we should stay here any longer than we need to."

"Oh, Andy," said Madison, "where is Julie?   In all the confusion, I forgot all about her."

By this time they were all nearing the gazebo by the beach and Evan was walking toward them and as soon as he came within earshot, Jack asked him to end the party as soon as possible.

Evan could tell by the tone in Jack's voice that something was terribly wrong, so he asked Aimee to help him get all the guests together so that he could make an announcement.

"Listen up everyone, I'm sorry to have to end this party so early but we have a family emergency."

"For those of you that are not yet ready to end the evening, I suggest you continue your celebration at La Petit Bistro."

"Thank you all for coming and Happy Halloween."

Everyone wanted to know if there was anything they could do to help but Evan assured them that they had it all under control.

"I do apologize and I hope to see everyone again."

As soon as everyone was in their cars headed toward the gates Evan wanted to know what had happened and who this strange man was.

Madison began filling him in on what and who she and Andy found in the secret passage but before she could finish, Evan interrupted and asked where Jack and Andy were.

"Jack has gone to find Beatrice so that she doesn't discover that Renee` is missing and Andy went along to find Julie."

"Maybe I should go see if they need some help."

"Actually I need you, Aimee and Renee` to go with me to find out what secrets Beatrice has hidden in the old servants quarters."

"Martha and Franklin, you need to keep a watch out in case something goes wrong."

"I just don't get it, sis, if Beatrice kidnapped Renee` then why don't we just call the police and have her arrested?"

"Because she is a loose cannon, Evan, and we have no idea what else she has been hiding. If we have her arrested, she may clam up and never tell us what we need to know."

"She called Jack Renee` tonight and that's why he has gone to find her. Martha told him where to find the sedatives so he can slip one in her tea."

"Why do you want to knock the old girl out, sis? Are you hoping she talks in her sleep?"

"No, silly, we are going to slip Renee` back into the passageway and follow her in the morning when she goes in to feed him and take him for his exercise."

"He said she mentioned the treasure to him and that she knows exactly where it is and if Renee` is gone, we will never find it and no one will ever own Willow House."

"Well is that so bad?"

"Yes, Evan, it is. Our great grandfather caused a lot of pain for many people and our mother was one of them. I believe it's time to rid Willow House of Tempest Bienvenue once and for all."

"But what if she has already discovered that Renee` is missing?"

"I thought the same thing but Jack said she was in no shape to go that far into the secret passage tonight and besides; Renee` said she brought his dinner to him earlier and that she never comes back to check on him until morning."

As Jack and Andy walked up the steps to the front porch of

Willow House, Andy said he would search the downstairs for Julie while Jack went upstairs to check on Beatrice.

"Beatrice," said Jack, as he gently knocked on her door, "are you there?"

Julie opened the door and said that Beatrice was in the bathroom changing into her nightgown.

"She doesn't feel very well, Mr. Bloom, so I made her some chicken broth and brought it up for her."

"That was very sweet of you, Julie and I will make sure she gets it, but I need you to do me a big favor."

"Certainly, Mr. Bloom, what can I do for you?"

"Go downstairs and find Andy. He will explain it to you."

"But shouldn't I tell Miss Beatrice goodnight? She reminds me so much of my grandmother."

"I'll tell her for you, Julie, please hurry and find Andy, okay?"

Just as Jack close the door behind Julie, Beatrice came out of the bathroom in her robe and slippers.

"Oh Renee`, I didn't expect to see you. I thought you might be having dinner with your father."

Jack realized that she had slipped back into the past and that she mistook him for Renee`, so he played along.

"Of course not, my dear, I knew you were not feeling well so I brought you some nice chicken broth and some tea."

"Just climb into your bed and I will bring it over to you."

As Beatrice took off her robe and climbed into bed, Jack took the sedative from his pocket, opened the capsule and emptied into her tea.

"Here you go, my dear, some nice warm broth and some hot tea."

But before he could set the tray down on her lap, she looked at him and screamed.

"What are you doing in my room? Get out, get out right this minute."

Chapter Forty Six

Andy heard the scream all the way in the dining room downstairs and as he ran into the living room, he saw Julie headed upstairs.

"Julie, stop. Please don't go up there."

"But I heard Ms. Beatrice scream."

"Julie, please come back down here. I know that Jack is with Beatrice and I promise you that she is alright."

"But she screamed and I'm afraid that…."

"Julie, you have known me for quite some time and you know that if someone were in trouble, I would be the first to go to them right?"

"Yes sir I do know that. Mr. Joe and Ms. Angela are always saying such nice things about you but…"

"Then trust me, Julie. Beatrice is not well and Jack is the only one that can help her right now."

"Please just come out onto the front porch with me for five minutes and I will explain, then if you still want to go up and check on her, I will go with you."

Andy didn't know if Beatrice had her speaker turned on in her room, but he didn't want to take any chances. He knew that Jack could control Beatrice, but he couldn't be sure of how she would react if Julie showed up.

As soon as Andy stepped out onto the front porch with Julie, he noticed that Madison was headed toward the house.

Thank God, he thought, *I can't imagine how I would ever explain any of this to Julie.*

He then told Julie that Madison had something very important to speak with her about and t after she spoke with her, she would understand what was going on at Willow House tonight,

"Madison, I thought that you were all going to check out the old house."

"Yes, Evan, Renee` and Aimee are there now."

"I thought I should check and see if Julie was okay."

"What do you mean check and see if I was okay?" said Julie "What is going on here, please tell me."

"Madison, I need to go up and see if everything is alright with Jack so if you will please explain everything to Julie."

"Yes, please do check on my brother."

"Julie, I have to ask you some questions. I have a strong suspicion that you are a descendent of Tempest Bienvenue and if that's true, the last place you need to be right now is with Beatrice."

Meanwhile Jack was trying to calm Beatrice down.

"Beatrice, what is the matter? Why are you so upset?"

"Mr. Bienvenue, what are you doing in my room? Get out or I will tell Renee`. I do not think he would like the fact his father was in my room, do you?"

"Beatrice, it's me Renee`. I just brought you some broth and tea."

I knew you were not feeling very well and I just wanted to make sure that you had some nourishment."

As Jack walked toward her with the tray, Beatrice began to relax a little.

"I'm sorry, my dear, the light is rather dim and I am so very tired. I think I shall just rest."

"Yes, my love, I do believe that rest is what you need but please take a sip of tea, it will make you sleep do much better."

Beatrice was so exhausted that she didn't resist Jack when he gave her the tea   and it was only a matter of minutes before she was out like a light.

As Jack opened the door to leave Beatrice's room, he saw Andy in the hallway, headed toward him.

"Everything went according to plan, Beatrice was exhausted so the sedative didn't take long to take effect, but what did you do with Julie?"

"She's with Madison. Evan, Aimee and Renee` are out at the old servant's house so I think we need to go find them and take Renee` back to his cell.

Beatrice should be out all night, but just in case she walks in her sleep, it might be a good idea if Renee` is where she left him."

Jack said that he agreed, but that he really hated to put Renee` back into that room.

"The poor old guy has had his first taste of freedom in such a long time and it just seems ashamed to have to lock him up again."

"Jack, he is so happy that he has you and Madison and Evan that he is willing to do anything to make things right for all of you."

"I know that, Andy, but now we have to break his heart all over again. He thinks his daughter is alive and I just don't know how we are going to tell him that she was killed in a car wreck less than a year ago."

Chapter Forty Seven

Evan and Renee` were trying to find a way into the old house when Madison and Julie arrived.

"Aimee" said Madison "I cannot believe they haven't found a way in yet."

"I know it seems strange Madison but it looks as if there is a brick wall on the inside of the house."

"What do you mean a brick wall inside the house?"

"Well you know that all the doors and windows were boarded up so Evan got a crowbar from the tool-shed to pry them off and it seems that there is brick behind every opening in the house."

"But that just doesn't make sense Aimee. If someone put a brick wall up inside the house, then how did they get out?"

"Think about it sis" said Evan as he walked up behind her with the crow-bar in his hand.

"That's where the secret passageway leads isn't it?" said Madison "But why would anyone want it bricked up?"

"That's exactly what we are going to find out before we leave Willow House" said Evan.

"But Renee`, you have lived here your entire life" said Madison "Didn't you know the secret passage led to the old house?"

"Sweetheart, I didn't even know there was a secret passage."

Evan said that the best thing they could do at this time was go find Jack and Andy and decide what to do next.

"That won't be necessary" said Jack as he and Andy arrived at the old house.

Evan, Andy, Renee`, and I will go back into the secret passage and find out why Tempest had the brick wall built.

"That's fine" said Madison "Julie, Aimee and I will wait for you in Beatrice's room, but what about Franklin and Martha? Does anyone know where they are?"

"We are right behind you" said Martha "We are in this together, right Franklin?"

"That's Right Martha. For the first time in my life, I have a family and no one will take that from me.

Martha and I will go through all the other closets in the house and see if there are any other entrances to the secret passage."

"Yes because it doesn't make sense that Beatrice would have the only entrance to the secret passage in her room" said Madison.

"Well actually it does" said Franklin "You see, that was Renee's room until he disappeared and it was Tempest's room before that so Beatrice must have known about the secret passage and that is why she chose that room.

She may have already checked to see if there were anymore openings, but I'm going to check for myself, just to be sure."

As everyone headed back up to Willow House, Renee` asked Franklin what he meant when he said that he finally had a family and that no one was going to take them away from him.

Franklin looked over at Jack as if to ask if it was okay to tell him and Jack just nodded his head up and down so as they continued their walk, Franklin told Renee` the real history of Tempest Bienvenue and Willow House and how the two of them were actually brothers.

Though Renee` was surprised, he was also happy at the thought of having a brother and as he stopped and put his arms around Franklin's neck, he said.

"I believe you are the best of the Bienvenue men because you did not know that Tempest was your Father."

"My God Renee`" said Franklin. "How can you say that? You turned out to be a very fine man in spite of knowing Tempest was your Father. That truly speaks volumes about you."

The two men then just burst out in laughter and Jack, Evan and Madison realized just how much alike they were.

Madison was thinking about her Mother and what a kick she would get out of seeing her Father and her Uncle together at last.

I'm sure she would get a kick out of just hearing laughter coming from anyone that lived in Willow House she thought.

As Madison, Julie and Aimee walked back to Willow House, Julie asked Madison why she thought she might be a descendent of Tempest Bienvenue.

"I can't tell you exactly why sweetie but I promise we will find out.

Have you any idea who you were named after?"

"Yes, my Grandmother said that I was named after a very beautiful lady named Juliette but she never told me who she was."

"I'm almost afraid to ask this question but what was your Mother's name?"

"Her name was Renee`, just like your uncle Renee`."

And Renee's wife was named Juliette Thought Madison *A little more than coincidence I think.*

Chapter Forty Eight

After Jack, Evan, Andy and Renee` made sure that Beatrice was still asleep, they opened the closet and headed back to where Beatrice had been holding Renee` prisoner.

"I have never been Closter phobic Jack but this is pretty hard for me right now. I never thought I would ever see daylight again and technically I haven't, but I also never would have believed I would willfully go back into the place I have been held prisoner in if I every escaped. I must be a lunatic."

"No you are not a lunatic" said Jack "You are someone my Mother would be very proud of."

"It's a little late Jackie. If only I could go back and change the past."

"You know my Mom called me, I mean calls me Jackie so maybe she is somehow here and telling us that it's never really too late Uncle Renee`"

Evan looked at the two of them and just shook his head.

"I thought I was the smooth talker in the family but it seems that I was wrong."

"Oh don't worry Evan" said Jack "You are still the smooth talker, it's just that I have listened to you for so many years that I became half-way decent at it myself."

"In other words, you learned at the foot of the Master?"

"Yes Evan, I learned at the foot of the Master."

"Okay, if you put it that way."

By this time they had reached the room that Renee` had been held prisoner in and Jack and Evan stood on either side of him and promised him that they would make sure that this would be his last night without freedom.

Jack then said that it wasn't necessary that Renee` stay all alone.

"In fact, Beatrice won't be awake until morning so we should all stay together and find out if the secret passage leads to the old house.

Renee`, you said that Beatrice always brought you to a place that you could see daylight through your blindfold and you could smell fresh air right?"

"Yes but it couldn't be the old house, because there were no walls and windows, remember?"

"That's right, but that doesn't mean that the secret passage ends there now does it?"

"Jack" said Evan "people in this area don't build underground to start with so…"

"I know what you are about to say Evan but it doesn't mean it never happened. There is an underground tunnel in downtown New Orleans that people walk though from a parking lot to a casino and New Orleans is below sea level."

"And you know this how?"

"It doesn't matter how I know this Evan, I'm just suggesting that there is a possibility that Tempest Bienvenue could have built an underground tunnel and that it could very well lead from the secret passage to the old house."

"I say we check it out boys, after all we have plenty of time before Beatrice wakes up and I have spent quite enough time in this room."

As the three men made their way through the secret passageway, Rene` asked Jack and Evan if his daughter had a happy life.

"I'm afraid I didn't do much to make her life happy here after her mother died.

I spent so much time grieving that I neglected to see how much my daughter was grieving as well.

"I only hope she will forgive me."

"Our mother gave us a wonderful childhood Uncle Renee`.

Evan, Madison and I could not have had a happier, more loving Mother."

"You speak of her in the past tense Jack, why is that?"

Jack could tell that his uncle was getting a little suspicious so he thought that maybe he should go ahead and tell him that their beloved Mother, his daughter was gone, but he decided that the time was not right and after all, the old man had suffered so much in his life.

Yes, this could wait a little longer thought Jack.

"Look Jack."

It was Evans voice that interrupted Jack's thoughts.

"What is it Evan?"

"It looks like another doorway in the wall." And just as the words left his lips, the wall slid open and there stood Franklin and Martha.

Renee` began to shake his head very slowly and said "How could I have lived in this house for so many years and not have known about any of this?"

"I grew up in this house as well Renee`" said Franklin "and I never knew there were doorways leading to secret passageways. Don't you think that our Father took every precaution so that we never found out?"

"I know you are right Franklin still…"

Jack interrupted and asked Franklin what room he and Martha were in.

"This room belonged to your Mother Jack. As a matter of fact, after she left, Tempest insisted that it be kept exactly as she left it and no one was ever allowed to use it. I can see why now. We have been through all of the rooms in the house and this is the only other one that has a doorway to the secret passage."

"But why would her room have a door to the secret passage in it?" asked Andy

Chapter Forty Nine

Madison, Julie and Aimee brought some chairs into Beatrice's room and as soon as they were settled in, Julie began to question Madison about why she and her brothers thought that she might be a Bienvenue.

"Sweetheart, my brothers and I have grown up not knowing anything about our Mother's side of the family. It has just been since her death that we have learned that we even have relatives on her side. You probably know more about the Bienvenues than we do."

"Not really Madison, whenever my Mother brought their name up, my Grandmother just changed the subject. She said that the Bienvenue family was off limits as far as she was concerned. She said that they were very bad people and that she did not want her family anywhere near them.

I guess I was not that interested in them; however, my mother was totally mesmerized by them."

Madison realized that she needed to tell Julie everything she knew because she and her brothers needed all the help they could get at this point so she brought her up to date about the Bienvenue family history, at least as much as she knew.

"Wow, Madison, this is like something out of a sci-fi movie."

"I agree Julie, secret passages, unknown relatives, but hey, this is happening to me as well."

"I'm sorry Madison but this is Ocean Springs, Mississippi for God's sake, not Transylvania."

"We're not talking vampires Julie, just some very eccentric and in some cases, some very cruel people."

"Look, I know that I am not really involved in this family thing" said Aimee "But I have lived here my whole life and I was right there with Andy and the other kids every Halloween.

Willow House and the Bienvenues were always a mystery in this town.

I would think it would be a great privilege to find out that you are actually a part of the Bienvenue family."

"Aimee, my Mother was a Bienvenue and she was not very proud to be one so maybe Julie and I are not so privileged after all."

"You are absolutely right Madison. I had no right…"

"Stop Aimee, I'm the one that had no right.

I'm sure that Willow House seemed like a wonderful place to live if you grew up in Ocean Springs, but my brothers and I never heard of Willow House until our parents were killed in a car wreck so you can see why I don't think it's a very special place.

Actually, it seems like a place that my Mother considered a prison, and was very happy to escape."

"How about we just change the subject you two." said Aimee "in fact, here's a positive thought to ponder. If the guys find what they are looking for, Renee` won't have to stay in the secret passage tonight and Beatrice won't be a problem any longer."

"That is a nice thought" said Julie "but what will we do with Beatrice? She might just be my real Grandmother."

Suddenly the lights began to flicker and Madison remembered that she saw some candles in the kitchen pantry.

She told Aimee and Julie that she heard earlier that there was some bad weather moving in later tonight so she had better go and get some candles just in case.

"That's not necessary Maddie" said a voice that seemed to come out of nowhere and just as the three women were about to bolt from the room, the closet door opened and out stepped Martha.

141

"You scared us to death Martha."

"I'm sorry Miss Madison, it's just that I heard you say that you were going for candles and I wanted to catch you before you left. I guess I didn't think about how frightening it would be to hear someone's voice in the room, yet not be able to see them.

Please forgive me Miss Ma......"

"It's okay Martha, I'm not sure it would have been any less frightening if the door opened up before you spoke. I guess all our nerves are on edge.

Anyway, what did you mean that it wasn't necessary for me to get candles from the kitchen?"

"Oh, it's just that we keep candles in all the rooms. You wouldn't want to go roaming around Willow House in the dark.

Beatrice keeps candles in the drawer next to her bed in case her flashlight doesn't work. She has this phobia about being in the dark."

"Okay, at least we know where they are if we need them and by the way Martha, how did you get into the secret passage?"

"Franklin and I found another entrance from your mother's old room.

We ran into your brothers and Mr. Renee`, so they asked me to check on you and make sure everything was alright."

"Franklin went to close the storm shutters. He asked that I get some fresh linens; because the weather was going to be pretty rough and it would be safer for our guests to stay here for the night."

"I agree, Martha, if that's okay with Aimee and Julie."

"Hey ladies, we have a mystery to solve so I'm not going anywhere," said Aimee.

"Yes, and I may have found a family I never knew existed so storm or no storm, I'm…"

"My God, what is that sound?" asked Madison as she jumped from her chair and ran to the window. "It sounds like…"

"Like a freight train," said Aimee. "Help me get Beatrice into the secret passage, NOW!"

Chapter Fifty

As Jack, Evan, Renee` and Andy made their way through the secret passage, Andy said it felt as if they were beginning to go downhill.

Evan said they were probably descending into the gates of Tempest Bienvenue's hell.

Jack said he felt it also and Renee` said he had no doubt that they were going downhill because Beatrice took him on this walk daily and there was a portion of the walk that was downhill.

"We should be veering to the left in a couple of minutes and after that, and if I'm right, there will be another decline and if my sense of direction is right, we will arrive at our destination in about five minutes."

Martha had no longer made it to the linen closet when she heard a rumble that sounded vaguely familiar to her, and as she stopped to listen a little closer, she heard Franklin yelling for her to get inside the secret passage.

By the time Madison, Julie and Aimee got Beatrice into the secret passage, the house began to shake but the three continued to move deeper into the passage, dragging Beatrice along with them.

As they reached the area that Renee` was held captive, by Beatrice, they stopped and placed Beatrice on the very bed that Renee` was confined to for so long.

Madison said they should try and find Jack, Evan and Andy. Julie volunteered to stay with Beatrice while they were gone.

"Madison, I don't know for sure if she is my grandmother or not, but if she is, I need to be here with her when she awakens. I feel like she's a very, tormented soul, but I also saw the look in her eyes when she thought I might be her granddaughter."

"You understand, don't you?"

Madison noticed a pair of handcuffs and keys hanging on the wall so she told Julie that she would leave her there on one condition.

"I'm going to put one of these cuffs on her wrist and one on the bed. Before you protest, know that I'm doing this for her own good, as well as yours."

"I do understand, Madison, but I need for you to leave the key so I can uncuff her if I need to."

"Fine, but I want you to leave the key on this hook, unless you absolutely have to have it."

Aimee said she would be happy to stay with Julie, but Julie said Madison needed her help to find the others and Beatrice would probably sleep until morning anyway.

As Jack, Evan, Renee` and Andy approached the end of their journey, they all began to feel as if something was not quite right.

Andy said that there were some pretty strong thunderstorms out in the Gulf and they were probably entering the sound.

Jack said Franklin and Martha were taking care of everything on that end.

"Franklin has lived here his whole life and has weathered much worst weather than what we are expecting tonight."

"He has told me some hurricane stories that you would not believe, so I know the ladies are in good hands with him."

"This is it boys. This should be the end of the line for us."

"This can't be the end, Renee`" said Andy, "we are still in the passageway and it seems to be a dead end."

"Yes, but Beatrice did something to make a door open because I could hear it open and I could see the sunlight through my blindfold, so I suggest we all start looking for a way into that room."

As Franklin made his way up the stairs, he noticed that Martha was waiting for him at the top.

He yelled for her to get inside the secret passage but she refused to budge until he was safely by her side and they could take refuge together.

"What were you thinking, Martha? You could have been hurt."

"But I wasn't, and considering all the years we were unable to be together, I'm not about to abandon you now."

You know, Franklin, if Julie is Beatrice's granddaughter, and she really does know where the treasure is, she has probably been waiting all these years for her to grow up so that she would make sure that Julie was the Bienvenue that claimed the treasure and Willow House, as well, still I can't help wondering why she didn't have her daughter, Julie's mother, claim the treasure."

"I have no idea, Martha, but I suspect we are about to find out."

"I hope so, Franklin, for everyone's sake."

Chapter Fifty One

By this time Madison and Aimee had reached the end of the secret passage.

"What the devil, the secret passage dead ends at a wall?"

"I doubt that, Maddie, I'm sure there is either another room either behind one of these walls or under this floor."

"Hey, you're the spy here."

"Not really, Madison, it's just that Andy always says that if something doesn't make sense then there is a usually a reason and it just doesn't make sense that a secret passage would end nowhere and besides, if it did end, then where are the guys?"

"Now I'm beginning to worry, Aimee."

Franklin and Martha knew that Madison, Aimee and Julie had probably taken Beatrice into the secret passage when they heard the tornado, but they decided to make their way back toward Beatrice's room just to make sure they were okay.

Franklin said they probably would have taken Beatrice to the room where she held Renee` prisoner because it had a bed and any supplies they would need, but by the time they arrived, all they found was Julie, handcuffed to the bed with a gag in her mouth.

As Franklin pulled the gag from her mouth, Martha was searching everywhere for a key to the handcuffs.

"It's no use, Miss Martha, she took the key with her."

"What happened, Julie, where is everyone else?"

"Madison and Aimee decided to go find the guys and I said that I would stay here with Beatrice.

Madison insisted on handcuffing her to the bed but when she

left, but when she woke up and said that she needed to go to the bathroom I took the handcuffs off.

I honestly didn't think she would hurt me, but when she came out of the bathroom, she had a gun in her hand.

She made me handcuff myself to the bed and she put a washcloth in my mouth so that I couldn't call for help. As she left, I saw her put the key to the handcuffs in her pocket."

"Look, sweetheart. It's not your fault. Beatrice is mentally deranged. I'm just glad she didn't hurt you worse than she did, and by the way, how do you feel?"

"I'm okay, just a little shook up."

You two need to go find the others because there is no telling what Beatrice will do if she finds them first, especially since Mr. Renee` is with them."

"We can't leave you here alone, Julie."

"That won't be necessary, Franklin, I just found a spare key under a loose floorboard in the bathroom. It must have been where she kept the gun."

"Great, let's get Julie free and then I want you two to call the police and get in the car and go straight to the police station and wait."

"I'm not leaving you, Franklin," said Martha, "so please don't waste your time trying to convince me to go."

"I'm not leaving either," said Julie.

"I have a cell phone in Beatrice's room so you two go ahead and I'll wait for the police, otherwise it will take them too long to find the secret passage."

"Fine, but wait for them outside, please.

I know Beatrice went to find Renee` and the others, but I would feel better if you hide until the police arrive."

"I will, I promise, Mr. Franklin, and you two please be careful."

"Remember, she has a gun and you have nothing to defend yourself with."

"Let's pray that it doesn't come to that, my dear," said Franklin, as he and Martha hurried off to find Beatrice.

Chapter Fifty Two

"I give up," said Evan. "There are four of us here, and one of us is a detective. It would seem that if there really is a room on the other side of this wall, one of us would have found it by now."

"Don't be so impatient, my dear," said a voice that seemed to come out of nowhere and within seconds, the wall opened up to reveal Beatrice standing in the middle of a huge solarium with a gun pointed right at the four of them.

It was nighttime so all you could see through the glass was the storm raging outside.

"Do come in everyone."

"Jack, Evan. I see that you have met your grandfather Renee` and what a surprise it must have been for you, Renee` to find out that Franklin is your long lost brother, oh and look who else has arrived."

As Madison and Aimee entered the room, the wall seemed to close on its own.

"Beatrice? I thought you were---"

"Were what, Miss Bloom? Handcuffed to the bed?"

"Oh I'm much smarter than any of you gave me credit for."

"You see, Mr. Bloom, when you gave me the cup of tea, I pretended to sip some of it, but when you turned your back to go and sit in the chair I poured it all in the plant next to my bed."

"But you thought I was Tempest, and then you thought I was Renee`"

"Again just a trick to make you think I was losing my mind, why I'm as sane as you are, Mr. Bloom."

"I doubt that," said Evan.

"I suggest you refrain from your usual sarcasm, sir, or you might not live long enough to enjoy the surprise I have planned for you."

As soon as Julie reached Beatrice's room she quickly grabbed her purse to search for her cell phone.

Where is it? She thought, *I know it was in my purse when I left home.*

My God, could Beatrice have taken it from my purse when I went to make her some tea?

She remembered seeing a phone in the living room so she hurried downstairs as quickly as possible only to find that the line was dead.

She assumed the storm was to blame until she noticed the line had been cut.

I guess there's no point in checking the whole house, she thought, *I'm sure if there are other phones, she made sure that those lines were cut, as well, and I have no idea where anyone else's cell phone could be, I'll just have to drive to the closest neighbors house and call the police from there.*

Oh ,please, don't tell me she took my keys too.

The storm seemed to be getting worse and as Julie ran to the front door to see how much damage had been done on the grounds, she knew beyond a doubt that no one would be leaving Willow House tonight.

Chapter Fifty Three

Franklin and Martha were nearing the end of the secret passage and all they were hoping against hope that the police arrived before Beatrice harmed anyone.

"Franklin, I'm so worried that Beatrice might have hurt someone and I feel so guilty that I didn't realize sooner how deranged she is."

"Martha, it's not your fault. I knew she was a little strange, but it was not until she locked us in the attic that I began to realize that she was a little more than strange. Still, I never thought she would go so far as to keep someone locked away for months and that she would even resort to murder if she had to."

"You know, Franklin, it makes me wonder now if she had something to do with Miss Juliette's death."

"I wouldn't doubt it now, considering the extremes she went to in order to keep Renee` for herself."

"Look, Franklin, this is the end of the tunnel, now what?"

On the other side of the wall, Beatrice was almost ecstatic at the thought of having every last descendent of Tempest Bienvenue under her control.

As she continued to hold her prisoners at gunpoint, the floor on one side of the solarium opened up and she ordered everyone over to the opening.

"Please form a single line, everyone, and kindly descend the staircase in the floor, otherwise I will be forced to execute each one of you, beginning with the ladies."

Andy whispered that he didn't doubt that she would do exactly what she said and they were better off doing what she wanted, for the time being, so one by one they went down the stairs and as the last one arrived, the stairs folded up to the ceiling and the opening closed, leaving everyone in total darkness.

"I can't find any way to open the wall, Martha, so maybe this is just what it seems, a dead end."

"It can't be a dead end, Franklin; otherwise we would have run into someone on their way back."

"Yes, but we must have missed an entrance somewhere else, so I suggest we back track and see if we can find it."

"It just doesn't make sense though. Why would you build a passage that led to nowhere?"

"To throw people like us off, I guess.

Martha, you know that Tempest was a very strange man; however, he was an extremely intelligent man, also, so I can see him building a room that no one could find and we do know for a fact that there is a room because Renee` said that Beatrice took him to this room every day."

"But how did Beatrice find it?"

"I wondered when the two of you would show up"

Startled, Franklin and Martha turned to see the wall sliding open and Beatrice facing them, gun in hand and a look on her face that nearly caused Martha to pass out.

"What is it, my dear? You look like you've seen a ghost"

"Do come in, you two, and that is an order and please don't bore me with your silly question like the others did, I just don't have the time."

Again, the floor opened and Beatrice asked that Franklin and Martha to take their place with the others in the room below.

As the opening in the floor closed, Beatrice turned to face the opening to the tunnel, smiled and said "And then there was one"

Chapter Fifty Four

I know what I need to do, thought Julie, as she made her way into the Library.

If I am a descendent of Tempest Bienvenue, then most of those people in the secret passage are my family and I will not let them down, the way that my great grandfather did.

As the storm continued to rage, Beatrice felt as if her time had finally come because she was now in control of Willow House and all of the living descendents of Tempest Bienvenue, all except one and she would be arriving soon.

"Listen, someone's coming down the stairs," said Andy. "Everyone hide, if that's at all possible, just in case Beatrice decided to come down here and finish us all off."

"And what are you planning to do?" asked Madison.

"Maybe I can reason with her."

"Or maybe you are planning to use yourself as a decoy so that the rest of us can escape."

"Hey guys, are you down here?"

"Franklin, yes we are down here. Are you okay?"

"Yes, Madison, Beatrice and I are fine. Are the rest of you okay?"

"Yes but what about Julie, is she with you?"

"No, sweetheart," said Franklin, as he reached the bottom of the stairs and could finally see Madison's face. "Julie went back to call the police. She will be able to lead them to the secret passage, so it shouldn't be too long before we are rescued."

"Uncle Franklin, you know Beatrice better than anyone. Did you ever think that she was capable of anything so demented?"

"I'm sure he did," said Evan, "after all, wouldn't you stay in a house with someone that you felt was capable of kidnapping and maybe even murder?"

"I'm sorry, Uncle Franklin, Evan is right. That was kind of a dumb question. I know you would have gotten Beatrice some help if you had known that she was…"

"Yes I would have, Maddie, unfortunately Beatrice was a master at hiding her feelings. I guess she never got over Renee` and somehow faked his death so that she could have him all to herself."

"Well now, that's another matter, just how do you fake someone's death?"

"You know, Evan, now that I think about it Beatrice was always involved when someone from this family passed away."

"The afternoon that Rene` disappeared Beatrice said that he went for a walk on the beach and that was the last we saw of him. She said that he was very depressed because his beloved Juliette and his only daughter were lost to him forever. I guess she was planting the seed for suicide and of course his body was never found."

"Then there was Juliette. No one was around when she died either."

"Yes, but there had to be something left of the body in the attic."

"That's right, Jack, but now I wonder if Beatrice was the one to start the fire."

"The police said the attic door was locked when they arrived, which really didn't make sense at all, but I guess it eliminated the idea that foul play was involved."

Andy then asked Franklin what caused the fire and Franklin said that they determined that it was caused by a candle. They said that it must have caught her clothes on fire because all they found was a skeleton, a zipper from her dress and some jewelry."

"Well at least we know that she didn't fake our grandmother's death"

"I wouldn't be so sure of that if I was you, Evan, something is not quite right about Juliette's so called accident, in fact I would love to see the police report on that one, and speaking of the police, they should be here by now."

"That is if Julie was able to call them," said Madison. "Her cell phone could be dead and as far as I could tell there was only one phone in Willow House and it was a land line so it might be out also."

Andy said that rather than dwell on whether or not the police were coming, the best thing they could do was continue to look for a way out of there.

"You're right. Andy, I didn't mean to worry anyone; I guess I'm just worried about Julie and I'm hoping that she doesn't try and find us on her own."

Chapter Fifty Five

As Julie left the library, she couldn't help but wonder if her plan might just backfire and get everyone killed.

Stop it, she thought, *I just can't afford to let myself think that way because there are too many people depending on me.*

I can do this if I just stay calm.

But as she headed up the stairs to Beatrice's room, she felt as if she were going up against Tempest Bienvenue himself.

As she made her way through the door to the secret passage, she wondered where it ended and why it was built in the first place.

I sure do hope I'm not taking on more than I can handle, and as if on cue, Beatrice appeared, gun in hand and Julie's thoughts became reality.

"I thought you might be headed this way, since you couldn't call for help and I knew the storm would prevent you from leaving the house."

Julie knew that the only way she would be able to outsmart Beatrice was to play her game, she just prayed that she had armed herself with enough information from the family history books in the library to carry it off.

"Oh, I wasn't trying to go for help, Grandmother, quite the opposite, in fact."

"What do you mean by that? I heard you say that you were going to call the police, but of course you couldn't, could you?"

"That's right, Grandmother, I was going to call the police, but I soon realized that you made sure no phone calls would be made from Willow House tonight, and yes I did think about driving to the police station, but of course there were no car keys to be found anywhere."

"You have lived here long enough to know that it would be impossible for me to go anywhere, by foot, during a storm because of the rising water, not to mention the lightening."

"You know you are a very clever girl, Julie, but I do wish you would stop calling me grandmother."

"And why is that?"

"Because I'm not your grandmother, in fact I'm nothing to you and you are nothing to me."

"I beg to differ, Grandmother. I believe that your daughter was raised by your twin sister, Bernice, and I also believe you planned it all, so someday you would be able to use your daughter to claim Willow House as your own."

"Alright then, little missy, if that were true then just how do you think I would be able to claim Willow House for myself when there were other descendents that had the opportunity to claim it for themselves."

"Oh yes, they had the opportunity alright, but you were the only one that knew where the treasure was and you made sure that no descendent of Tempest Bienvenue would ever discover it and after everyone failed, you intended to produce this long lost daughter that belonged to you and Renee`."

"My goodness child, you really are a descendent of Tempest aren't you?"

"From my perspective, Grandmother, you seem more like a descendent of Tempest Bienvenue than I do."

"I don't think I like your tone, missy, and unless you are blind you must see that I have the gun, which makes me very much in charge, doesn't it?"

"Oh I know that you have the gun, Beatrice, but I have something you need, so I really don't believe it would be in your best interest to kill me."

"I am an old lady, Julie, and I am growing very tired of your games, so either tell me what you know or prepare to join the others."

"Very well, Beatrice, I will share what I know and then you will share the treasure with me."

"And if I decide not to share the treasure with you?"

"Then one of us will die."

Chapter Fifty Six

"Hey guys," said Madison, "come see what I found. It looks like more open passages."

"To God knows where, I'm sure," said Evan.

"At least be grateful the old loon didn't take our flashlights away from us."

"Oh yeah, that's right, Maddie, we should be grateful the old crone left us flashlights. She probably wanted us to find these tunnels cause they lead to a snake pit and that will save her the trouble of killing us herself."

Andy said that whatever reason Beatrice had for not taking their flashlights, he still thought exploring the tunnels would be better than waiting for her to shoot them like fish in a barrel.

He then decided they should split into four teams, one team for each tunnel and each team should have a man on it.

"Now I'm not being chauvinistic, ladies, it's just that…."

"I don't think you need to explain it to us, Andy," said Madison, "we are pretty smart females, after all, and I for one definitely want a male with me, you know, just in case of snakes or something."

"Okay, then it's decided."

"Madison and I will be a team, Jack and Rene`, Franklin and Martha and Evan and Aimee."

Franklin said he was sure that Beatrice put them in this basement for a reason.

"She must be sure that there is no way out."

"Yes, but I'm not sure there is no way out," said Andy. "I find it hard to believe that anyone as clever as Tempest Bienvenue would ever design a prison that he could become trapped in himself."

"But wouldn't Beatrice know if there was a way out?"

"Not necessarily, Franklin, you see Beatrice has probably been to just about every room that the secret passages lead to, at least the ones she could find."

"What if there are other rooms she never discovered?"

"Then I say what are we waiting for, let's find a way out."

"That's the spirit, Franklin, but before we split up, everyone remember to leave a trail so you don't get lost. Something tells me that may have happened to others before us."

"I don't doubt it," said Madison, "the tunnels that lead away from this dungeon remind me of the catacombs."

As everyone began to gather whatever objects they could find, to leave along their trail, Andy said that everyone should return in one hour unless someone found a way out in which case that team would return and wait for the others.

Jack said he felt that if one team found a way out, one could come back for the others while one went for help.

Andy said that would have to be a judgment call,

"If you really feel it's safe for one of your team to go for help, then by all means, make the call, otherwise we are better off staying together."

"Makes sense to me, Andy," said Jack. "Now let's get going before Aunt Bea returns looking for you and Opie."

"Very funny, Jack, see you all in one hour."

Chapter Fifty Seven

As Julie stood before Beatrice, she tried very hard to remain calm, but seeing the dead look in her eyes made it very hard to control the fear she felt inside.

I know she is an old lady, she thought, *but she does have a gun and from the look on her face, she wouldn't mind using it on me.*

I have got to remain calm.

"So, little missy, which one of us do you think will die?

It seems to me that I stand a much better chance of surviving than you do."

"Oh, I don't think you'll shoot me, Beatrice, because then you will have nothing."

"You must have everyone else held captive somewhere or maybe you have already done away with them and since my mother was your last hope, you have no choice but to partner up with me."

"You know there is another way that I can have Willow House *and* the treasure. As long as Franklin is alive, we can remain here until we die."

"Yes but where is Franklin now?"

"Just cut the crap, old lady. You know, as well as I do, that I am all you've got."

"Okay, just say that I do partner up with you, how do I know you won't throw me out as soon as you legally inherit Willow House?"

"Well that would be pretty stupid of me don't you think?"

"If I threw you out, then you would have nothing to lose and

I'm sure you would just love to tell the police that I'm not really a Bienvenue after all."

"What do you mean that you are not a Bienvenue?"

"I mean that I was adopted, well not really adopted."

You see, my mother's best friend became pregnant, but she didn't want me so guess who agreed to take me and raise me as her own?"

They never knew I was aware of any of this but I was such a little sneak that I listened in on their conversations and just before my so called adoptive mother passed away, I overheard your sister tell her that she was the daughter of Rene` Bienvenue. She said that he had gotten the housekeeper pregnant and when Tempest found out, he sent her away to have the baby and told her she could remain in his employ as long as she returned without the child and kept her mouth shut. I guess Renee` didn't want his wife Juliette to find out so he kept quiet as well."

"Well it seems that the housekeeper had a twin sister on the other side of town who agreed to take the child and raise her as her own."

"I guess my Mother wanted nothing to do with the Bienvenues because they gave her away."

"It was then and there that I decided that one day I would claim my birthright, but of course I don't really have a birthright do I?"

"So what's the point to all of this?"

"The point is that if I claim to be the daughter of Rene` Bienvenue and you back me up then we can both have the whole enchilada."

"I really don't want this old creepy place, but I do want the treasure."

"As the last of the Bienvenues, I will inherit Willow House and being such a kind and decent person I will sign the rights to the house over to the saintly lady that took care of my ancestors for so many years."

"I'm sure there will be a clause that states that if I pass away, the estate reverts back to you, right?"

"Beatrice, I am appalled. Have you not done your homework? The will clearly states that whoever inherits Willow House also inherits the bank account."

"All I have to do is sign away my rights to Willow House and any funds connected to the estate, and it is all yours, free and clear; no clauses whatsoever."

"Of course we know that the treasure is a separate part of the estate, and that no one knows about it except you and me and all I want to do is take myself and my treasure to a tropical island somewhere and party til I die."

"You know, Julie, you really are so much like Tempest Bienvenue that I'm sure he would have been so proud to call you his descendent; however, that is not important."

"I see no reason why we cannot strike a deal between the two of us. I do have the real birth certificate that proves that your mother was a Bienvenue."

"And I have a birth certificate that says I'm her real daughter also because my mother insisted that her friend put her name on the birth certificate so there would be no question that I was born to her."

"How did she…"

"Get away with it? She helped deliver me at home, so it was easy to pretend that she was the mother, so what do ya think? Do we have a deal?"

"Yes, Julie, we do have a deal, now come with me and I'll show you where your so called relatives are."

Chapter Fifty Eight

As Andy and Madison made their way through the tunnels, Madison said that if they ever made it out, she was going to write a book about Willow House.

"I believe it will be a best seller, don't you Andy?"

"There is no doubt in my mind that it will be a best seller, Maddie, no doubt."

"You called me Maddie and no one has ever called me Maddie except my family."

"Guess that means that I'm part of the family, that is if you'll have me?"

"Of course we'll have you, Andy. I believe that Jack and Evan already think of you as a brother."

"I'm not really asking if Jack and Evan will be my brothers Maddie, I'm actually asking if you will make them my brother-in -laws."

"Your brother – in…. oh you mean your brother – in – laws?"

"Does that mean you are asking me to marry you?"

"I am, Maddie. I know we have not known each other for very long but I do know that I have fallen madly in love with you. I feel as if I have been waiting for you my whole life and that is enough to convince me that we belong together."

"You know what, Andy?"

"What, Maddie?"

"I am also madly in love with you and YES I will marry you, or as you put it, I will make Jack and Evan your brother- in- laws, although you may want to rethink that one."

"I'm sorry I don't have a ring, sweetheart, it's just that I had no idea that I would be proposing to you tonight; however, I would like to seal my proposal with a kiss and worry about a ring later." And as Andy reached for Maddie, she lost her balance and fell back against the wall of the tunnel and as she regained her balance, the wall began to slide upward into the ceiling, revealing a very sterile room very much like a hospital waiting room.

Andy quickly grabbed Madison's hand and as they entered the room, they couldn't help but notice there were two small tables in the room and as they moved closer, Maddie recognized one of the magazines on the table as being the newest edition of *Southern Living*.

"Andy, someone has been in this room recently because that is a new magazine."

"You're right, Maddie," he said, as he picked the magazine up. "I can tell by the date that it's recent, but how did you know it was new before we got close enough to see the actual date on it?"

"I mean I'm not totally dumb, so I did notice that it had Thanksgiving stuff all over the cover, but that wouldn't necessarily mean that it was from this year."

"I'm beginning to feel paranoid about my profession or…. wait a minute, I get it, you're one of those psychics aren't you?"

"Think about it, mister, *I'm not totally dumb,* if I were psychic, would we even be in this underworld?"

Andy, *Southern Living* was my mother's favorite magazine so after she passed, I continued her subscription because it made me feel close to her. "

"This issue arrived right before we left Shreveport, so I brought it with me in case I needed something to read, ha, ha, ha."

"And here I thought you were just a better detective than me."

"Look, Andy, there's another room."

"Well, we've come this far, we might as well see what's behind door number two."

Andy noticed there was no door knob so he tried pushing it open, and even with Madison's help, it wouldn't budge.

"I guess this is another one of those doors that slides open, only we don't have any idea where the lever is that opens it."

"Let's not worry about it right now, Andy. We said we would meet back up with the others in an hour and the hour is just about up."

"I agree. Let's go see if they have discovered anything and if not, then we can bring them back here and we can all search for a way into the new secret room."

But as Andy and Madison turned to leave the room, the wall closed before they could get through and out of nowhere came a voice all too familiar to both of them.

Chapter Fifty Nine

Beatrice led Julie back her bedroom and when they arrived, she told Julie that she was about to show her the real brains of Willow House.

"Open the closet dear and pull the lever that opens the entrance to the secret passage."

Once inside the tunnel, Beatrice pulled a device from her pocket that looked like a small television remote.

Julie watched carefully as Beatrice turned to the left and pointed the device toward the wall. She then pushed the top left button and the wall slid open to reveal what seemed to be a video surveillance room.

"Quite impressive isn't it my dear?"

"My God, Beatrice, what is this place?"

"I'll explain later, right now I need to check on my guests, oh and if you have any thoughts of overpowering me and releasing my prisoners, think again."

"Without me you would never be able to reach them before they all died of asphyxiation."

"You see, every part of the underground quarter's air supply is on a timer that is controlled by me, and you, my sweetheart, have no idea how or when I reset it. I will tell you this though, you could never free them without help and by the time help arrived, they would be dead before they could figure out how to turn the generators back on down there."

"Listen, Bea, I don't care about those people, hell, I don't even know those people. All I want is the treasure you promised me and a one way ticket to anywhere tropical, that way we both win. You get to be the queen of Willow House and I get as far away from Willow House as possible."

"Very well, we can get started now that you understand that if you interfere with my plan, your plan to live in the tropics is history."

Julie noticed that Beatrice placed the remote back in her pocket and walked over to what seemed to be the brains of the surveillance equipment.

Boy I sure wish Andy could see this stuff, She thought, *I'm sure he could figure it out in a heartbeat.*

Suddenly, several of the screens in the room lit up and from where Julie was sitting, she could tell that there was a group of people on one screen and only two on another screen.

"Well, well, well, I certainly didn't think they would have found the special living quarters so quickly even if little Miss Bloom is as nosy as her mother, and her boyfriend is a detective."

"Come over here Julie and see what control I really do have over Willow House."

Julie watched as Beatrice closed the door to the room that Andy and Madison were in.

"How in the world did you close them in? I never saw you push a button."

"As I told you, little girl, I am in total control of Willow House so don't even try to second guess me."

Julie could see that Beatrice was getting a little too excited so she decided to try and lead her in another direction.

"I can see that you are in control of Willow House and it is as it should be."

"Just keep your mouth shut while I deliver a message to two of our guests.

"Well, Miss Bloom, I see that you and Colombo found the living quarters reserved only for our very special guests."

"What do you mean by very special guests, Beatrice?" said Andy.

"Patience, my dear, you will find out as soon as the others arrive."

This woman is totally deranged, thought Julie. *There is no way she's going to let me leave this house. I just need to keep my cool until I can come up with an idea.*

"Now it's time to for me to lead the others to their final destination."

"Not that I really care, but what are you going to do with everyone once they are all together, kill them?"

"Kill them, of course not, Julie, darling, if I kill them then I would have to find a way to dispose of them and it is so much more fun having them under my command."

"I am finally the Lady of Willow House because, there are no other Bienvenue descendents left to take Willow House away from me."

"So you are going to keep them as prisoners?"

"Prisoner sounds so harsh, my dear, I prefer to call them my special guests, besides they had an opportunity to leave here, so it's their own fault they ended up as my permanent guests."

"Yes, but have you thought of what you are going to tell the police when someone files a missing persons report."

"Of course I have, I'll just say they all went out in the boat and never returned."

"What boat?"

"I have no idea, Julie. You see, there are several boats in storage on this property that have not been used in a very long time. I'll just say I have no idea which one they went out on and that I don't even know how many were stored here because it was not my business."

"Don't you think it's going to look strange that Franklin and Martha went along on the trip?"

"Not at all, my dear, in fact it makes perfect sense. Franklin always went out with Renee`, so he knew how to run the boat and he was also very familiar with the waterways in the area."

"I'll say they went out deep sea fishing and Martha offered to go along and prepare lunch for them. She did love the water and Renee` would often allow her to accompany him and Franklin on their fishing trips. Renee` would act as if they needed her along to make sandwiches and serve them but I knew he brought her along because he felt sorry for her."

"But Beatrice, everyone was here last night for the Halloween party."

"I know that, my dear, but the storm will be over soon and I'll say they left at daybreak, after the storm passed and you are going to be my witness."

"You are going to say that Andy asked you to call his parents and tell them he went out deep sea fishing and would be in touch when they returned."

"You'll say that you stayed here for the night because of the storm, and the reason you didn't go along with them was because you get seasick."

"My God you really have thought of everything, haven't you?"

"Yes and I'll bet you are wondering if I'm going to keep my side of our bargain or throw you in with the others."

"As a matter of fact I was worried about that until you said that I was going to be your witness that the others really did go out on a fishing trip."

"You can't very well do away with me, not after I vouched for you because that would look very suspicious, wouldn't it?"

Chapter Sixty

Everyone returned from the search, but Andy and Madison, and Renee` was getting very worried.

Aimee reminded him that she was in good hands with Andy, but he knew, first hand, how devious Beatrice could be and he was worried that she might just have plans to hurt Madison, because she was his granddaughter.

"Look, I 'm very concerned About Madison and I think we need to go and look for her."

"I agree with you, Renee`," said Franklin. "They should have been here by now."

"Look at them," said Beatrice, as she and Julie watched everyone enter the tunnel in search of Andy and Madison, "they are so predictable."

"I don't really care how predictable they are Beatrice, I just want to make sure that you don't intend to put me in there with them."

"Of course I won't put you in there with the others, dear. I would draw way too much attention if you went missing, so soon after the others, besides if you decided to develop a conscience it would be way too easy to blame you for the entire plan."

Julie knew that Beatrice probably could convince the police that she was an innocent old lady because she was certainly conniving enough.

"I guess we do have to trust each other to a point, but I would feel much better if I could have the treasure, like you promised me."

"In due time, dear, it would look pretty suspicious if you

took off for parts unknown before talking to the police. You know they are going to want to speak with the last two people that saw our guests alive."

"Beatrice, what will you do if one of your guests gets sick or hurts themselves?"

"I thought you didn't care about those people."

"I don't, I was just curious."

"Yes, well I don't have to tell you what curiosity does, do I?"

I noticed that Beatrice never took her eyes off the screen as she talked to me and as soon as the group had almost reached the area where the entrance to the special guest quarters were, she pulled the remote out of her pocket and pushed a button.

The door that was previously locked, in the room where Andy and Madison were being held, suddenly opened up and Beatrice ordered them both to pass through the door.

"Why should we?" asked Andy.

"Because your friends are just outside, and I can't allow them to enter until you are safe and sound in my holding room. You see it's sound proof, so they won't be able to hear you in there, but don't worry, I'll let you out as soon I let them in and if you refuse, I'll just cut off the air supply in the tunnel."

Julie thought this would be the perfect time to let them know that she was alive and well.

"Hey she's not kidding, people, she has quite a little control room up here and she can see and hear everything you do, so if I were you, I would do what Aunt Bea says."

"How dare you speak to my guests without my permission, I am the Lady of Willow House now and what do you mean telling them about my computer room?"

Julie realized that Beatrice was so upset that she forgot to turn the microphone off so she knew she must choose her words carefully so that Andy and Madison would realize that she was doing her best to set them free.

"I'm sorry, Beatrice, I just wanted them to know you meant business. It's not like they know where the generator room is, that the computer system runs off of, though I think it's underneath that outside room you boarded up. You know the one I'm talking about, don't you, Beatrice, the one that everyone was trying to get into last night?"

Beatrice seemed to calm down a little and with a glazed look in her eyes and a slightly wicked smile on her face she said that Julie had no idea what she was talking about.

"Why that's just an old storage room that we no longer use, miss know it all, besides, it's none of your concern as to where the generators are stored, just remember who's in charge, I've waited many years to be in the position that I'm now in and no one is going to take Willow House from me, not even you."

"Then why were the windows boarded up?"

"Well, certainly not to hide the generators, do you think that the all knowing Tempest Bienvenue would have huge generators stored above ground for all to see, of course not, Tempest might have been the most vile human on the planet, but he was a genius, never the less, actually it was me that had the room boarded up because I discovered the whole operation after following him, but that is another story, now if you will excuse me, I need to get back to my guests."

"So, Mr. Bergeron, Miss Bloom; are you going to enter the holding room or do I suffocate your friends and family?"

Andy and Madison looked at each other and without a word they entered the holding room and as their door closed, Beatrice opened the door to the tunnel so that the other guests could enter.

Franklin suggested that Evan and Aimee stand watch in the tunnel just in case this was a trap.

"You know me better than I thought, Franklin, because this is a trap and if the whole group doesn't do exactly as I say you will never see your niece again."

"What have you done to her, Beatrice?"

"Take it easy, my love. Now walk over to the door on the other side of the room and look through the small glass pane.

You will see that Mr. Bergeron and Miss Bloom are quite safe and will be released as soon as all of you are inside, otherwise I will be forced to cut their air supply off and they will expire in a very short time."

Franklin walked over to the door and as he peered through the pane and saw that Andy and Madison were okay, he motioned for everyone to enter the room.

"Good boy, Franklin," said Beatrice. And after everyone was inside, she closed the door to the tunnel and opened the one to the holding room and as soon as Andy and Madison emerged, the door closed once again.

The group was finally all together again and knowing that Beatrice could hear their every word, they chose to greet each other with smiles and hugs. No words were really needed.

Chapter Sixty One

"Well isn't that special," said Beatrice, "half those people just met and they're acting like long, lost friends."

Julie wanted to say what she really felt, but if she did, Beatrice might really lose it and kill everyone.

"I agree with you, Beatrice, but let's not worry about those fools, according to my watch its morning and I am ready for phase two."

"Slow down, Missy, remember who is in charge here. We can't report anyone missing until tonight, so we need to get busy and get rid of the purses and cell phones that we know the ladies would have taken with them. You also need to call Andy's parents and I believe you need to call the *View* restaurant and tell them that you are not feeling well enough to come in today."

"Hey, they were here at the party last night so they will think that I'm just hung over or something."

"What do you care? You're leaving anyway and I don't believe you're going to need their references with the amount of money you will have."

"Oh, that's right, I forgot all about the treasure. So, Aunt Bea, just how much money is in the hidden treasure? It is money, isn't it?"

"First of all I find it very hard to believe that you forgot about the treasure when you speak of it incessantly, but to answer your question, its money and jewels, Julie dear, is that okay with you?"

"Perfect, Beatrice, just perfect, oh and in case you do get any ideas about snuffing me out, I have to tell you that I did forget to tell you one little detail about my life."

"What is that, my dear?"

"Well I guess I forgot to mention that I have a brother in Shreveport."

"What do you mean you have a brother in Shreveport?"

If I can make her believe this story, thought Julie, *then I might have to think about becoming a writer, as well as an actor.*

"Well, you see, my mother really did have a child before me and I guess he really is a Bienvenue, but he went to live with his father, in Shreveport, after high school and the last I heard he was about to graduate from Louisiana State University in Baton Rouge."

"Why didn't you tell me this, young lady?"

"Look, Beatrice, he doesn't know his heritage and he never will, so I just didn't see the need to tell you before."

"Then why are you telling me now?"

"Because I wrote a letter to him right after I found out that my mother was a Bienvenue, but I never mailed it."

"Why not?"

"Because my grandmother and my mother didn't want him to know that he was a Bienvenue. My grandmother told my mother that Tempest was the devil himself and that his son Rene` was just as evil, so they made a vow never tell him that he was a descendent of the Bienvenues."

"So was your mother ever married?"

"Of course she was married, but her husband was killed in a car accident a few years after my brother was born and she never married again. She moved back in with my grandmother. I guess my mother felt sorry for me because my biological parents didn't want me, any more than hers, wanted her."

"So what did you do with the letter, Julie dear?"

"Oh I stuck in my keepsake box and it's with most of my things that have already been shipped to my aunt's house in Shreveport, but don't worry, I will destroy it as soon as I...."

"I know, as soon as you get your treasure."

"Look, Beatrice, the way I look at it is that I'm honoring my grandmother and my mother's wishes. They didn't want him to know that he's a Bienvenue so when I get the money, I'll send him a check and tell him I won the lottery; however, if you get any funny ideas about throwing me in with the others, just remember that my brother will have access to my personal belongings and that could cause real problems for you."

"I told you, young lady, that I don't need the treasure because there is more than enough in the estate to take care of me for two lifetimes. I should be the one that's concerned. What if you decide to turn me in and tell your brother he is a Bienvenue?"

"The will states that a Bienvenue has to find the treasure in order to claim the estate. If you give me the treasure and I turn you in, the bank will claim ownership of Willow House and all the assets of the estate because the treasure was not found by a Bienvenue and if I turned you in before you give me the treasure, you would make sure no one ever found the treasure and again, the bank would still win, so what the hell do I have to gain by turning on you? Besides, you said if I contacted the police you would turn your guest's air supply off, so the way I figure it I'm keeping them alive by keeping my mouth shut."

"Alright, Julie, I'm a little tired of all of this. We both agree that this is a win, win, situation for both of us and if either of us turns on the other then we both lose and all the guests expire, so I guess we just have to trust each other from now on, right?"

"Easy for you to say, Bea, you have the gun and I have to tell you that it does cause me to wonder if I can really trust you at all."

"Oh for God's sake, Julie, take the gun, but before you do, remember that I still have the treasure and I do control the fate of our guest's and I would rather you shoot me than have to go to prison at my age."

Beatrice knew that if Julie was really after the treasure, she wouldn't shoot her because she would never get her hands on it and on the other hand, if she were trying to help the others get free, she couldn't afford to shoot her until the others were free.

As Julie took the gun from Beatrice she knew that she would have to make some sort of gesture in order to really gain her trust so she emptied the chamber and put the gun in her pocket.

"Okay, I have the gun and you have the bullets, now let's get rid of those purses and cell phones okay?"

Chapter Sixty Two

"Oh Jack, Evan, I'm so glad to see you. How did you find us?"

"I don't think we found you, Madison, I believe we were led here by Beatrice."

"You're right, Jack," said Andy "she told us to go into the holding room so she could let the rest of you in and she said if we didn't do what she said, she would cut the air supply off in the tunnel. I guess she wanted us all together so she could keep better track of us."

"What scares me is that it seems as if she has done this before," said Evan. "I mean why else would you have a holding room unless you needed to gain access to this room without risking the escape of your prisoners?"

"Oh I prefer to call you my special guests"

"Beatrice, please don't do this."

"So Rene`, what would you have me do? Set everyone free so they can turn me in to the police?"

"Beatrice, I promise that no one will turn you in. I will personally get you the help you need."

"That comment doesn't even warrant a response. I know you think I'm insane, but do you think I'm stupid as well?"

"Look, Beatrice, we both know that Tempest Bienvenue was a cruel man but there is no reason to take it out on his descendents."

"Oh my dear, Franklin, do you really think I am trying to punish the descendents of that demon? I have kept Rene` safe for quite some time now, until those meddling Blooms descended upon us."

"Have you not been paying attention to what I have been saying?"

"All I want is Willow House. I want to be in charge of everything that goes on in this house. I want to finally rule the Bienvenues instead of them ruling me."

"Beatrice, what are you talking about, Tempest is the only Bienvenue that ever ruled in this house. My mother was very good to you as was Juliette and myself."

"Oh yes, sweet Juliette, the love of your life. Ashamed she had to suffer such a horrible death, but life does go on doesn't it Rene`?"

"I just don't understand why you are being so cruel and why you kept me captive for so long."

"It doesn't really matter much now, does it Rene`."

You have joined sides with your relatives so you shall suffer along side of them."

"Beatrice, where is Julie?" asked Madison.

"Strange girl, that Julie, seems that all she wanted was the treasure all along, isn't that right, Miss Julie?"

Julie knew that she had to find some way to let the others know that she was playing double agent here so she chose her words very carefully.

"That's right, I've been playing you all along, in fact, I've already called your parents, Andy, and told them that you went out deep sea fishing and of course they have no idea that you will be lost somewhere in the Gulf of Mexico."

"They did tell me to give you a message though. They said they are having dinner at your supper club tonight and your brother and his wife are in town and they would love it if you and Madison could join them."

Andy turned away from the camera and walked over to a chair and sat down.

Madison followed him and as she sat down beside him and put her arms around him; he whispered something in her ear.

Madison then stood up and shouted at the camera.

"Julie, I cannot believe that you used us."

"Yeah, well, Madison, not everyone was as pure and sweet as you were in high school. I loved it when you said that you were considering becoming a nun. It was all I could do to keep from laughing right in your face."

"I told you that because I thought we were friends."

"I don't do friends, Madison, the only friend I have right now is the hidden treasure of Willow House, oh and remember that anytime we enter this room we can see you and hear you so don't think you can plan an escape."

"Hey, Beatrice, let's go have some breakfast, or is it lunch time now?"

"I do feel quite hungry, my dear, and after we eat, we can bring our guests some food as well."

"Did you hear that people? Please try and relax and Julie and I will bring you some sandwiches very soon."

Chapter Sixty Three

Andy noticed that the lights on the camera changed depending on what Beatrice was doing. If she was talking to them, the light was red and when they answered, it was green, and Andy knew enough about surveillance equipment to know that when it was off, there were no lights at all; however, he thought it best to do a little test just to be sure.

"Hey, Aunt Bea, could you maybe bring us some coffee? Or maybe a secret code to get out of here?"

"What are you doing, Andy?" whispered Madison."

"Oh I don't think it's necessary to whisper now sweetheart, you see Beatrice and Julie really have gone downstairs to the kitchen and they can only see or hear us when they are in the control room."

"So we were right when we thought that Beatrice had the house bugged and could hear us as long as we were inside?"

"Yes, you were right, but she could only hear you if she was in the control room."

"So what do we do now?" asked Jack.

"There's nothing we can do except wait, but at least we know that Julie is on our side."

"And we know this how?" asked Evan.

"Because Julie said that she called my parents and they said my brother and his wife would be in town and they would meet us at my supper club tonight and it just so happens that not only do I not have a brother, but the restaurant is closed tonight and the reason Julie knew is because…."

"Oh let me tell them the reason, Andy," said Madison. "Last night Julie asked me if Andy had any brothers in her age range."

"And I walked up about that time and told her that my parents had only one child because I was so perfect that they didn't need to try for another one."

"Can you believe he said that?" asked Madison. "But you know Julie also sent me a message that she was on our side when she said that I told her that I was thinking about being a nun."

"But sweetheart you went along with her. You said that you had shared that in confidence."

"Yes I did and it seems that I not only convinced you, but my brothers as well."

"Not me," said Evan, "I knew she was on our side when she said you wanted to be a nun."

"This is all very entertaining folks but I suggest we figure out what to do next," said Jack. "I happen to be a little cloister phobic."

"I agree Jack," said Andy, "the room we are in now is kind of like a waiting room and of course the other room was a holding room, so it stands to reason that there are actual living quarters down here."

As Beatrice and Julie made their way downstairs, Julie thought she should test Beatrice to see just how far she would go to protect her secret.

"I almost feel sorry for the guests, Beatrice, but when I think about the treasure and what a fun life I am going to have, I really don't feel that bad."

"It's not like you're going to torture them or deprive them of food or anything, are you?"

"Of course not, dear, they will all be as snug as a bug in a rug; however, you do know that there will be police investigations going on for a short period of time and I think that you should stay around long enough for them to be satisfied that there was no foul play involved in the disappearance of our guests."

"Aunt Bea, would I leave you in your time of need?"

"Julie, my dear, it is also your time of need."

"The police are going to want to question you, as well as me, and if you took off for parts unknown, well that would just look very suspicious, wouldn't it?"

"Hey I'm cool, Beatrice. I will answer all the questions that they ask of me and then I'll disappear. I promise not to leave you until the police are satisfied that everyone went out on the boat and never returned. That should take what, a day or two at most?"

"It could take a week or two, Julie; I just don't want you to trip up and cause someone to get suspicious."

"I promise to behave, Beatrice."

"That's good, dear. You know I will almost miss you after you leave Willow House."

"It's funny you said that because I was thinking the same thing. I almost feel like you *are* my grandmother. Maybe it's because we are so much alike."

"What do you mean by that?"

"Hey, it's not an insult; I just meant that we both have a soft spot for the underdog."

"And what underdog are you talking about?"

"The special guests of course. I know that you threatened to suffocate the whole bunch of them if I went to the police, but I really don't believe you would have done it."

"Really? Well that's where you are wrong because I would have no problem getting rid of everyone of them if it meant that I would have to leave Willow House."

"Whoa, chill, Bea, I get it and it really was a dumb thing to say because there will never be a reason to do away with them, besides, just think of how much fun it will be to boss the whole bunch of them around."

"Still, it's too bad you can't find a way to make them help out with the housework."

"Oh they'll help out alright, much more than you know, that is if they want to continue breathing."

I have no desire to touch that, thought Julie, *what I really need to do now, is focus on to get everyone out of* Willow House *Down Under.*

Chapter Sixty Four

"I give up," said Evan, "there is no way out of this room; this really is the twilight zone."

"Never give up, Evan, if there is a way in than there is a way out, we just haven't found it yet, but we will."

"Remember when Julie said she thought the generators were underneath the outside building that we were trying to get into?"

"Of course I remember, Andy, it was only about thirty minutes ago, although it does seem like a few weeks."

"Well it did seem really strange that the building was boarded up, because when we tore the boards off and looked through the bars on the windows, there was nothing inside."

"That's right, Andy," said Jack, "that's when we decided we could probably reach the room through the secret passage, but we never got the opportunity to try and find the room."

"Yeah, because we got caught."

"Little brother, you really are the voice of doom and gloom."

"I prefer to call it the voice of reality, besides, what difference does it make, we can't get out of this room, much less look for another one?"

Andy noticed the light on the camera was on so he motioned for everyone to be quiet.

"So how are my subjects doing? Have you figured out how to escape yet?"

"No, Beatrice, we were just discussing the fact that we are all starving and wondering where we were going to sleep tonight?"

1

"Oh, my dear, Franklin. It just so happens that Julie and I made you all a nice big picnic lunch and we will be bringing it down momentarily and as for where you will be sleeping tonight, well you're just going to have to wait and see what I have in store for you."

"That's what I'm afraid of."

As Julie followed Beatrice to the special guest quarters, she tried her best to memorize the way. She had already memorized which button Beatrice pushed on the remote to open and close the waiting room and which one was for the holding room, but getting hold of the remote was something she had not figured out yet.

"Look, the light is off again, which means that Beatrice is on her way down here to bring lunch."

"That's right, Martha, and I'm glad that you noticed. Hopefully we won't be here that long, but as a precaution, I suggest that we all pay attention to the camera."

"Okay boys and girls," said the all too familiar voice of Beatrice, "you know the drill." And as everyone entered the holding room, Beatrice pushed the button on the remote to open the door to the waiting room, and after she and Julie emptied the picnic basket, Beatrice pushed yet another button which opened a door on the opposite side of the room.

"Good God, Beatrice, you scared me again. I did not expect to see another secret door open. How the hell can you remember which one is which?"

"Practice, my dear, lots of practice."

Julie had always been frightened of Beatrice, but now she was actually terrified of her, after seeing what control she had over Willow House, both above and below ground.

"Calm down, dear, it's really not that complicated. Tempest taught me everything."

"But why you, Beatrice?"

"Because after I found out about the room, I went snooping around when Tempest was away and I found some papers hidden in the computer room that could put him away for a very long time. I made copies of them and put them in a safety deposit box to be opened, in case of my demise. I then made him teach me everything about his underground hideaway. My next step was going to make him change his will and leave Willow House to me, but the old devil had a heart attack and died, so here I was no better off than before; that is until I came up with my plan to eventually take over Willow House and have the Bienvenues work for me."

For a while it seemed as if nothing was going right. Juliette died, then Camille left and Rene` became very despondent and I feared that he would leave Willow House as well, so I began giving him small amounts of a drug that caused him to be confused most of the time and when he spoke of visiting Camille, I would cause him to become so ill that he couldn't go."

"Camille wrote to him for several years and I would help him answer her letters and promise to visit, but he backed out so many times that I guess she thought he didn't care about her and when he stopped answering her letters we never heard from her again."

"How come he stopped answering her letters?"

"Because they never quite made it into his hands."

"Eventually I had to stop giving him the medication because I was afraid it would kill him, so that's when I came up with the plan to fake his suicide. I notified Camille but she said she just couldn't bring herself to return to Willow House. Tempest was a very cruel man and Camille always blamed her father for not taking her and her mother far away from Willow House and of course right after she graduated from high school, her mother passed away.

"I can still hear her parting words as she walked out the front door. She said, *"Father please come with me, because if you don't I'm afraid I will never see you again. I don't believe I could ever step foot inside* Willow House *again."*

"But she did come back, didn't she?"

"Yes, but that's another story and right now we need to leave so our guests can have their lunch and get settled in their new living quarters. We can bring their clothes down later when we bring their evening meal"

Chapter Sixty Five

After Beatrice and Julie were back in the passageway, Beatrice used her remote to open the door to the holding room and after everyone was back in the waiting area, she and Julie left.

Madison and Aimee were the first ones to open the basket of food.

"Hold on, you two, don't you think we should check it out first to make sure the old bat didn't poison us?"

"What difference does it make, Evan," said Madison, "if we don't eat we'll starve to death, at least our last memories will be of food."

"Or excruciating pain."

"Evan's right, Madison, Beatrice could have put something in the food although I really don't think that she wants us to die."

"Why not, Andy?"

"Because she could have cut our air supply off and we would be dead by now, no I think she has other plans for us."

"I can't imagine what, it's not like she could sell us all to a traveling circus."

"Well, all of us, except you, Evan, I'm sure they could use you as a companion to the monkeys."

"Yeah and you could certainly clean up elephant…."

"That's enough, you two, I can't believe you can still find things to fight about, considering the situation we are in."

"Come on, bro, you know by now that Madison and I just bicker to entertain you."

"Hello again, special guests, I see you haven't eaten your lunch."

Hearing Beatrice's voice caused everyone to become silent.

Trust me, darlings, I didn't put anything in your lunch that could harm you in any way, on the contrary, I want you all alive and well for your big surprise."

"In a moment I will open the door to your suites, but first I want you to know that Julie and I will return later with some clothes for all of you when we bring you your evening meal."

Julie watched as Beatrice pushed another button and as the door to the suites opened, everyone walked through it like programmed robots.

"Now, my dear, why don't we go and gather some things for our guests before we have afternoon tea, oh and by the way, I will be taking my usual rest this afternoon so please make yourself at home, in your room of course."

"What are you going to do, Beatrice, lock me in one of the guest rooms? I thought we had a deal."

"We do, dear, it's just that I don't want you having access to my home while I am resting."

"Are you kidding me, you are really going to lock me up while you nap."

"I'm sorry, my dear, it's just that I will rest much better if you're not roaming around, perhaps trying to find the treasure."

As soon as the last of the group entered through the door, it closed behind them.

"It's a good thing I brought the basket of food cause it looks like we are going to be here for a while."

"That was a smart move, Evan, thanks for thinking of it."

"See, Maddie, Andy thinks I'm smart."

"Wait till he gets to know you."

"Look at this place, these suites are nicer than many of the ones I have stayed in," said Andy, as they all went from room to room "and best of all there are no cameras, at least none that I can see."

"There are six suites with bathrooms down here, what do you suppose Tempest used them for, Franklin?"

"Again, my dear Maddie, I have no idea. I still can't believe Beatrice found out about all this."

"Well you know, Franklin, Beatrice has always been very suspicious of Tempest and I guess that suspicion, combined with her curiosity and greed caused her to pay much more attention to what Tempest was up to than any of us did."

"You are right, Martha, everyone else stayed as far away from him as possible and I don't think any one of us cared what he was up to as long as it didn't involve us."

"I'm sorry Rene` I had no right to say those things about your father."

"You mean our father, Franklin, and you have every right to say whatever you please, I should be the one apologizing."

"I should have left Willow House long ago, before Camille was even born."

Juliette would probably still be alive and I would have been able to watch my grandchildren grow up."

"Please don't be sad, Grandfather, you have us now and we have you. I just wish our mother was…."

Okay you two," said Jack, "there will be time for reminiscing later, right now we have got to put our heads together and figure out how to get out of here."

"Yeah, right after we eat," said Evan.

Chapter Sixty Six

After Beatrice locked Julie in one of the guest rooms, she returned to her own room for a much needed nap.

"*Now what,* thought Julie. "*I have got to figure out a way to get everyone out of this house. I just hope they found my note.*

"Look what I found."

"What is it, Andy?"

"Well, Jack, let's just say that it's our first ray of hope in our quest for getting out of this place. It's a note from Julie. I guess she hid it in the bathroom when she and Beatrice brought our lunch down, it says *Not much time to write, doing my best to help. Will try and get more info from Bea about layout of underground & escape routes. Can't go to police, said she would cut off your air supply. No cameras or microphones in suites. Leave note for me in same place.*

"This girl is pretty clever."

"So what are we going to write back to her?"

"I guess we can start with asking her to learn as much as she can about which buttons do what, on that remote of Beatrice's. If she can get hold of that thing, we might have a chance. Even if she could surprise Beatrice and get it away from her while the two of them are down here, she could open the door long enough for one of us to grab the old girl."

As Andy began writing all this down on the back of the paper that Julie left, Madison was thinking about her mother and how much she missed her. For some strange reason she felt that her mother was very near. *Maybe it's because I miss her so much,* she thought, *or it could be because I am about to be with her again.*

"We have got to find a way out of here, Andy. I know that your family and Aimee's family will be heartbroken when Beatrice tells them that you never returned from deep sea fishing and I can't bear to think of what it will do my daughter, Camille."

"Don't worry, Rene`, there is no way we will let Beatrice hurt another soul. I promise you, we will get out of here and soon."

Madison knew she should tell Rene` the truth, but she just couldn't do it and as she looked at Jack and Evan, she could tell that they were thinking the same thing.

"Alright, everyone, the note is written and put back where Julie left it, now I think we should search every little corner of these rooms."

"What, in particular, should we be looking for?"

"Too be honest, Martha, I really don't know, but it's not as if we have anything else to do and who knows what we could find."

Julie must have dozed off because it seemed like only a few minutes had passed since Beatrice locked her in and yet here she was standing at the foot of her bed staring at her.

"You startled me, Beatrice, don't you believe in knocking?"

"Why knock, you couldn't open the door if you wanted to remember?"

"Oh yeah, you locked me in, didn't you?"

"It's time to get moving, little girl, we have lots to do. We have to gather a few clothes for our guests, but not too many because the police will wonder where all their things went. We already got rid of the purses and cell phones because they would have taken them with them on the boat."

Now when the police come, I'll tell them that you came back over this afternoon because we were planning a fish fry when everyone returned and you offered to help me get things ready."

"What things?"

"I don't know, silly, appetizers, cole slaw, desserts."

"I'm scared, Beatrice, what if they get suspicious?"

"Of what, that an old lady and a young girl lined seven people up, executed them and buried them in the back yard?"

"There are eight of them, Beatrice."

"But they don't know about Rene`, remember? Have you gotten suddenly dumb in the last few hours?"

"No, I didn't get suddenly dumb, Beatrice, I just forgot that you had the poor guy locked up for what probably seemed like a thousand years to him."

"Just go splash some water on your face and let's get busy. We also have to make dinner for our guests."

"Well I'm afraid that you will have to take that job on because I don't cook."

"Fine, then you can clean up the kitchen."

Chapter Sixty Seven

Andy watched as Madison slept and he couldn't believe that so much had happened in the short time he had known her.

For the first time in my life I have fallen in love and I end up locked up in an underground Holiday Inn with her and her entire family.

"What are you thinking about, Mr. Bergeron?" asked Maddie as she sat up in bed.

"That I wish we were already married and that this was our honeymoon suite."

"underground Willow House as a honeymoon suite? Remind me not to let you plan our honeymoon, that is, if you still want to marry me."

"And why wouldn't I want to marry you, Miss Bloom?"

"Oh, I don't know, maybe because you had one date with me and ended up in Bienvenue House of The Living Dead."

"Oh, I'm so glad that you still have a sense of humor, my love. That will come in handy when you and I get married."

"Oh, well he still wants to marry me, must be because of that lobotomy that we performed on him when he arrived."

Andy fell on the bed next to Madison and began mimicking Count Dracula when Evan walked in and asked what blood type Andy would like for dinner.

"Oh I've already chosen my blood type, in fact I will be having this same blood type for every meal."

"Hate to break up your party, Count, but I need Egor to help me with something."

"Jack, you know Egor was with Frankenstein, not Count Dracula."

"Franklin thinks there may be more in the generator room than generators."

"That's right," said Franklin, as he entered the room "That outside room was used as a kind of retreat. I remember that Juliette used to go out there and read sometimes because it was near the water and she could feel the breeze because there were so many windows."

"I wonder if my mother ever went out there to be alone."

"She did indeed, Madison. She used to say she felt like she was a thousand miles away from Willow House when she was out there."

"She would pretend it was her yacht and she would sail away to a different island each time."

"I guess my mother felt close to you even though she didn't know you were her uncle."

"I suppose she did, sweetheart, and I adored her as well. When she left, it broke my heart because she was the only light left in Willow house."

"I'm sorry, Evan, you said that you needed me for something."

"Yeah, it seems that Franklin thought that you and Jack and I should put our heads together and see if we can remember any little thing that our mother may have told us about her childhood."

"I told him that she never spoke of it except to say that she was an only child and her parents died when she was very young. She said that she was raised by an old aunt who had passed away."

"You know, now that I think about it, when I was very young, mom would tell me a story about a princess that lived in a castle near the water. She said that the princess was so very lonely that she dreamed that a handsome prince would come and rescue her, but he never did so she decided to sail away and find him herself."

"Of course she said the Princess did indeed find her prince and they lived happily ever after, then she would tell me that the moral of the story was that I should never wait to be rescued because, I, just like the princess, I didn't need to be rescued. She said that all I had to do was decide what I wanted and go after it."

"She was talking about herself, wasn't she, Uncle Franklin."

"I'm afraid she was because she was a very lonely little princess."

"Hey, I remember a story that she used to tell Jack and me. It wasn't about a princess, of course; it was about a mean old pirate that hid underground."

"She said that there was a family that lived near the sea and that they were a very happy family until the mean old pirate came out of the underground and made their lives very miserable."

"She said they had a son that loved to play on the beach and he had a special place near the water that he pretended was his ship, but in reality was nothing more than a building with lots of windows in it that the family members used as a retreat, until the son told his family that a mean old pirate appeared from below and told him never to come there again or he would harm his whole family."

"I guess mom knew that Jack and I needed to hear some action stories. I never dreamed that she was talking about her own childhood. Do you suppose the old pirate was her grandfather, Tempest Bienvenue?"

"It does make sense," said Andy "If your mother was in the outside building near the water, she could have witnessed Tempest come out of a wall from the secret passageway, or from underneath the room."

"But Andy, why would he have taken a chance on being caught?"

"I have an idea but it does seem farfetched. What if he knew that Camille was there and he wanted her to see him?"

"Your mother was young enough to believe him if he said that she must do as he said or he would hurt her father and mother."

"Yeah but what could he have wanted from her?" asked Madison.

"Maybe an accomplice, one that would do as he told them but keep their mouth shut."

"But why would my mother do that?"

"Who knows, maybe he threatened to hurt her mother and father. I have seen cases like that before, Julie. It's much easier to put fear in a child and make them believe that you have more power than you really do."

"If that's true, Andy, then I could see why my mother left Willow House and never returned."

"But she did return, sweetheart, and we need to figure out why."

Chapter Sixty Eight

As Beatrice prepared dinner for the guests, Julie wracked her brain to come up with a plan that would ensure that everyone would survive, even Beatrice.

"Beatrice, when do you think Andy and Aimee's family will start getting worried?"

"Well Julie, I would hope that two grown children, living on their own would not have their parents breathing down their necks."

"We, on the other hand, will have to be the ones that are worried."

"As soon as the sun sets we will call and say that we are concerned because they left at dawn and said they would be back by sunset."

"The police, of course, will say that maybe they are just a little late because they have caught a bunch of fish or maybe because they are having so much fun."

"We will then call Andy's family and express our concerns. They will in turn call Aimee's family and the next thing you know there will be a full fledged search."

"Naturally they won't be found and everyone will assume that they were lost at sea."

"Which would probably be better than being prisoners of Willow House."

"Julie dear, you are so very cynical and I really can't imagine why. I told you that our guests will be well cared for."

"I just don't understand how you will be able to take care of that many people by yourself. How can you cook for them and wash their clothes and what if they get sick?"

"I have a surprise for my guests this evening and the surprise will answer all of your questions."

"Won't the executor of the estate become suspicious when suddenly the food bill becomes so much bigger than normal, especially when you are the only one left at Willow House?"

"Not at all, dear, because as soon as you sign the estate over to me, I have total control of the money in the estate. No one will see the bills except me."

"Well all I can say is that you have certainly done your homework."

"Madison, what is it that you are not telling me?" asked Rene`. "I walked in just in time to hear Andy say that your mother came back to Willow House. I need to know when that was and just why she came back."

"I think it's time we told him, Maddie."

"Please, Jack, I can't…"

"You don't have to, it's my place to do it anyway."

Jack asked Rene` to sit down and by the look on his face, Rene` knew that the news couldn't be good.

"What happened to my daughter, Jack?"

"We really don't know what happened. All we knew was that our parents went on a trip and said they would call us when they arrived. They never said where they were going just that it was a much needed getaway and that they would keep in touch."

"They called several times to say that they were having a great time and would tell us all about it when they returned."

"But they never returned, Grandfather," sobbed Madison, "and I believe that Beatrice had something to do with it."

"What do you mean they never returned?"

Andy held Madison close to him and asked Jack to continue.

"Maddie didn't want to tell you just yet and I think it's because she really wasn't ready to re-live what happened and if we told you then she would have to go through the grieving process all over again with you."

"My daughter is gone, isn't she?"

Suddenly the door to the waiting room opened and Evan ran out to see what must have been their evening meal on two rolling carts

Madison ran into the waiting room and yelled out to Beatrice.

"I know you can hear me and I want you to know that I know that my parent's death was because of you."

"Just calm down, Madison, I was going to save your little surprise for after dinner, but since you seem to have gone mad I guess I will give it to you as an appetizer, although I so much wanted it to be your dessert."

By this time, everyone was standing in the waiting room and when the door to the holding room opened, no one had a clue as to what was about to happen.

Chapter Sixty Nine

"What are you doing to these people, Beatrice? I can't stand this any longer."

"Julie, my dear, you are much too high strung. Maybe I should take my chances and throw you in with the rest of them."

"I don' think so, Beatrice, because I have spoken with Andy's parents and they know that I didn't go with the others and besides, you need me to verify that I am the last of the Bienvenues or you are out on the street."

"You're right, Julie, but you also need me. Beatrice then pushed a button on her remote and said.

"May I please have your attention everyone? As you can see, I have opened the door to the holding room, but what you don't know is that there is another door on the other side of the holding room. I did want to wait until everyone had eaten and Julie and I had spoken to the police about your unfortunate boating accident; however Madison and Julie's untimely outbursts have caused me to believe that I should present you with your surprise a little early."

"Now, if everyone would please enter the holding room I will show you your surprise, and if any of you choose not to enter the holding room, well you know by now that I can control whether or not you take another breath."

After everyone entered the holding room and the door closed Beatrice said that she just wanted to go on record as saying that she was not totally responsible for what they were about to encounter.

"You all must know by now that Tempest was a vile man and

it's because of him that I had to do what I did; however, I want you to know that I have never really physically hurt anyone, at least not yet."

"Grandfather, Uncle Rene` please tell me what my great grandfather did that not only drove my mother away, but also drove Beatrice crazy, and let's not forget the fact that everyone was so terrified of him that they dare not make a move to stop him."

"Grandfather, how could you stay in a house that your own daughter hated so much? She obviously had a terrible childhood. Didn't you know how unhappy she was?"

"Every time we brought up her childhood she would either change the subject or say that she didn't remember that much and though she tried very hard to hide it, we could tell the subject was very upsetting to her."

"I felt very sorry for my mother, Grandfather and so did Jack and Evan so as we got older, we spoke less and less about her childhood"

"Madison, you have every right to be upset with me over what happened to your mother and I cannot blame anyone but myself and now it seems that my actions or lack thereof have trickled down to my grandchildren."

"You know, Madison, your mother didn't always hate Willow House, in fact her childhood was pretty normal until her last few years of high school. She stopped having friends over and she acted as if she couldn't wait to get away from here."

"Juliette and I tried to talk to her about it but she would just say that she had outgrown her friends at school and that her education was more important to her than having fun and if we pushed too hard she would say that she just didn't like living at Willow House and then she would ask if we could move away and I guess we would just make up excuses why we couldn't move at that time."

One day I finally told her that Willow House was my home

and I had no intention of ever leaving it and after that she never asked again."

"When she left, she told me that she wished that I had taken her and her mother away because if I had, she might be alive right now."

That hurt me terribly, Madison, and we didn't speak for several years then suddenly I began getting letters from her and the rest is history."

"I'm sorry, Grandfather, I didn't mean to blame you for everything. I know that you loved my mother, it's just so frustrating because I want to know what happened here that made her feel that she had to get away from here and never come back."

"My mother was so happy and content, yet she did come back here last year and we have no idea why."

After about fifteen minutes in the holding room everyone began to get a little cloister phobic.

"Hey, Beatrice," yelled Evan, "did you nod off and forget about us? It's getting pretty warm in here."

"Not hardly, Mr. Bloom, although you are quite forgettable, I just got so caught up in preparing your surprise that I didn't think about how warm the holding room could be."

"I'm just about ready, so be prepared for the surprise of your life."

As the holding room doors opened behind them, everyone turned to find the most startling scene they could ever have imagined.

Chapter Seventy

Madison was the first to move and Jack and Evan were close behind her.

"Mother, Daddy?"

"Yes, Maddie, it's us."

Rene` seemed to be unable to move and Franklin knew why. He looked at Andy and said, "It's Juliette, Rene's wife."

Hearing Juliette's name spoken seemed to bring Rene` back to the present and as he moved toward his beloved wife, he whispered, "my life just began again."

No one spoke for at least five minutes because they were all so busy looking at each other and hugging each other. Finally Madison asked if this was heaven and Evan said, "Of course not sis, if it was, do you think Beatrice would be in charge?"

"I heard that, Mr. Bloom, and I'll thank you to keep your insults to yourself. "

"Now I'm sure you will all want to get reacquainted so I'm going to leave you alone for awhile. Julie and I have to make a missing persons call to the police."

"My God, Beatrice, who are all those people you have locked up down there?"

"I can't take credit for all of them, Julie, just Camille and her husband, oh and Juliette, of course."

"Rene's wife? I thought she...."

"Burned to death? Well she didn't. I told you that I wasn't a murderer; now let's get out of here so that we can get ready for the next scene."

"This certainly does seem like a very low budget film to me, now if I could just wake up and find out that it's a nightmare I would feel much better."

"Yes and you would be much poorer also, wouldn't you?"

The door in the holding room that led to the waiting room opened up and Andy noticed the camera lights went out.

"Franklin, I think that Aimee and I will go back to our quarters so that Madison and her family can get reacquainted."

"Yes, I believe Martha and I will join you."

"No, please don't go, Andy, after all, you are about to become a member of my family and Uncle Franklin, you already are a member. I guess we'll just have to adopt

Martha and Aimee."

"Are you sure, Madison?"

"Quite sure, in fact I believe that whatever has been happening at Willow House is of concern to all of us."

"Maddie is right, Andy," said Jack. "We are all involved in this so I believe we should all take a seat and let our parents fill us in on how they ended up down here. From the looks of things I believe there will be plenty of time to catch up on what has been going on in our lives."

Zachary Bloom was the first to speak,

"I have no idea where to begin except to tell you how we ended up down here and then I believe Juliette can fill you in on what happened to her and the others that came before her."

"First of all I want my children to know that before we came to Willow House, your mother was ready to tell you about her childhood. She felt she owed you all that much; however, she felt she should return to Willow House once more before she spoke with you because she felt she needed to face her demons first before she spoke with you about them."

"A couple of years ago, Camille received a letter saying that her father had disappeared, and it was believed that he had committed suicide and there would be no memorial service."

"Your mother secretly grieved because she had never shared

her childhood with anyone except me and she made me promise not to ever tell anyone else, especially our children."

"Eventually she began having nightmares and it all became too much for her to bear, that's when she said she wanted to return to Willow House and find out once and for all if the nightmares were real memories or if she had just made them all up. I guess she had suppressed those memories for so long that she wasn't sure if any of them were real."

"Let me tell them the rest, Zach"

"Are you sure you are up to it?"

"Oh I'm up to it, alright, in fact it is long overdue."

"First, I want to apologize to my children for keeping my past a secret from them. My life was just so perfect and I was so afraid that if I spoke of Willow House, they might just want to go there someday and I could not risk that happening."

"As time went by, I watched you grow into such wonderfully responsible adults and I knew that it was time that I shared that part of my life with you, but only after I made the trip back first so that I could come to terms with my past."

"When we first arrived, Franklin was so happy to see me but Beatrice acted like she couldn't wait for me to leave. I guess she thought I was there to take over Willow House but of course that was the farthest thing from my mind."

"After a few days and nights in Willow House with no negative memories, I decided it was time that I brought my children here for a visit. I began to feel as if my past wasn't that bad after all and that maybe my mother's death affected me much more than I realized."

"One night I began to roam around the house when I thought everyone else was asleep because I wanted to see if I could bring back the memories of Christmas and summer vacations because I knew they must be buried somewhere deep in my subconscious."

"The only thing that made me feel a little fearful was the building down by the water, so I walked down there to see if it would jog any memories that would help me understand those parts of my past that I seem to have blocked."

"The closer I got to the building, the more afraid I became, then suddenly the memories came flooding back and I froze right there in my tracks for what seemed like an eternity."

"The next thing I remember was someone putting their hand on my shoulder and calling my name. I guess I started coming back to reality because I could vaguely hear her saying something about it being awfully late to be outside and that I should go back to bed and get some sleep, but I told her that I couldn't sleep because I finally remembered why I left Willow House and why I never told my children about my family."

"I told her that I wanted to go inside the building because there was an underground tunnel that led to that room and I wanted to find out what was down there."

"She said she knew about the underground and she promised to take me and Zack in the morning. She said that it was very easy to get lost so I shouldn't attempt it alone. I thought she sounded genuinely sincere so I went back to bed and early the next morning she woke us up and said that we should come to her room right away."

"I guess she didn't want Franklin or Martha to know what she was up to but I thought nothing of it at the time."

"When we got to her room, she brought us through the wall in her closet and led us right down here where we have been held captive since."

"Mother, this is all so bizarre, what did you remember when you went outside to the building?"

"I remembered my Grandfather Tempest coming up through what seemed to be a door in the floor in the building one afternoon when I was playing there. He wanted to show me the *underground city* as he called it. I was always a little afraid of him but the look he had on his face as he reached for me was terrifying."

"He must have seen my mother approaching through one of

the windows because he grabbed my arm and said that if I spoke of this to anyone, he would bury my mother and father in the underground city."

"I guess that I passed out from fear because the next thing I knew, my mother was kneeling over me, calling my name."

"I heard my grandfather tell her that he walked in and found me on the floor and when she asked me what happened, I said I didn't know and at that time I really didn't know. I knew that something was terribly wrong but I couldn't remember what it was. Now I realize that my fear of my grandfather's threat must have caused me to block the incident from my memory."

"I hated Willow House after that and I didn't really know why and until I grew up and moved away, I stayed as far away from Tempest as I could get because somehow I knew he was evil."

Chapter Seventy One

"Juliette, my darling, I cannot believe you have been down here all these years. I thought you were dead. I thought Beatrice was pretty obsessed with me but she is more than obsessed, she is a monster."

"Yes she is pretty deranged, Rene`, but it really didn't start with her. Yes she was the one that faked my death and put me down here but Tempest built this place and these other people you see are part of your family also."

"I don't understand, Juliette."

"Well it seems that Tempest built this underground city in order to keep the Bienvenue family in Willow House for eternity. The man was truly insane but also a genius and you will see why in a while."

"But why would he want to keep his family in a prison?"

"Because he wanted to have his own empire to rule."

"But most of these people are very young and there are children here, I just don't understand how that can be."

"Rene`, your father faked the deaths of several of his relatives and then kidnapped what he thought would be suitable mates for them. He also kidnapped several couples from other cities so that they could have children that would mate with the children of his family because he thought his plan would work. I guess he believed that he could pass the throne down to his descendents."

"When Beatrice found out about this place, she faked my death and threw me in here. She told me that Tempest was going to change his will and leave everything to her but she knew that he hoped to eventually bring you over to the dark side and throw her down here with the rest of us so she kidnapped you and faked your death so that Tempest would have no one to depend on except her."

She loved to torment me by telling me that she was keeping you near to her so that you would come to realize she was the one you truly loved."

"Needless to say, Beatrice had no intention of growing the population down here; however, she has kept us alive. There have been those that have died of old age, but thanks to your father, we have had wonderful health care. One of his kidnapped victims was a very young doctor and he has trained some of the others to assist him and a few are as knowledgeable as he is."

"We have all the medical supplies we need and surprisingly Beatrice continues to supply us with whatever we need so we have managed to stay in pretty good health."

"She was so delusional that she believed that someday, the two of you would rule the underground city together."

"My father was truly insane, wasn't he? What if one of you needed to be in a hospital?"

Juliette turned and addressed everyone in the room.

"I believe we have explained about as much as we can without showing everyone how extensive Willow House underground really is, but before we start the tour, I would like to introduce everyone to the two most inspirational people they will ever know."

"John and Maggie are the last couple that Tempest brought here and Maggie was pregnant at the time. Everyone that lived here prior to them has passed on."

"We all have so much respect for John and Maggie because they have managed to give everyone hope in spite of the fact that some of these people have never even seen a tree. Their own child grew up and wed one of the Bienvenue descendents and had children of their own and these children, their grandchildren are now adults."

"I know it almost seems like an Adam and Eve story, but Tempest Bienvenue could hardly be considered a God, though I'm sure he believed that he was."

"John, Maggie, would you mind taking our new residents on a tour of underground Willow House?"

"It would be our pleasure, Juliette."

Chapter Seventy Two

Beatrice appeared to be very distraught as she repeated her story to the local police department and Julie knew that she would have to play the game for a while longer or everyone in the underground city would die.

"You know that the Coast Guard is doing everything they can, Miss Beatrice, and there is nothing you can do at this point so why don't we go into the kitchen and I'll make you a nice cup of tea."

"That would be lovely, Julie, and maybe we could put on a pot of coffee for all these nice policemen as well."

"That won't be necessary, Miss Beatrice.," said the officer that had been questioning her."

"Of course it will be necessary, won't it Julie?"

"Yes, please allow us to at least provide your men with some hot coffee while you conduct your investigation."

"If you are sure it's not too much trouble, miss."

"No trouble at all, in fact I'll bring it out to the front porch as soon as it is ready."

Julie noticed that the officer that had questioned Beatrice was quite young, so she asked him how long he had been with the department."

"It actually seems like my whole life," he said, "you see my father is the chief of police and I can't remember a time when I didn't want to follow in his footsteps."

"Well I think that is very refreshing officer…."

"Michael, my name is Michael."

"And my name is Julie."

"It's very nice meeting you Julie; I only wish it was under different circumstances."

Julie was about to tell Michael that it was nice meeting him also when she noticed that Beatrice was glaring at her.

"You know I really should go and get the coffee started."

"Thank you, Julie, you know I do appreciate all the help you have been to me today, said Beatrice. "I just don't know what I would have done without her officer Michael."

As Julie made her way toward the kitchen she could hear Beatrice telling Officer Michael how she spent the night because of the storm and that after everyone left she offered to stay and help clean up from the party the night before.

"She is such a sweet young lady and to think that if she were not prone to sea sickness, she would be out there, lost with the others."

I really do feel sick to my stomach just thinking about what that old woman is capable of, thought Julie, as she went into the kitchen. As soon as the coffee was ready, she filled a couple of coffee carafes and hurried back out to the living room.

"I was only able to carry the coffee out so I'll have to go back to the kitchen for the mugs."

"Oh please, let me help you, Julie, my partner here can finish speaking with Miss Beatrice."

"I will not hear of it, Officer Michael, I will help Julie myself."

"Please, I really don't mind, in fact I insist.

I can tell you are pretty shaken up and my own grandmother would think I was pretty rude if I didn't offer to help."

There wasn't much that Beatrice could do to keep Michael from going to the kitchen with Julie so she just smiled sweetly and thanked him.

I guess I shouldn't worry so much, thought Beatrice, *that little girl stands to lose a fortune if she blabs and she knows that I could cut the air supply off and suffocate the underground guests before the police could figure out how to get them out.*

No, I don't believe she will say a word, especially after I told her that if she turned against me, I would have the police believing that she was my accomplice.

As Michael helped Julie gather the mugs and place them on the tray, he noticed that she was a little jittery.

"Julie, I know you must be pretty concerned about your friends, but you know they could have had mechanical problems and docked at one of the islands out there. It's really not an uncommon thing around here."

"Maybe the radio could have even gone out and they haven't been able to contact anyone."

Julie couldn't believe how concerned Michael seemed to be and it really upset her that she couldn't tell him the truth.

She knew that as long as she went along with Beatrice, everyone would remain safe, but if she made one wrong move, it could result in everyone's death and she knew that she could not live with that guilt, no, she would have to think of some other way to make sure that everyone came out of this situation alive.

"Thank you for your reassurance, Michael, and I know that you are right, I guess that I'm just a little tired."

"No, I think it's more than that, Julie, I think that you are hiding something."

Chapter Seventy Three

As John and Maggie led the new comers through the underground city, no one could believe their eyes.

"This really is a city," said Jack.

"It's sci-fi city," said Evan.

"It's fantastic," said Madison.

"How can you say it's fantastic?" asked Evan.

"Because I can see that our parents were not tortured."

"Well, ya got me there, sis, they were certainly not tortured; that is unless you understand that there is more than one way to torture someone, like not letting them go home to their family."

"I know what you are saying, Evan, I just meant that I'm so relieved that our parents were not tied up and beaten, that type of torture."

"Maddie is right, Evan. It was torture being down here, knowing that you thought we were dead and it was torture not being able to see our children, but your mother and I had each other, at least, and it could have been much worse."

"Oh, Daddy, I'm just so happy that you are both alive."

"I can't believe this place, Dad, it's totally self contained."

"It is that, Jack. There is everything down here to maintain life, everything, that is, except contact with nature."

"We grow all our own food, practically and Beatrice brings our paper products and such."

"As you can see, we have many bed rooms, a huge kitchen and dining room, a recreation room and everything else that your everyday mansion would have."

"You know if your Grandfather had built this underground

dwelling for a different reason I would say that he was a genius, but he built it to keep his descendents all together, dead or alive so that means he was completely insane."

Evan made some remark about genius bordering on insanity and said that if he ever came up with any outrageous ideas he wanted to be locked up.

"Oh, did I say locked up? Too late, I'm already locked up."

Zach began to chuckle.

"Evan, you have always been able to make me laugh, even under the worst of circumstances, and these are about as bad as they have ever been."

"I'm sorry, Pop, I guess jokes are not really appropriate right now."

"Hey, we're not dead, son, even if we do live underground."

"Now I know where I get it from," said Evan, as he put his arm around his father.

By the end of the tour Camille noticed that her children and their friends seemed exhausted.

"I'm sure are all hungry and tired so why don't I fix you something to eat."

"Actually we could use some food, Mom," said Madison. "Beatrice and Julie brought us some dinner but we didn't really have time to eat."

"Who is Julie, sweetheart?"

"Well, Mom, she is probably our only hope of ever getting out of this place."

Chapter Seventy Four

"Michael I don't know what you mean, what could I possibly be hiding?"

"Julie, I know I haven't been in law enforcement very long but I learned a lot from my father and the look of fear in your eyes tells me that you know something and are just too afraid to tell anyone."

"I know we just met but you can trust me, I promise I will protect you."

"Excuse me you two," said Beatrice, "are you finding everything okay?"

"Everything is fine, Miss Beatrice, Officer Michael and I were just on our way out."

Michael offered to take the tray out to the other officers and as soon as he was on the front porch, Beatrice grabbed Julie's arm and said that she had better be very careful about what she said to Officer Michael because she was not only playing with the lives of her friends, she was also facing prison time as an accomplice.

"Look, Beatrice, if you would just hand over the treasure, I would be on an island by tomorrow morning."

"Well, you know that's not going to happen, Julie, I told you that you would have to stick around a while until everything dies down, besides, you must certainly have some loose ends to tie up before you go."

"What do you mean loose ends?"

"Your house, your belongings, my sister's belongings; I would at least like to have a few of her personal things to remember her by."

Julie wanted so much to tell her that she didn't deserve to have anything of her sisters and thank God they were nothing alike, but she couldn't afford to upset her and cause her to do anything crazy, not that what she had done wasn't crazy enough.

"Oh, I think that can be arranged, Beatrice. The house has already been sold and most everything has been shipped to Shreveport; however I did leave some of my mother's and grandmother's keepsakes out to pack with my own things."

"You mean your adoptive mother don't you?"

"Look, Beatrice, she took care of me and loved me as if she was my biological mother and your sister was a wonderful grandmother, as well. I just wanted more material things than they could give me and that will never change, so lighten up okay?"

Before Beatrice could answer, Michael walked through the front door and into the living room where Beatrice and Julie were standing.

"Miss Beatrice, do you know which boat the group took out this morning? I have the coast guard on the line and they need some sort of description of the boat, they don't seem to find any recent boat licenses in the Bienvenue name."

"Oh, my dear" I have no idea. It has been so long since anyone used any of the boats and I never really paid that much attention to them. I'm not much of a water person myself."

"Well I'm sure he kept the paperwork on the boats, can I see his files?"

"Rene` evidently destroyed all his personal papers before he disappeared. For the life of me I can't imagine why he would do such a thing."

"What about his will? I'm sure there must be a copy of that somewhere."

"There would not have been a need for a will, Officer Michael, you see Rene` had nothing of his own."

"Tempest made sure that Willow House would never be sold to outsiders. His will stated that his family could live here as long as they wanted and they would be taken care of financially; however, if they left the house, they would never be allowed to return and they would not receive a dime."

"You mean he had no money of his own?"

"Technically he didn't, but he had access to any amount of money he wanted as long as his father was alive. I guess it's a little hard for you to understand this, Officer Mi…"

"Please, just Michael."

"Alright Michael, I'll try and explain the situation the best that I can."

"Tempest Bienvenue was a great inventor and his son, Rene`, worked right alongside his father ever since he was a young man."

"Rene had several pretty impressive inventions of his own but his father convinced Rene` to allow him to introduce them so they would have the recognition they deserved. I don't think Rene` really cared about the recognition or the money, he just enjoyed inventing things that made other people's lives easier, and I'm sure that he believed he would inherit everything anyway."

"You know, Michael, as unfeeling as Tempest could be, I believe that Rene` saw something in him that no one else could and I don't think he ever completely gave up hope, that someday Tempest would soften up and becoming the loving father he had longed for his entire life. Of course it never happened. Even after his wife died and his daughter left home, Rene` stayed by his father's side, until the day he died and as time went by, he became more and more depressed and then one day he just disappeared."

"Yes, I remember the story, but how is it that you knew about his financial situation?"

"I've lived here many, many years, Michael and I became a friend to Juliette, René's wife, and she confided in me because she had no one else."

"I'm sorry, Miss Beatrice, I didn't mean to offend you. I know you must be very worried about your husband right now, so I'll just finish checking the grounds and be on my way. Thank you for the coffee and it was nice meeting both of you."

Julie wanted nothing more than to stop Michael from leaving but she knew that if she did, Beatrice would lose what little sanity she had left and kill everyone in underground Willow House so she just smiled and said goodbye."

Chapter Seventy Five

"We don't know this for sure, Mother, but we think that Julie could be the granddaughter of Beatrice."

"Oh my God, Danielle had a daughter," said Juliette.

"Mother, who is Danielle?"

"Oh, Camille, I didn't want to tell you any of this because you have missed your own children so much and I knew that pain all too well."

"This is going to be very hard for me to talk about because your father doesn't even know about Danielle."

"Juliette, what are you talking about, who is Danielle?"

"Danielle is your other daughter, Rene`"

"You had the baby down here?"

"There is so much that this woman has stolen from me," said Juliette. "My husband, my daughters and my grandchildren, what kind of woman does this to another woman?"

"Camille, I probably would have gone to my death without ever telling you about Danielle."

"I'm so sorry, Juliette, I haven't even digested the fact that you are still alive, let alone that you gave birth to our baby down here."

"I understand, Rene, this is quite a shock for all of us."

"What I am about to tell you is very painful so I'm going to ask that you all remain very quiet until I am done, please?"

"When Camille was a senior in high school, I found out that I was expecting a baby and I was torn between excitement and fear because I knew that Camille wanted to leave Willow House as much as I did."

"I finally convinced Rene` that if we didn't leave Willow House, we would lose Camille forever because once she left, she would never come back."

"Yes, I remember, Juliette, and I also remember that you said you would not raise another child in Willow House but before we could tell Camille that we were going to leave, you died, or so I thought you did."

"I was so crushed that I didn't tell her about the baby because I was afraid that it would upset her even more, so I decided to release her and let her live her life free from what seemed to me to be a curse, the Bienvenue curse."

"Yes, well it turned out to be the *Beatrice Curse,* Rene`, because she overheard me speaking to my doctor on the phone. He had just confirmed what I already knew in my heart. I was expecting another child, though I was told that I would never have any children at all."

"I had no idea that she knew, until she walked in on me in the attic polishing Camille's cradle."

"She said that she heard me on the phone with my doctor and that she knew I was expecting another baby, but that she could not allow that to happen."

"She said that she was in love with you and that I had been a thorn in her side for too many years and that it was time that she took control."

"I was stunned, so I tried to reason with her but she grabbed me and put something over my face and I passed out. When I woke up, I was down here."

"Everyone took care of me and I had a healthy baby girl but the joy was short lived because less than a week after my baby's birth, Beatrice came and said that Franklin was gone and she and Rene` were together the way it was meant to be. She said that shortly after I died, he turned to her in grief and that she convinced him she was pregnant. She said that she faked the pregnancy and when it was time to deliver, she made sure that she was at her aunt's house in another city. Of course, she had already taken my baby from me and when she returned from her aunt's house she had the baby with her."

"I named her Danielle and she looked so much like you, Camille. I had already lost you and your father and when Beatrice said that I had to give Daniel to her, I felt as if my life was finally over. At first I refused but she said that if I didn't give her the baby, she would turn off our air supply and all of us would suffocate, even the baby."

"Everyone was so supportive and begged me not to let her have my baby but I couldn't let her die so I gave her my Danielle and I made her promise to take very good care of her. My only consolation was that she would be with her father."

"I don't even know what to say, Juliette," said Rene`. Beatrice lied to you about everything."

"Oh she eventually told me the truth, Rene`, because I begged her every day to let me see my baby and one day she just lost it and told me that she gave my baby to her sister as insurance that she would never lose Willow House. She said that she lied about the two of you being together."

"It seems that she told her sister a lie, as well, but with a different twist. She told her that she was afraid that Tempest would try and take the child from her if he knew that it belonged to his son, so when Danielle was born, she brought her to her sister's house and said that she hid her pregnancy from Tempest and Rene` for as long as possible and that she stayed with friends until her baby was born."

"She and her sister agreed that the only contact they would have with each other would be through mail that would be sent to a post office box that Beatrice had secured, just for that purpose, and for many years she brought me photographs of Danielle and would give me updates on her life, but one day she stopped bringing me pictures and giving me progress reports and when I asked her why, she said it was because her sister had stopped sending them. Her sister told her that she had come to think of

Danielle as her own daughter and that she thought it best to stop all communication."

"I remember that Beatrice was furious with her sister, for a while, but she soon calmed down and said that it didn't really matter because in time she would tell Danielle the truth; that she was a Bienvenue and in her deranged mind I guess she thought that it would all work out according to her plan."

"She told me all about the will and how no living Bienvenue descendent would ever be able to claim ownership to Willow House because she had the treasure."

"She also knew that our children were the last of the Bienvenue descendents who may try and claim the House; however, she wasn't concerned because she knew they would never find the treasure and that after she got rid of them, she would tell Danielle that she was her mother and she would allow her to find the treasure and claim Willow House for the two of them."

"Well, whatever became of our daughter, Danielle?"

"I have no idea, Rene`"

Chapter Seventy Six

Julie noticed that Beatrice looked exhausted so she suggested that they both turn in and get a good night's sleep

"That sounds good to me, Julie; I'll walk you to your room."

"That's fine, Beatrice, but don't even think about locking me in this time. I think I proved to you that I could be trusted when I didn't turn you in to the police."

"I won't completely trust you until you call me from some tropical island and tell me how much fun you are having."

"Believe me I can hardly wait, now if you don't mind, I am worn out and I think that we both need some sleep if we are going to face the police again tomorrow, not to mention the families of the victims that are lost at sea."

"Oh, and by the way, I'm going to have to run home tomorrow and get a few more clothes if I'm going to be staying at Willow House for a while."

Beatrice nodded her head and stood there as if she was waiting for Julie to close her door so that she could lock her in.

"Beatrice, I am going to take a nice long bath and then I'm going to put on one of those nice flannel gowns you supplied for me and then I am going to get into that big comfy bed and sleep for at least twelve hours, but if you lock my door, all bets are off, is that clear?"

"As a bell, my lady, and if you need anything else, get it yourself."

Julie stood in the doorway and watched Beatrice until she turned the corner at the end of the hallway, she then closed the door to her room and made a mental note to remove the door knob from her door if she had to stay her another night.

As she walked over to the window, she saw a light flash.

What the heck was that? She thought and just as she was about to walk away, she saw a ladder appear outside her window and the next thing she knew, Michael was standing at the top of the ladder, smiling as if the two of them were about to elope.

As Julie opened the window, Michael stepped in and Julie put her finger to her lips. She grabbed a pen and paper from the nightstand and wrote, *please do not speak, these rooms are bugged.*

Michael then wrote

"I hope I didn't frighten you, I just couldn't shake the feeling that you wanted to tell me something.

"Michael, if Beatrice catches you in here she will..."

"Hey, don't worry, she won't catch me. I was very quiet."

"But how did you know this was my room?"

"Because the only room upstairs that had a light on was this one so I looked through my Binoculars and I saw you talking with Beatrice and when she walked away, I knew it was your room.

I figured I should get up here pretty quickly before you decided to go to bed."

"I don't believe you. You're like a young Colombo, but with a Zorro flare."

I have an idea, lock the door to your room and we can go back out the window so that we can talk. My hand is cramping up from all this writing."

As soon as the two reached the ground Julie asked Michael if he had recently lost his mind or if he had always been insane.

"Hey, I told you that I had good instincts."

"Look Michael, I don't know you very well, but I have to assume that you are one of the good guys and the only reason I took my life in my hands coming down that ladder is because I had no choice."

"Willow House is bugged, but as far as I know, it's not against the law to bug your own house and from what I hear, Tempest Bienvenue himself had it done many years ago."

"I don't care about that, Julie, I just don't happen to believe this boating accident thing and I think you know what is really going on."

"Then why didn't you just arrest me?"

"Because as I said before, I believe that you are afraid of something or someone, and I believe that someone is Beatrice."

"Michael, please, you don't understand. I am afraid of Beatrice but not because of what she will do to me, but because of what she can and will do to the others."

"Then explain it to me, Julie, because the way I see it, you don't have much choice. You will either have to tell me what is really going on, so that I can help you, or I will have to get a search warrant and go through Willow House with a fine tooth comb."

"Please don't, Michael, there are too many lives at stake here. I'll tell you the truth but you have to promise not to bring anyone else into this until we figure out what to do to keep my friends from being hurt."

"I promise that I will do everything I can to keep your friends safe, Julie, but you are going to have to trust me."

"I do, Michael, I don't know why, but I do."

Julie told Michael about everything that had happened since she arrived at Willow House.

"Michael, there is absolutely no doubt in my mind that Beatrice will follow through with her threat to kill those people if she thinks, for one minute, that she would be taken away from Willow House, it's like some kind of obsession."

"You know, she told me that Tempest was about to tell Rene` all about his underground project because he felt that Rene` had remained loyal to him, by not leaving when Juliette died, and he wanted him to take over where he left off, but before he got a chance to meet with his son, Tempest just mysteriously dropped dead of an apparent heart attack."

"You should have seen the look on her face as she was telling the story. She said that she was the only person in the room with him when he collapsed and by the time the paramedics got there he was dead."

"Michael, I think she killed him or at the very least didn't try and save him."

"Julie, I don't think you should go back inside that house."

"I have to, Michael, or she may very well torch it just t keep anyone else from being the *Lady of the Manor* as she calls it."

"I'll be okay as long as I play her game and it will also buy us some time to figure out what to do next."

"This is against my better judgment, Julie, but I'm going to keep this between you and me, for now, even though I could lose my job over it."

"Yes, but you could be saving the lives of those people being held prisoner, by Cruella Deville, besides; if you do lose your job, there will be one very grateful private investigator that will probably make you his partner, Andy Bergeron is one of prisoners."

"I haven't even seen the list of the missing, yet, because Beatrice said that everyone's relatives had been contacted and she indicated that they were visiting from out of town."

"I've met Andy a few times, my Dad thought highly of him."

Come to think of it, having Andy down below might make our plan a lot easier."

"What plan? Do we have a plan?"

Chapter Seventy Seven

Madison saw the look of hope on her grandmother and grandfather's face and she knew that she had to tell them that Danielle died before Beatrice told them.

Jack and Evan saw the look on their faces, as well, and when Madison looked over at them, Jack shook his head no and motioned for her to come to him.

"Madison," he whispered, "I think I should take this one."

Madison was only too willing to let Jack break the bad news to her newly found grandparents because she wasn't quite sure if she could.

She watched their faces as he told them that Danielle had been ill for quite some time and had recently passed away.

"Your granddaughter, Julie, told us about it after we told her that we suspected that she was, in fact, a Bienvenue herself."

"Her mother's name was Danielle, so that pretty much proves that Julie is your granddaughter."

"I'm so very sorry to tell you this and especially tonight, but we were concerned that Beatrice might tell you, since she just found out herself."

"Please don't feel badly about telling us Jack, you did the right thing by not waiting for Beatrice to tell us, in a way that I'm sure would have been very cruel, at least your grandmother and I can grieve in peace."

Later that evening when Andy and Madison were alone in her room, Andy said that he was going to have to write a note to Julie and hopefully she would be able to retrieve it when she came down with Beatrice tomorrow.

"I might not have another chance after tomorrow, Maddie,

because Beatrice said that she and Julie would bring some more personal supplies to us in the morning and who knows when we will see them again, since Beatrice won't have to bring us our meals anymore."

"What are you going to tell her to do?"

"I'm going to ask her to get in touch with an old friend of mine, Mike McCrary."

"Who is Mike McCrary?"

"Mike is the recently retired Police Chief, who happens to be an old friend of mine. We worked together on quite a few cases and I trust him with my life."

"Mike has a son on the police force, I've met him a few times but I don't know him that well, so I'm going to have to ask that he not bring him into this. Mike is retired now and has nothing to lose by not giving the department the information; however, his son would stand to lose his job if he knew about this and didn't share the information."

"Andy, I can't even imagine how terrified I would be right now if you were not here with me. I actually think I'll be able to sleep knowing that because of you, we might just have a chance of getting out of here alive."

"You sweet talker you, does that mean I can stay in your room tonight?"

"Just try and leave."

"Are you sure, Maddie?"

"Andy, we have no idea when and if we will ever get out of here and though I do have faith in you, I don't believe that this is the time to worry about appearances, in fact I'm sure the last thing anyone in my family is concerned about is my virginity."

"Excuse me, did you say virginity?"

"I did say that, but remember, you did propose to me, so that's as good as being married as far as I'm concerned and besides, think what we'll have to tell our grandchildren."

"I don't think we'll share this part with them," said Andy, "I want this night to be mine and yours alone and as soon as we get out of here, I promise to take you on a real honeymoon, right after the real ceremony."

As soon as Julie was back in her room, she began writing a note to Andy, letting him know that she and Michael were working on a plan to free everyone.

Michael had taught her a few tricks he had learned from his father about causing a distraction in order to get a job done and she knew that she had better get it right the first time because she might not get another chance.

Later, as she lay in bed, it dawned on Julie that her mother had finally found out that she was a Bienvenue.

What she asked me to do makes sense now.

The next morning, Julie was out of bed, showered, dressed and downstairs before Beatrice even woke up, so she decided to make some breakfast and bring it up to her room, but just as she was about to leave the kitchen with the tray, Michael appeared at the kitchen door.

Julie quickly put the tray back on the kitchen counter and went outside to find out what Michael was doing there so early.

"Michael, I thought we agreed that you would not come around until later in the day so that Beatrice would think that everything was going as planned."

"We did make that agreement but I was worried about you."

"Well good morning, Officer Michael, what are you doing here this early? Please tell me that you have found the boat and that everyone is okay."

Julie turned around to see Beatrice standing on the other side of the screen door and she prayed that she didn't look as scared as she felt.

"Beatrice, you frightened me, I was just about to bring you a tray when Officer Michael showed up."

"Yes, ma' am, I'm sorry that I came over so early but I heard that the Coast Guard had rescued a group of people that were stranded on one of the islands and I'm pretty sure that it's your people."

"Well, that is good news, Officer Michael.

Julie, you should have invited Officer Michael in."

"I know Beatrice but I knew you were exhausted and I didn't want to wake you."

"Thank you, sweetheart, I do appreciate that but since I'm already downstairs, why don't the three of us have breakfast together and Officer Michael can tell us about the rescue."

"I appreciate the offer, Miss Beatrice, but I need to get to the station and find out the particulars about the rescue. I probably shouldn't have even told you about it until I knew for sure but I just had a good feeling about it."

"I'll be in touch when I know for sure."

"Thank you, Officer Michael, please do."

As soon as Michael was in his car, Beatrice began to laugh.

"What an idiot, he just came by to see you, that was so obvious."

"Look, I don't think the man would make up a story about a rescue just to see me again, besides, he's not my type."

"You're right about that, sweetie; you are definitely on opposite sides of the law, now where's that tray you were bragging about.?"

"It's on the counter, Aunt Bea, I swear, between you and Deputy Barney, Horn Island is looking good to me right now."

"Cute, you can commune with nature since you would be the only human being living there, now let's get the rest of the supplies together and deliver them to our guests."

"How are you going to justify spending so much money on supplies when you are the only one left in Willow House?"

"It won't be a problem dear because Franklin always gave me signed checks to get what I needed and no one ever questioned what I spent and now that you will be the legal owner of Willow House, I'm sure that you won't mind signing a document stating that I can write checks for whatever I need will you, beside, they grow most of their food organically and they don't go out in public so their wardrobe is very limited."

"Tempest might have been a bastard; however, he was a brilliant bastard."

Chapter Seventy Eight

Madison helped her mother and her grandmother prepare breakfast for everyone and after everyone had eaten, Andy filled everyone in on his plan to slip a note to Julie.

"I know that some of you have been down here for many years and some have been here your whole lives and I'm sure you have tried to think of anything and everything you could do to escape, but we do have one thing now that you never had before and that is Rene` and Juliette's granddaughter, Julie, and though I haven't known her for very long, I know that she loved her mother and grandmother very deeply and I'm sure that she will do everything that she can on her end to get us out of here."

"I agree," said Madison, "Julie is family and in the time I spent with her, I could tell that family was most important to her."

"Well, people, family or not, I have a very good feeling about Julie," said Franklin. "She reminds me very much of you, Madison, and I feel much more hopeful knowing that she is on our side."

Suddenly the red light came on and everyone stopped talking.

"You people are so predictable," said Beatrice. "If Tempest was alive, I'm sure he would have invented a camera that didn't light up when it was on, but he's not alive is he? And neither will you be if you don't do exactly as I say."

"Julie and I will be bringing the rest of the newcomer's supplies down in a few minutes."

"Martha, I want you to bring the dishes and trays from yesterday out to the holding room."

"You won't be hearing from me for a few days so if any of you need anything, now is the time to tell me."

"I know that this might sound very trivial to you, Beatrice," said Madison, "but I have been keeping a journal since I was a little girl and if you could please bring it to me, I would be very appreciative."

I just started a new one and it's in my suitcase."

"Forget it, Madison," said Julie, "find something else to write on."

"I guess you must be forgetting who the Lady of Willow House is, Julie. I don't think that getting Madison's journal is such a big request, do you?"

"Well if you put it that way, I guess not."

"So what's keeping you, child? Go get the journal."

I sure hope you really have a journal, Madison, because if I return without one, Lady B might just think we are up to something.

"I trust that my people are doing well," said Beatrice after Julie left the room.

"We are doing quite well, Lady Beatrice, thanks to you," said Juliette.

"And how are the newcomers faring?"

"Well, they will have to adjust to their new environment, just as we did and in time, I'm sure they will come to love this place as much as we do."

"Wonderful, now in a moment Julie and I will be delivering the supplies to the waiting area, but before we do, I am going to open the door to the holding room so that Martha can bring the dishes and trays out that we brought in yesterday. No sense in breaking up a beautiful set of dishes, especially when they are part of a collection from the Bienvenue family."

Andy decided the best way to keep Beatrice from discovering his note to Julie would be to wad it up and put it in with the used napkins.

I just hope that Julie is as smart as I think she is.

"Well, my dear, it took you long enough to find the journal, now if you don't mind, I'll take a quick look at it."

As Beatrice grabbed the book from Julie and shook it, Julie was glad that she had decided not to put her note inside until they were inside the waiting area.

"Why don't you read every page, Beatrice, just to make sure that I didn't write something inside the book?"

"Don't be snide, dear, I'm just very suspicious by nature."

"Well please ease up on me a little. After all, what could I tell those people that they don't already know?"

"I couldn't help them if I wanted to so why should I try?"

"I'm actually doing them a favor by doing nothing because if I even thought about going for help, they would be dead before anyone could reach them and I would be poor again, so the way I look at it, I get the treasure and they get to live."

"I love the way you rationalize, Julie. I think I will lighten up on you a little."

If I get away with convincing Beatrice that I am as greedy and uncaring as she thinks I am, I am going to consider going to Hollywood, thought Julie.

"Hey, do you mind if I wait out here while you bring the supplies in?"

"Now who's being suspicious, my dear? What are you afraid of, that I'll lock you in with the others?"

"I told you that I can't afford to have you disappear before this investigation is over now get in there and help me."

Once inside the waiting area, Beatrice noticed that Juliette left a list of personal things that they would need soon and while Beatrice was reading the list, Julie slipped her note inside Madison's journal, but soon had second thoughts about placing it there.

What if Beatrice checks the journal again, she thought, *I should have hidden it in some of the other supplies*

Her fears were quickly extinguished when Beatrice asked her

to get a move on because Officer Michael would probably show up again at lunchtime.

"Yeah, with the bad news that the family that was rescued was not ours," said Julie, as she walked back out into the passageway.

"And though we must appear to be very heartbroken, we must also remember that our guests are safe and sound."

Chapter Seventy Nine

As soon as Beatrice and Julie left the waiting area, the doors opened up to allow everyone in.

Juliette said she and Zack would go out and retrieve the supplies because it would seem more natural than letting the new comers take over so quickly.

"That's fine, Mom," said Madison, "just make sure my journal is there."

"I will, sweetheart, I remember how important my journal was to me when I was young."

"It's not that, Mother, it's just that I feel like Julie might have placed a note inside."

"I acted like it was vital that I have my journal and she did get to know me well enough to realize that I would not be so shallow as to worry about my journal when my life was in danger."

"I think it must be true that each generation is smarter than the one before."

"Maybe more knowledgeable, Mother, but never wiser."

"I did raise a very respectful young lady, didn't I?"

As soon as Beatrice and Julie returned to the computer room, the red lights went on indicating that the cameras and microphones were on.

"Hello again, my family and friends. Things seem to be going quite well, don't you think?"

"I have your list, so Julie and I will make sure you have everything you need, in a few days."

"Juliette, I'm sure you know by now that Julie is your granddaughter and that Danielle is no longer with us; however,

Julie does intend to carry on the family tradition, at least the one that Tempest started. She is going to make sure that I have her power of attorney so that I will be able to finally be the Lady of Willow House and since there will be no more Bienvenue descendents since Julie is unable to bear children, this house will remain in my charge until I die."

"Which cannot be too soon, as far as I'm concerned."

"I heard that, Franklin, and I'm not the least bit offended. I suppose I deserved that, but look on the bright side, you can finally acknowledge that you are a Bienvenue and accept your place with the rest of your family, in the basement."

As soon as the camera lights went out, Martha surprised everyone with her comment.

"What a complete bitch she is. I only wish I could get my hands on her right now."

Franklin burst out in laughter and said that he wished he had a camera so that he could take a picture of the look on Martha's face.

"I don't believe I have ever seen you so angry, my dear."

"I suppose I was always too afraid of Beatrice to let myself get angry."

"It's a good thing too because if you had ever looked at the old girl the way you are looking at me right now, she would have left Willow House long ago."

It took Martha a moment to realize that Franklin was teasing her and as she began to laugh, so did everyone else.

"Laughter, that's what has been missing in our lives," said Juliette, "and you know, it actually does sound like music."

By the time Beatrice had entered the kitchen, Julie had already gone through all the trash and found the note from Andy, but before she could hide it in her pocket, Beatrice asked to see what she had in her hand.

"It's a napkin, Beatrice. I didn't have a Kleenex and I needed to sneeze so I used a napkin, but I'll be very glad to give it to you, better yet, why don't you retrieve it from the garbage." And as soon as Julie threw the napkin in the garbage, Michael showed up at the kitchen door.

"Hope I'm not interrupting anything, ladies."

"Of course not, Officer Michael, please do come in, Julie and I have been expecting you."

"Looks like you had some company while I was gone."

"I beg your pardon."

"From the looks of all the dirty dishes, I just assumed you had company."

"Oh, the dishes, well no we didn't have company, Officer Michael, they were dishes left from the party the other night."

"Julie and I took a walk down to the beach after breakfast. I guess we were both hoping that the boat would have miraculously appeared and that everyone on board would be safe, but all we discovered was a pile of dishes left over from the Halloween party, which was really a blessing because it gave us something to do while we waited to hear from you."

"Well, since you seem so anxious for information on the people that were rescued, I…."

"Don't you dare act as if we were not concerned about those people."

Beatrice has been beside herself worrying about her husband, Franklin, not to mention her long time friend, Martha."

"This poor lady is sleep deprived and is not thinking clearly."

"I'm very sorry, Ms Beatrice, Ms Julia, I didn't mean to be so cold, I just thought…"

"No you didn't think and that is your problem. You need to have more compassion for people."

"That's enough Julie, I'm sure Officer Michael didn't mean to offend me, he was just trying to do his job."

Julie pretended that she was very upset and began pacing up and down the kitchen, and as soon as she was out of Beatrice's view she motioned to Michael to get Beatrice out of the kitchen.

"Oh my God, I'm so sorry, Ms. Beatrice I guess I do have a lot to learn about compassion."

"No harm done, Officer Michael, just tell me that you rescued my family."

"I wish I could, Ms. Beatrice, but the people that the Coast Guard rescued were from Mobile, Alabama."

"That doesn't sound very promising, does it?"

"You know, Ms. Beatrice, it really is too soon to give up hope; in fact we have helicopters flying over all the other islands, as we speak, not to mention volunteers that are searching the islands by foot."

"Several civilians have put together their own search parties and are using their own boats to help find and rescue your family."

"I just don't know what to say, please thank everyone for us and thank you so much for stopping by."

"Oh, before I go, I do need to speak with you in private for a moment."

"Would you mind stepping outside?"

Beatrice was caught off guard but before she could come up with an excuse, Michael said that it would only take a moment and that he really couldn't discuss this with anyone else present.

Chapter Eighty

"Well, is there a note in the journal?" asked Andy.

"Yes, but I'm almost afraid to read it out loud. What if Beatrice really does hear us, even when the lights are off?"

"Then Julie would probably be down here with us by now. Trust me, Madison, she can only see us and hear us when the red light is on. This is all Tempest's creation and he never felt a need to hide the cameras or listen in to the conversations at all times. He knew these people weren't going anywhere so why would he have to spy on them?"

"The cameras were placed in certain areas just so that he could see that everything was running smoothly and the microphones were placed here strictly for communication between him and his prisoners."

"I guess I am being paranoid, I'll read the note from Cousin Julie.'

'Plese hng n thr, wrkng wth Mchl, frnd of Andy. Wil gt u ot asap."

"I guess she was in a hurry or just used to texting her friends."

"Mchl, Michael, that's my old friend, Mike's son, on the force. He must have told her that his father was a friend of mine."

"I'm sure that the police have been around, questioning Beatrice and Julie about our disappearance. Michael must be one of the investigating officers."

"Well, so much for leaving him out of the loop. I just hope that he contacts his father after he sees my note. This is way too much for him to handle on his own."

"So while we're waiting for our super heroes to rescue us, what do we do?" asked Evan

"We continue our investigation," said Andy. "Everyone that came here before us was unaware of how they got here."

"We have had the opportunity to explore some of the tunnels before we were locked up and from the size of this underground manor, there has to be many more tunnels that even Beatrice has no idea about."

"Okay then, Commander, where do we start?"

"At the beginning, Evan, always at the beginning."

As soon as Michael and Beatrice had stepped outside, Julie began riffling through the garbage to find the note from Andy.

Luckily she was able to retrieve it and stuff it into her pocket before the two came back inside.

"Thank you, again, Officer Michael, and please call us no matter what time it is, day or night."

"Of course, Ms. Beatrice, and a pleasant evening to you both."

"Well that was insulting," said Julie, as she poured herself a cup of freshly brewed coffee. "I was going to offer Officer Michael a cup but seeing as he was so rude…"

"Oh get over yourself, Julie, he was just doing his job."

"And what was so important that I couldn't hear it?"

"Oh Julie, he just wanted to know how much I knew about you."

"It was really quite sweet because he was concerned that you might be taking advantage of my hospitality, but don't you worry, my dear, I assured him that you were a very nice young lady and only concerned for me."

"Yeah, well it was best for both of us that you make Officer Michael trust me, wasn't it?"

"It was indeed, Julie, and I assure you that I did a fine job of convincing him that you were no less than my Guardian Angel."

"Oh, by the way, did you find any notes in the trash when you were cleaning up?"

"As a matter of fact I did find one. It said, *Please make sure that no one ever finds us down here because we would rather deal with imprisonment than old lady Beatrice.*"

"Not very funny, Jules, our guests could very well have slipped a note to you, hoping that you would find a way to rescue them somehow."

"You're right, Beatrice, but why should I look in the trash for a note pleading for help when I have no intentions of helping anyone at this point except myself."

"You know, I wish that I had met my real mother because I'll bet that I am a lot like her."

As Beatrice and Julie were finishing up in the kitchen, Beatrice suggested that the two of them go shopping that afternoon.

"You know it will do us both some good to get away from our guests for a while and you do need some clean clothes don't you?"

"Yes, and I was about to tell you that I needed to run home and get a few things but I'm really not in the mood for shopping."

"I knew you would want to get some of your things from home and I was hoping that I could go with you and maybe bring back a few of my sister's mementos."

"Oh I am not ready for all that, Beatrice. When this missing persons search is over and I have my treasure, you can have all of your sister's mementos; besides, everything is packed away."

"I'm pretty tired right now from all this stress. All I really want to do is run to the house, get some of my things and come back and soak in a nice hot bath."

"I'm pretty tired myself and a nice hot bath does sound wonderful.

"Hey, I'll even stop and pick up Chinese for our dinner tonight."

"We'll get a good night's sleep and in the morning we can

go shopping and then I'll treat you to lunch, how does that sound?"

"I've never eaten Chinese food and no one has ever taken me out to lunch so it sounds a little strange to me."

No wonder she's so strange, thought Julie, *It's as if she has been living in underground* Willow House *all these years.*

"Well Beatrice it's high time you tried Chinese food and let me say that I am would be honored to be the first person to ever take you to lunch."

"Hey, don't play me, little girl, I never tried Chinese food because I just didn't want to and going out to eat has always seemed like a waste of time and money."

"I am quite happy to prepare my own meals right here in my royal dwelling."

"Excuse me for trying to do something nice, Miss Thing, now if you will excuse me, I am going to pick up my things and I'm bringing Chinese home weather you want it or not."

Chapter Eighty One

"I still can't believe how massive this underground facility is," said Andy, as he and the other new comers completed their tour. "I can't imagine what Tempest was thinking when he built it."

"I know that some of you have been down here for many years; however, I do believe that Tempest incorporated an escape route in his plans we just have to find it."

"Please don't think that I feel I am smarter than any of you, it's just that this is my expertise, although I have to admit that I've never encountered anything even close to this."

"Andy, most of these people have never really felt the need to escape, this is all they have known and the others have adjusted over the years."

"Camille and I have only been here a year and I have tried my best to figure out how to escape, so that we could get back home to our children, so I for one, hope like hell that you are smarter than me."

"I have to assume that Tempest only told Beatrice what he absolutely had to, so that she wouldn't turn him in and I would be willing to bet that if he had not died when he did, Beatrice would be down here with the rest of us."

"There is no way he would tell her about escapes routes when he fully expected her to be one of his prisoners."

"You are a pretty devious man, Andy Bergeron," said Evan, as he lifted one eyebrow.

"I prefer to be called clever, if you don't mind, Evan Bloom."

"Then clever it shall be, my good man."

Camille was the first to laugh and in no time, everyone in the room was laughing as well.

"I guess it's true that laughter is contagious," said Camille. "Now on a more serious note, Beatrice has decided to leave the doors to the holding rooms open so that we can visit back and forth."

"You mean so that she doesn't have to bring meals to us every day."

"Well, yes there's that, Madison, but for whatever reason she did it, I'm happy because I can see my children anytime I want to."

"You're right, Mom, I guess I need to let go of the need to judge Beatrice because nothing matters except that we are all back together as a family."

Andy noticed that the red lights were back on so he turned his back to the camera and tilted his head up in such a way that everyone knew that they were once again being watched.

"Hello again, my people, I just wanted to tell you that Julie and I will have everything you need in a few days."

"I can't tell you how excited I am to have another generation join our family, in fact I am thinking about recruiting someone else to assist me, since Julie will be leaving us soon."

"I actually believed that you and I would be Lord and Lady of Willow House someday, Rene`, but all you wanted was your family back. Well now you have them back, grandchildren and all."

"Oh and if you're wondering why Julie is leaving us, well it seems that she is not a Bienvenue after all, she was adopted."

"It doesn't really matter though, because her birth certificate says that she is legally the daughter of Danielle so that makes her a descendent by law."

Oh, and you want to hear the best part? Danielle has a son that lives in Shreveport and has no idea that he is a true Bienvenue descendent."

"Hate to burst your bubble, Beatrice but we already knew

that," said Andy. "I did a quick background check on Julie when we suspected that she was related to the Bienvenues and we found out about her big brother, though she never bothered to mention him at all. Now I know why."

"Clever one isn't she? More like Tempest than any of his own family."

"I honestly hate to see her leave, now back to business."

"I will be hiring new help soon to replace Franklin and Martha, and since neither one of them knew about my subjects below, nothing really has to change, except for the fact that I will be spending more money on food and supplies and no one will question how much I spend when Julie signs a paper saying that I am in charge of Willow House and have the right to spend whatever I deem necessary."

"I must go now, my people, and I won't be seeing you for a few days, but you know what to do if there is an emergency so until I return, enjoy yourselves."

Chapter Eighty Two

As soon as the red light went out, Evan began strutting around the room and in a very shrill voice he said,

"Hello, my little peons, I hope you grow to love living in the dirt because you will never be able to dig your way out."

"Evan, some of these people may take offense to that."

"You're right, Maddie, I'm sorry if I offended anyone, I was just trying to lighten the mood a little."

"Please don't apologize," said Jim, one of the residents that had never lived anywhere else, "I like a good laugh as well as anyone and even though I have been here my entire life, doesn't mean that I wouldn't want to see what life is like above ground."

"Juliette and some of the others have told me stories about life on the outside but it's just so hard to imagine."

"I've read stories about children that grew up and wanted to leave their home town to explore other cities in the United States and stories about people in the United States that set out to explore the world and hey, I've read about people that have actually left this planet and walked on the moon, a moon that I can only picture in my mind but have never even seen, so please joke all that you want to Evan because I think I speak for the others like me that have never been above ground, we need all the laughter and stories and happiness that you have to offer."

"Wow, I have never been so well received in my life."

Once again, everyone burst out laughing and Juliette said that she was so happy that there was a comedienne in the family.

As soon as everyone had settled in for the evening, Andy told Madison that her grandfather was way ahead of his time, but that it was too bad that he didn't use his genius for the good of humanity.

"I hate to say this but I'm afraid that our best bet in escaping really is going to be Julie."

"I need to be in the waiting room when Beatrice returns to bring the supplies."

"But she always makes sure that the doors are sealed before she enters."

"Right and that is why I slipped a note to Julie, asking her to get in touch with Mike."

"There is something I didn't tell you about Mike, before. He was an undercover agent with the Government for many years before he retired and returned home to be with his wife and watch his young son grow up."

"Does Michael know?"

"I have no idea, but after what I wrote in the note to Julie, he will have many questions for his father, if he didn't know."

"Michael? Thank God you answered. I'm going home to get some of my clothes but I'm afraid that Beatrice might follow me so please do not show up."

"I do have a message for your dad from Andy Bergeron though so…"

"What is it ?"

"It just says that he wants your father to be contacted as soon as possible."

"My dad is calling Beatrice, as we speak, to ask if he can meet with her."

"Just go to your house and I'll call you as soon as I know what's going on with Beatrice."

Beatrice was having second thoughts about letting Julie leave the house alone.

I just don't trust her completely, she thought. *I should have insisted on going with her. I know she wants the money but what if she gets cold feet.*

That's it, I'm going after that little…

But just as Beatrice was about to go for her car keys, the phone rang.

"Hello, Ms Beatrice?"

"Yes, who is this?"

"Miss Beatrice, this is Chief Mike McCrary with the Ocean Springs Police Department and I just want to do a follow up on a missing persons report."

"Look, Chief McCrary, I've already spoken to…."

"Yes ma' am, I know, Officer Michael is my son and he told me that your husband is one of the people that went out on the boat, he also told me that a very dear friend of mine, Andy Bergeron was along as well, so if you don't mind, Miss Beatrice, I would really like to come by Willow House and speak with you."

"Well, I was just about to run to the store."

"Well then would you mind stopping by the station, I won't keep you very long."

"Never mind, Chief McCray, I have a friend staying with me for a while, and I'm sure she won't mind running a few errands for me.

When can I expect you?"

"I'm on my way, Miss Beatrice."

As soon as Beatrice hung up from talking with Chief McCrary, she called Julie on her cell phone but when it went to voice mail, she was livid, but she realized that she must be very careful when choosing her words.

"Julie, sweetheart, please call me as soon as you get this message.

I'm sorry to disturb you dear, but I'm just not feeling very well."

The moment Beatrice hung up the phone, it rang.

"What is it Beatrice, are you okay?"

"Yes, I'm okay, but you may not be if you don't get back here pretty quickly."

"Beatrice, I was just trying to call you but your line was busy."

"Don't you have call waiting or voice mail?"

"No, Julie, I don't and why were you calling me anyway?"

"I was trying to reach you to see if you wanted anything from the grocery store.

I have a craving for strawberry ice cream and I…"

"Forget the ice cream, Julie, Officer Michael's father, Chief Mike McCrary is coming over to question me and the worst part is that he is a very good friend of Andy Bergeron."

"Look, Beatrice, don't panic, just make some coffee and I'll be there as soon as I can."

"You can handle this, can't you?"

"I can handle most anything, Julie; besides, Chief McCrary is at the front door as we speak."

Chapter Eighty Three

"Michael, I just spoke to Beatrice and your father is there now."

"I know, I just spoke to him and if you open your front door, I'll be standing on your porch."

As Julie hung up her cell phone and was walking toward the front door, she couldn't help but smile.

I can't believe that in the last few days, I have found out that I have a family that I never knew existed and met a man that I believe I have fallen in love with.

I must be out of my mind.

As soon as Julie opened the front door, Michael took her in his arms and kissed her as if he might never see her again.

Julie was taken aback by his actions, but she was also pleased.

I can't believe that two seconds ago I was questioning my sanity because I thought that I might be falling in love with a man that I have known for less than twenty four hours and the next thing I know…

"Julie, I'm sorry, I guess you think I'm some sort of freak."

"I don't know what came over me."

"Don't give it a second thought, Michael, and no I don't think you're a freak, in fact, I rather enjoyed that kiss and under different circumstances, well that's a conversation for another time."

"Hey, I'm just glad you didn't throw me out."

"I'm going to finish packing some things to take back to Willow House while you look at this note from Andy okay?"

"Sure, I'll be right here when you come back."

Michael couldn't believe his eyes as he read the note from Andy.

What is he talking about, thought Michael, *my father is the Chief of Police, not James Bond.*

"Chief McCrary?" asked Beatrice as she opened the front door.

"Yes ma'am and you must be Miss Beatrice."

"Yes, please, do come in Chief, I just made some fresh coffee for us."

"I usually drink tea in the afternoon but I know you fellas love your coffee. Sorry I don't have any fresh donuts but I did make some homemade beignets."

"You make homemade beignets? I'm very impressed."

"Oh there's nothing to it, Chief, you see, I grew up in New Orleans and my mother taught me to make most of the traditional dishes and besides, I have nothing else to do except wait, do I?"

"Well let's hope you don't have to wait much longer, Miss Beatrice."

"I really do believe that they are safe on one of those islands out there and that we'll be hearing from the Coast Guard any minute."

"I certainly hope so, I'm very worried about my husband and I'm sure that Andy and Aimee's family are worried as well."

Chief McCrary noticed that Beatrice had a look on her face that he had seen numerous times in his career, it was the look of someone that bordered on insanity.

Her eyes were cold and empty of any concern whatsoever and though she spoke as if she really cared about her husband and the others, her mannerisms said something entirely different.

I was a profiler for too many years to not recognize the sort of person this Beatrice really is, he thought. *She may never have had to kill anyone before, but she could kill in a heartbeat if she needed to.*

"Chief, are you okay?"

"Oh I'm sorry, Miss Beatrice, I'm just a little tired and I know you must be worn out so I'll get on with my reason for being here."

"As I told you on the phone, Andy Bergeron is a friend of mine so I have taken a personal interest in this case. I just want to assure his family that I am doing all that I can to bring him home."

"I do understand, Chief; however, I told your son everything I know, don't you think I want my husband back just as much as Andy's family wants him back?"

Chief McCrary could tell that Beatrice was becoming a little irritated and that was not a good sign, considering the fact that she was holding lives in her hands and if he did or said the wrong thing, she might just decide to burn the house down and be done with it.

"Iapologize,MissBeatrice,Iknowyoumustbefranticwithworry aboutyourhusband.IguessIshouldgobutIhateleavingyouallalone."

"Oh she's not alone sir, whoever you are."

"Oh, Julie this is Chief McCrary, that nice Officer Michael's father. Julie is a friend of mine and will be staying with me for a few days."

"I'm sorry, Chief, I didn't know who you were and…"

"That's quite alright, Julie; as a matter of fact I'm relieved that someone is staying with Miss Beatrice. This is not a good time to be alone. I'll be leaving for now, but I want to thank you first for the coffee and beignets, they were the best I have ever had, truly."

As soon as the Chief was inside his car, Beatrice lost it.

"Don't you ever leave me here alone again, Juliette; that is, if you know what's good for you."

"First of all, my name is not Juliette and secondly, you know I had to get some of my things."

"You should be happy that I didn't turn you in, I could have, you know, but I didn't so that should finally prove that I'm on your side."

"Oh you're not on my side; you are strictly in it for the money."

"If that were true, couldn't I just turn you in and let you kill those people below like you said you would if I called the police? My brother could claim this place because he is a Bienvenue."

"You really are a dumb blonde aren't you? He might claim his birthright, but he would never find the treasure, so he would never own Willow House. The bank would continue taking care of the upkeep and the two of you could live here for the rest of your miserable little lives. You couldn't sell this house or collect the millions that Tempest left to take care of Willow House, I think we have been through this before."

"You're right, Miss B, we have been through this before so you must know, by now, that all I want is the treasure and all you want is this miserable old mausoleum."

"We are on the same side, so please get off my back."

Chapter Eighty Four

Michael was parked a little ways down the road and as he saw his father leaving Willow House, he called him on his cell phone.

"What, ya got eyes in the back of ya head like your mother?"

"You must mean like my father, Mr. Bond"

"What the hell are you talking about Michael?"

"Just meet me at my place, dad and we'll talk."

As soon as Chief McCrary arrived at Michael's apartment, he realized that he was going to have to share some things with Michael that he never thought he would.

"I assume you read the note from Andy?"

"Yes, Dad, I did and frankly I'm completely baffled."

"I guess Andy didn't think that anyone else would read it besides Julie and me."

"Look, Dad, I know that this is not the time to go into detail about your past but I would like to know one thing."

"I owe you that much, son, so what is it?"

"How come Andy knew and I didn't?"

"Son, a couple of years ago, Andy began consulting with me on some of his cases and one of his clients turned out to be someone that my agency had been after for many years."

"I won't go into detail about Andy's case but I did get a glimpse of his client, as he was leaving Andy's office, and within about five minutes, this man was in custody."

Needless to say, Andy found out that I had been undercover for many years, but he promised he would never utter a word to anyone. He kept his promise; so we continued to work on cases together."

"Your mother knew I was involved in the protection of our country and she handled it extremely well, but when you started school, I felt that I needed to be with my family on a daily basis, so we made a pact that we would never tell you, until you were married and had a child of your own, just in case espionage was in the genes."

"We didn't want you running off to some foreign country because of my past."

"You know, Dad, I feel like I'm in some kind of Disney movie, you know the movie where the kids save the parents from being destroyed by aliens"

"Sorry son, this ain't no Disney movie, but there are people that need to be saved."

"Wow, I always knew that one day I would share my past with you, I just didn't think it would be this soon."

"Dad, did you really believe I would have become a spy, just because you were one?"

"I don't know, son, you became a police officer, didn't you?"

"I fell right into that one, didn't I, so what's our next move?"

"Follow me to the station and we'll talk there."

"Okay, and um, Dad, when this is over…"

"I'll tell you all about the life I lived as Sean Connery."

"Very funny, Dad."

Madison watched as her mother and grandmother began preparing dinner for everyone.

"What can I do to help, Mom, Grandmother?"

Hearing Madison call her grandmother, Juliette smiled.

"Grandmother, I never thought I would ever hear those words."

"I never thought I would ever hear those words either," said Rene`, "in fact I never thought I would hear the word *dad*, again."

"You know, it just amazes me as to what good health everyone is in."

"Well Andy, I guess Dr. Tim has just taken very good care of us."

"That he has, Mr. Bloom."

"Andy, please call me Zach and after you and Madison are married, we'll see how you feel about calling me dad."

"Thank you, Zach, and I just want to say that I love your positive attitude, because we will be out of here soon and Madison and I will have the wedding of her dreams, whenever and wherever she desires."

As Zach and Andy shook hands, Andy asked Zach if there was a chance the two of them, along with Jack and Evan could have a little private time before dinner.

"No problem, son, I'll let everyone know.

Listen up everyone, Jack, Evan and my soon to be son and I would like to have a little time together before dinner, if it's okay."

"I believe that is a wonderful idea, this will give my daughter and me some time alone together."

"Something is off here, Zach," said Andy, as soon as they were out of hearing distance of the others.

"We agree, Dad, Evan and I have noticed that the people that have been down here since birth, seem to be much healthier than they should be, given the circumstances."

"I noticed that as well, Jack, but it's not like there is anything sinister going on down here, these people have welcomed us and treated us with the utmost respect since we arrived."

"Sir, I'm sure that these people are nice people, but just to be safe, I wanted to meet with you and Jack and Evan in private and I'm not excluding Franklin or Rene`, I just wanted to speak with the three of you first."

"I understand, son, but Juliette is the one you should be talking to. We have only been down here a year."

"I know and Juliette has been down here for well over twenty years and she looks remarkably young, considering the stress she must have been under. She was cut off from her family, and had her new born taken away from her. That's enough stress to push anyone over the edge and on top of all that, she was told that she would remain here for the rest of her life, yet she seems just as happy and healthy as the others, as a matter of fact, Zach, you look pretty damn good for a man that's been cut off from his family and friends and so does Camille."

"You know, Andy, I never really thought about it. I guess having Camille with me helped me adjust to being here and you have to admit that we don't really want for anything down here."

"Yeah, other than family, friends, fresh air and freedom."

"Good one, Jack," said Evan "leave it to you to give the F word a new meaning."

"God I've missed my boys, guess I had forgotten how much until now."

Chapter Eighty Five

As Beatrice and Julie sat down to dinner, Julie asked Beatrice if she believed that Tempest told her the truth about why he built the underground, I mean it just doesn't make sense that you would build a prison to make sure that the Bienvenue name never dies, he had to know that he would die someday.

"I have no idea what went on in that man's mind, but knowing his secret gave me the power to live in Willow House for as long as I lived and after a while, I came to care for the families in underground Willow House and that is why I continue to take care of them. They are my family now and they depend on me to stay alive."

"I have to admit that you do take excellent care of them, Beatrice, because they all look so healthy." "Of course they do, they grow organic foods and I provide them with everything else they need."

"Where do they grow their food?"

"Look, I've never been any further than the waiting room and the rest I have only seen through the cameras. I'll show you the entire site after dinner if, you like."

"Yes, please, it would be a lot less boring than reading magazines that are older than me. You really should get a television, Beatrice; you have no idea what you're missing."

After Mike briefed his son about his past life as a profiler for the government, he asked that he try and understand why he never shared this with him before.

"I will tell you more about my past after we rescue everyone."

"Dad, I just can't believe that you were able to keep your past such a secret all these years."

"Michael it's called secret service for a reason."

"And yet you never lost your wonderful sense of humor.

Okay Dad, you win, but when this is all over, I expect a blow by blow of your life as a…"

"James Bond wannabe?"

"I didn't say that, Dad."

"Alright then, Mikie, let's go kick some butt and save some folks while we're at it."

After dinner, Beatrice and Julie went to the control room and Julie watched very carefully as Beatrice flipped switches, trying to commit everything to memory.

"How can you remember what switch is for what Beatrice? I can't even remember where I left my car keys."

"Well to begin with, I don't drink and party like you do, besides, I've been doing this for a very long time."

One by one all the screens lit up in underground Willow House and Julie was dumbstruck.

"It's like a small city down there; this property doesn't seem that big."

"Oh trust me it's that big, Julie."

"I'm sure you've noticed that Willow House is the last house on the road and that there is nothing but woods on the other side."

"Yes I've noticed, but I just assumed the property belonged to someone else."

"No, sweetheart, it doesn't belong to someone else; it's part of this estate."

"Tempest had many offers to buy the property, but he refused, and you can see why, can't you? He certainly didn't want anyone building on top of his little metropolis could he?"

"I guess not, though can't you see some construction crew digging a little too deeply and landing right in the middle of underground Willow House's rose garden?"

"No I can't see that at all, Julie, and neither could Tempest, that's why he didn't sell the land."

"I'm sorry, Beatrice, please continue the tour."

"Very well, my dear, now as you can see, there are no cameras in the bedrooms or bathrooms, for obvious reasons."

"I can't believe that Tempest would have enough respect to make the bedrooms and bathrooms camera free unless he knew *that* those rooms were…"

"We're what, Julie?"

"I was about to say dark, but that didn't really make sense, so I guess Tempest had a little self control."

Julie realized that Tempest might have built escape routes throughout underground Willow House, but none of them would have been above a bedroom or a bathroom and that is why he didn't feel the need for cameras.

I cannot wait to see Michael tonight, thought Julie.

"Watch this, Julie."

"Hello everyone, I do hope you had a wonderful reunion dinner and that everyone is adjusting to their new quarters."

"Julie is here with me and she is amazed with the size of underground Willow House."

"Hey Ya'll, I really was amazed at the size of your living quarters because it's so much bigger than Willow House but then Beatrice informed me that your little city is built underneath the woods surrounding Willow House and…"

"That's enough, Julie, say goodnight."

"Okay, well goodnight everyone, have fun."

As Beatrice and Julie left the control room, Beatrice said that she would never share anything with Julie again.

"You just go on and on, don't you?"

"What are you talking about, Beatrice?"

"Some of those people have never even seen trees yet you rattle on about their city being built underneath the woods."

"Beatrice, I'm quite sure that Juliette explained trees to them many years ago and I shudder to think about what Jack, Madison and Evan have shared with them."

"I'm quite tired, Julie, so if you don't mind…"

"I don't mind if you go to bed; however, I am not ready to settle in so if, you don't mind, I am going to go for a walk on the beach."

"Just lock up when you come back inside, Julie."

That seemed way too easy, thought Julie, as she walked down the steps, on her way to the beach.

Chapter Eighty Six

After dinner, Andy asked Franklin if he would mind meeting with him in his quarters.

"Madison wants to spend some time with her mother and her grandmother and Jack and Evan will be with their father and their grandfather, so the timing is perfect for me to try and dig deep into your subconscious and see if there is anything you can remember about Willow House that might give me a clue as to how to get us out of here."

"Andy, I don't know what I can tell you that I haven't already told you but I want out of here as much as you do so I'll do whatever you need me to do."

"Thank you Franklin, that's all I can ask," and as soon as the two reached Andy's room, Franklin broke out in a huge grin.

"Franklin, I don't believe I have ever seen you smile that big, in fact, I don't believe I have ever seen you smile at all."

"What could possibly have happened to cause this?"

Franklin chuckled and said that he could remember back when he was pretty young and he and Rene` would sneak a bottle of Tempest's homemade wine, put it in a brown paper bag, kind of like the one you're holding right now, and sneak down to the beach.

"We would pretend we were cow boys and that the wine was whiskey.

I remember we would chew a couple of pieces of Bazooka chewing gum and pretend it was chewing tobacco."

"We would pass that bottle back and forth and by the time it was empty, we were both on our knees, worshiping Oceanus, the son of the earth Goddess, Gaea."

"Oh, so basically, you were throwing up in the Mississippi Sound, right?"

"Exactly, but you know, as miserable as that feeling was, Rene` and I did it again and again and I have to believe it was because it was our time together as brothers, even though we didn't know this at the time."

"So I guess I didn't disguise my little surprise too well, did I, cowboy?"

"No, Andy, but you did bring back some memories that I have not thought about in many, many years."

"That's good because I'm hoping that after a few gulps of this fine cow boy whiskey, you might just conjure up a few more memories."

I guess Tempest built a winery down here to keep the prisoners relaxed and happy."

"That or he intended to eventually live down here himself."

"Franklin, you're a genius."

"Thank you, Andy, but I have no idea what you're talking about."

"Franklin, why would Tempest go to all the trouble of building such an elaborate residence, complete with its own winery, unless he intended to live down here himself."

"Come to think of it, Tempest used to say that someday he was going to leave Willow House and travel all over the world. He said that Beatrice and I could continue to live here for as long as we lived because he would never sell Willow House."

"I thought it was kind of a strange thing for him to say because he never went anywhere. All he did was read and do what he called research."

"He would lock himself up in his room for days and Beatrice would deliver all his meals to him."

"I asked him, once, what he was researching and he said immortality."

"Needless to say, I never asked again."

"Well at least you know why he locked himself up for so

long; he was busy with his underground kingdom, I just wonder when he actually began building it."

"I know that Tempest inherited Willow House from his parents so he could have built the underground before he married Bedelia or maybe his father built it. He couldn't have built the underground while other people were living in the house, there would have been too much noise and I once overheard him tell Bedelia that he wished his father had bought more of the land surrounding Willow House before it was developed because he didn't like neighbors living so nearby."

"I thought that was strange as well because Willow House is surrounded on three sides by acres of wooded land that belongs to the estate and the nearest neighbor is not even in walking distance."

"It does sound like the underground community was built by Tempest's father and that Tempest added updates as needed, like the computer room."

"You know, Andy, I haven't thought about this in quite a few years, but Tempest used to receive deliveries quite often and some of the boxes were very large. I didn't pay that much attention, at the time, because I felt it was none of my business; however, I always wondered what he did with all those deliveries because they were never brought indoors. Tempest always had the delivery men put them in his private storage building."

"Tempest always went inside the building after a delivery and would be gone for hours, yet he never came back carrying anything."

"I never understood what he did with all those deliveries because the building was not that large, but again, it was none of my business so I kept it to myself."

"Franklin, I think you just might have provided the answer to how we're going to get out of here, now I've got to figure a way to get this information to Julie."

Chapter Eighty Seven

As Julie walked along the beach, she spotted a figure headed toward her and just as she was about to turn around and head back to Willow House, she heard Michael's voice call out to her.

"Julie, it's me, Michael."

"Michael, thank God, for a moment I thought maybe Tempest Bienvenue's ghost was coming for me."

"A ghost we can handle, Beatrice is another story, anyway, I told you that I would meet you on the beach tonight."

"I know but it just didn't look like you and I guess I got spooked."

"Where's your dad?"

"Prowling around the grounds, I told him we would meet him at that little storage building behind Willow House."

"Michael, I can't take a chance on Beatrice seeing us."

"She won't see us, Julie; surely I've inherited some spy skills from my father."

"Michael, I'm sure you have your own skills, it's just that Beatrice might have followed me."

"She didn't"

"How do you know?"

"Because I saw you leave the house and I watched you walk all the way down to the beach with no sign of Beatrice, or even Tempest behind you."

"You see, you do have skills of your own."

Chief McCrary waited behind the storage building and as soon as Michael and Julie arrived, he took Julie's hand and told her that it was a pleasure to meet her even though the circumstances were not ideal.

"Chief McCrary, It would be a pleasure to meet you under any circumstances."

"She's a charmer, this one, Mikie."

"That she is, Dad, but if you don't mind, please call me Michael in front of other adults."

Julie and Mike looked at each other and broke out in big grins.

"Obviously you two have the same sense of humor, but if you can stop grinning long enough, we have some people to rescue."

"His mother never found me that amusing either Julie, but he is right about getting on with this mission."

"Michael, I do feel that everyone will remain safe as long as Beatrice doesn't suspect anything, and right now the only person that Beatrice is suspicious of is Julie."

"I know, Dad, and that scares me, a lot."

"I know what your dad is trying to say, Michael. I told Beatrice that I was going for a walk on the Beach and I'm sure that she is waiting up for me so I need to go back to Willow House before she suspects anything."

"I have gotten to know Beatrice pretty well, Michael and I can handle her, but if she thinks I am betraying her…."

"I don't even want to hear the rest," said Michael, as he walked Julie back down to the beach.

"You told Beatrice that you were going for a walk on the beach so if she's watching for you, her eyes will be fixed in the direction of the beach.

Call me as soon as you are safe inside your bedroom, okay?"

And before Julie could answer, Michael pulled her into his arms and held her as if he were afraid to let her go.

"Michael, I can't call you from inside the house, but I can text you." And as she kissed him gently on the lips, she told him that he owed her a first date.

Michael smiled at Julie as she turned and headed back toward Willow House, but inside he was terrified because he knew that Beatrice was pretty stressed out right now.

It seems crazy. he thought. *but the safest place for Julie right now is inside* Willow House *because as long as Beatrice knows exactly where she is, the calmer she will remain.*

The moment Michael returned to the storage building, he asked his father to call Beatrice first, thing in the morning, and tell her t they called off the search because the Coast Guard felt there was really no hope of anyone being alive at this point.

"Julie said that there were no televisions or radios in Willow House and they didn't subscribe to the newspaper, so I'm sure Beatrice doesn't know anything about search and rescue protocol."

"Just tell her that you will be in touch with her as soon as you wrap up the loose ends."

"That could buy us some time to finish searching the grounds."

"It could also buy Julie some time to snoop around a little more."

"Dad, I don't want Julie snooping around at all. Beatrice is a dangerous woman."

"Julie is no dummy, Michael, if she was, then Beatrice would be onto us by now."

"I know that, Dad, but I don't want to chance anything happening to her."

"Nothing will happen to Julie because I'm going to have her sneak me into the tunnels while you keep Beatrice busy, and before you object, I have made up my mind."

"One of us needs to be on the outside and one inside and since I'm the oldest, I get to choose, now let's finish searching this storage building before we go."

Chapter Eighty Eight

"Where have you been?" said Beatrice as Julie walked in the front door.

"I had a craving for a Hurricane so I went to Pat O'Brians in New Orleans, and what the hell business is it of yours anyway?"

"I told you that I won't be comfortable with this situation until the search is called off."

"I understand that Beatrice because I am in this as deeply as you are, but I handle my stress in a different way than you do."

"The water has a calming effect on me so you might as well get used to me taking my walks, at least as long as I have to remain here, and by the way, you are perfectly welcome to come with me, walking is good exercise."

"I don't like the water or the beach, Julie, besides I get my exercise cleaning this big old house, especially now that Franklin and Martha are not here to help."

"You know, Beatrice, you could have Franklin and Martha back with you again; all you have to do is threaten to let everyone below die if they leave you or turn you in and you know that neither of them would allow that to happen."

"And how do you suggest I explain their being alive to Chief McCrary?

You did give me an idea though."

"I'm afraid to ask."

"There are people down there that no one knows. I could bring them up here to help me."

"That's perfect, Beatrice. I'm sure they would never say a word to the police because they would be responsible for their friend's and family's demise; not to mention they would have no one else to take care of them."

"You know what, Julie? I feel better already. As soon as the search is called off, I am recruiting help from my underground subjects."

"That sounds like a plan, Beatrice, and believe it or not, I am happy for you."

"Goodnight, Julie, I'm sure I'll sleep so much better, knowing that you care."

The moment Julie entered her bedroom she locked the door and sent a message to Michael, filling him in on her conversation with Beatrice.

Michael answered immediately, letting her know that his father was going to notify Beatrice in the morning that the search had been called off and *that* he wanted Julie to sneak him into the tunnels.

Julie messaged back to Michael that she didn't know how she would be able to sneak his father in the tunnels, but that she would meet him on the beach in the morning and they could talk about it.

"So, did you and Franklin have a nice evening? I really enjoyed spending time with my mother and getting to know my grandmother."

"You know, Andy, I would never say this to my mom, but my grandmother doesn't look much older than my mom and I don't understand that, considering the grief she must have suffered all these years."

"No one down here looks any worse for the wear, Maddie."

"What do you mean?"

"Everyone down here looks way too healthy."

"I know they grow foods organically and they don't have exposure to the elements, but from what Juliette says, the only deaths down here seemed to be from natural causes and she also said that none have occurred since she arrived."

"So what are you saying, Andy, that my grandmother is magic or something?"

"No sweetheart, I'm saying that I don't know what is keeping these people so healthy and why there have been no deaths in all these years."

"Anyway, that's not really important right now."

"Franklin gave me some information that might just help us escape but I need to get the information to Julie."

But before Madison could reply, an alarm went off.

"Let's go, Maddie, I have no idea what's going on, but I don't want to leave you alone."

"You don't have to worry about that, honey I have no intention of staying here without you."

Juliette was in the waiting room by the time Andy and Madison arrived.

"I was afraid that the alarm might frighten you so I got here as soon as I could.

Beatrice said the alarm is just a test that her system uses to make sure everything is working; however, I have never heard it go on for so long."

"Okay, but just to make sure that it's just a random test, I think we need to speak with Beatrice."

"Is there a way to summon her?"

Juliette said there was a button they were supposed to push in case of emergency.

"I don't believe anyone has ever had to use it, but I'll show you where it is."

As Andy pushed the button, he realized that this might just be his opportunity to get another message to Mike.

"Beatrice, this is Andy and I'm afraid something is wrong down here."

Chapter Eighty Nine

Julie heard the alarm and the first thing she did was run to Beatrice's room.

My God, she thought, *if this is a fire, I cannot allow her to let those people die.*

"Beatrice, open the door, it's me, Julie."

"For heaven's sake, Julie, calm down."

As Julie entered Beatrice's room, she said that she was afraid there was a fire and she wanted to make sure she was okay.

"Why do you care if I'm okay, Julie?"

"Look, Beatrice, not only do I care if you're okay, I also care about those people below, so if there's a fire, we need to get them out."

"There's no fire, Julie, but the alarm system is quite sensitive."

"Andy has already summoned me so I feel safe in saying that the newcomers are not trying to escape."

"Come with me to the computer room and I'll turn it off."

As the two entered the computer room, Julie noticed that a computer screen in the far corner of the room was flashing.

"Why is that screen flashing?"

"Good question, Julie I've never seen that happen before."

"Andy, can you hear me?"

"I hear you, Beatrice, what's going on?"

"I don't know, Andy, maybe you should tell me what's going on."

"Maybe this is some kind of trick to get me to let you out because it has never happened before."

"Beatrice, I understand why you might think that, but I assure you I have done nothing to set off any alarms; just check it out and make sure that there isn't a fire somewhere."

"The alarm that is sounding is not the fire alarm, Mr. Bergeron, so I assure you that everyone below is quite safe."

"If it's not the fire alarm, then what is it?"

"Mr. Bergeron, please don't question me. I am in charge and I will see to it that everything runs smoothly, but if you push me, I will push back, is that understood?"

"Completely."

"Beatrice, what was the alarm for? Are those people really safe down there?"

"What if someone in the area hears the alarm and calls Chief McCrary?"

"We do not need him sniffing around, not when I'm so close to getting everything I want."

"Shut up, Julie," said Beatrice, as she shut down the underground communications. "We never share what goes on up here with my subjects below."

"I'm sorry, Beatrice, I didn't know they could hear me."

"Forget it, they can't do anything about it anyway."

"So what was the alarm for?"

"I really have no idea, Julie, but trust me, if underground is threatened, there will be more than one alarm going off, that much I did learn from Tempest."

"I've checked all the gages and their air supply is fine, so I don't think we have anything to worry about."

When Julie returned to her room, she texted Michael about what had just taken place.

Michael's reply was that he and his father would be there first thing in the morning to speak with Beatrice about the search being called off.

"Please don't worry, Julie, this will all be over very soon."

Then she saw the words, *I Love You.*

"And I love you, Michael."

Chapter Ninety

"Maddie, did you hear what Julie said about Chief McCrary?"

"I did hear her, Andy, and I believe she must be related to me because she is so clever."

"And I'll bet she is just as humble as you"

"Hey, I'm just glad that I have a female cousin that I can pal around with. God knows I've had to deal with male relatives long enough."

"And speaking of male relatives, I need to gather all of yours together, cause if Julie is able to sneak Mike into the tunnels, we need to be ready for him."

"What can you do from in here?"

"It's really not what we can do from in here, Maddie, but what he might be able to do from out there, and if he can figure out a way to get us out of here, the window of opportunity might be very small, so I just want to make sure that your father, brothers and uncle Franklin are ready to help me move everyone out of here as quickly as possible."

Early the next morning, as Julie was pouring herself and Beatrice a cup of coffee, the doorbell rang.

"Who could possibly be ringing the bell at this time of the morning?" asked Beatrice, as she headed for the front door.

"Maybe it's about the missing guests."

"Right, Julie, maybe they actually found them, stranded on Gilligan's Island."

"Duh, we both know they couldn't have found them and where the heck is this Gilligan's Island, anyway?"

"It's the name of an old television series, Julie, and yes there were actually televisions here in Willow House, that is until

Tempest decided to get rid of them and I can't say that I blame him."

As Beatrice opened the front door, she saw Michael standing before her with his head slightly bowed.

"Ms. Beatrice, Ms. Julie, I'm sorry to have to bring you such sad news, but the Coast Guard has called off the search."

"Would you mind if I came in for a moment?"

"Of course not, Officer Michael, in fact Julie just brewed a fresh pot of coffee."

Julie couldn't help but notice the look of relief on Beatrice's face as she turned and headed toward the kitchen.

As Julie poured Michael a cup of coffee, she wondered how Michael was going to pull this whole thing off.

"Ms. Beatrice, I am so sorry about your husband and believe me, if it was up to me, I would not have called off the search, in fact I have one more theory that might prove the Coast Guard wrong, but I need you to help me with this one."

Julie knew that Beatrice couldn't refuse to cooperate with Michael or he might just become suspicious.

"Of Course I will help you, Officer Michael, just tell me what I need to do."

He is pretty good, thought Julie, *though not nearly as good as I am.*

"Michael, would you mind coming back in an hour or so?

This is a pretty big shock for Beatrice and it would be nice if she could have some time to process the fact that she will probably never see her husband again."

"No, no, Julie, Officer Michael has been a great help to me and if he feels that there is a chance that my Franklin could be alive, then I will do whatever it takes."

"Ms. Beatrice, I don't want to get your hopes up, it's just that I believe that if there is any way we could find out what kind of boat the group went out on, the Coast Guard might be willing to give it a while longer, at least they would know what type of craft it was."

"Officer Michael, I told you that I have no idea which boat they took out."

"I understand that but maybe if you come with me to the boathouse, something will jog your memory; it's worth a shot isn't it?"

"Of course it is, officer."

"Miss Julie, would you mind staying here? My father wanted to come with me but he was summoned elsewhere. He said that if he wrapped up in time, he would meet me here."

"No problem, officer, I'm not going anywhere, so take your time."

Show time, thought Julie, and as soon as Michael and Beatrice were out of sight, Chief McCrary appeared.

As Julie opened the door to let him in, he told her they should do this as quickly as possible.

"I'm sure that Michael will keep Beatrice with him as long as he can, but we can't any chances."

Julie quickly led the Chief up the stairs to Beatrice's room and from there, they entered the tunnels.

"Chief, this is the computer room here on the left. I watched Beatrice several times, so I know how to turn the communication switches on."

"Okay Julie, let's start this rescue mission."

Chapter Ninety One

As soon as the camera light lit up, Andy knew it must be Mike.

"Hey big guy, if I had know you wanted to go underground so badly, I would have recruited you long ago."

"Very funny, Chief, but all I want right now is to see the sun shining on the Mississippi Sound, so I hope you have a plan."

"Unfortunately, my friend, I don't have a clue as to how I'm going to get you out of this place, but I'm sure that between the two of us, we will find a way."

"Chief, I really need to get back downstairs in case Beatrice shows up."

"I drew you a map that will take you to the underground city and there are no cameras in the tunnels so you'll be safe in here."

"When you get to the entrance of the place where Andy and the others are being held, there is a button you can push to speak with them, but the only way in, is with a device that Beatrice keeps with her at all times."

"I don't believe Beatrice will be going down to underground Willow House for a day or two; however, if you hear anyone coming, there is a small cove around the corner that you can hide in."

"What if I just wait for her to show up and take the device from her?"

"Because there is a code that no one knows except her."

She said the oxygen is on a timer and if she doesn't reset the timer every twenty four hours, well you get the picture."

"Once she caught me looking at the device in her hand and

she said that if I had any thoughts of taking it away from her, underground, and everything above it would go up in a blaze of glory before the device even left her hand."

"Okay, sweetie, I get the picture.

"Tempest Bienvenue must have been some kind of mad scientist to be able to, not only design and build something so high tech, but keep it a secret for all these years."

"I know, Chief, I'm still trying to process it all, by the way, how am I going to get you out of here?"

"Michael will fill you in on that part, now hurry back downstairs before he and Beatrice return."

As soon as Chief McCrary reached the entrance to the waiting room and found the speaker button, he pushed it and asked if Andy Bergeron could come out and play.

"Mike, thank God you are here."

"I've got everyone watching all the cameras, just in case Queen Beatrice decides that she wants to speak with her subjects."

"Okay, so fill me in on the layout inside."

"Mike, you wouldn't believe it if you saw it, this place is the size of a small community."

"I know there must be an escape route, but I haven't been able to find it yet."

"Just take your time because that is something we have plenty of."

"I know that's easy for me to say, but the truth is, you are not in any immediate danger."

"I'm not so sure about that, Chief."

"What do you mean?"

"We heard an alarm go off last night. Beatrice said that it wasn't the fire alarm and when I asked her what it was, she said that she really didn't know, since it had never happened before, in fact she accused me of setting it off in order to escape."

"That does change things, Andy, your mission is to recruit everyone and I mean everyone. Let them know it's extremely important they search every little nook and cranny for a way out."

"Andy, I know they will tell you and probably already have told you, that they have searched everywhere they could, to find a way, out so it's up to you to let them know, without scaring them too much, that living in underground Willow House is no longer an option. Meanwhile, I'll search the tunnels."

"Wait, Chief, Camille had a memory of her grandfather coming through a door in the floor of the outside building near the water. It's sealed from the outside, but maybe you can find a way to get in from the tunnels."

"I don't really believe there is anything in there; I just think Tempest sealed it up so that no one ever found the entrance to the tunnels, but you never know."

"Camille was pretty traumatized because her grandfather tried to take her prisoner, and when her mother showed up, he threatened to kill her parents if she told them what happened. She totally blocked it out, until recently, so my guess is the old man just didn't want to take any chances, just in case Camille regained her memory and busted him."

"There might not be any clues inside that building, Andy, but it sure would be nice to have another way into the tunnels besides Beatrice's room."

"That's the other thing I wanted to tell you. There is another entrance to the tunnels from Camille's room. Julie doesn't even know about that one, yet."

You needed to see the computer room first, so it was best that Julie took you through Beatrice's room."

"That's great, Andy, you can give me directions to the entrance that leads to Camille's room and I can run my operation from there."

"I feel better already, Chief, so let's get this mission underway."

Chapter Ninety Two

"Oh, Beatrice, you scared me," said Julie as she turned around to see Beatrice standing in the doorway.

"Please, Julie, I'm not that ugly am I?"

"I didn't mean it that way, Beatrice; I was hoping I could have breakfast ready before you returned and I suppose I got a little caught up in what I was doing."

"I'm not the greatest cook in the world, but believe it or not, I have been watching you when you prepare meals and I have to say that I have learned quite a bit from you."

"Julie, I am impressed, it almost makes me wish you were not leaving me."

"Well, don't keep me in suspense; tell me what officer Michael had to say."

"He didn't really have much to say after I told him that nothing in the boat storage jogged my memory."

"So he's gone then?"

"Yes, he's gone, and I would say for good this time."

"Thank heavens, now we can both get on with our lives."

"Yes, but you do understand that we cannot act too quickly, don't you? We need to give them a couple more days to declare everyone dead and then there's the local reporters to deal with."

"I understand that, Beatrice, and I'm willing to wait another week or two for this to become old news."

"Big of you, Julie, considering you are about to come into a rather large amount of money."

"What do you want from me, Beatrice? I am doing everything I can to keep the two of us from falling under suspicion."

I don't want to go to prison any more than you do."

"Calm down, little missy, the worst is over, and you will be gone before you know it."

Julie didn't like the way that sounded, but she pretended she didn't notice.

"You're right, Beatrice, let's have some breakfast and discuss our next move."

After breakfast, Julie told Beatrice that she was going for her walk on the beach and asked her once more to join her.

"I told you, little girl, I don't do walks on beaches or anywhere else for that matter."

"You go on and take your walk while I get this kitchen cleaned up."

As she went out the door, Julie could hear Beatrice muttering something about young people not having a clue about cooking and cleaning.

If I didn't know better, I would think that I was listening to my grandmother, thought Julie.

"Psst, Julie, over here."

"You don't have to whisper, Michael, Beatrice wouldn't be caught dead near the beach; probably that thing about witches and water."

"What thing?"

"Don't even tell me that you never saw the Wizard of Oz."

"I saw parts of it."

"Which parts, the flying monkeys? Never mind, fill me in on what transpired with Beatrice and more importantly, how I'm going to get your father out of the tunnels."

"Beatrice was just as unaccommodating as ever and I was just as charming as ever, now what more do you want to know?"

"Please, move on to the part about your dad."

Michael began to laugh as he and Julie both plopped down in the sand.

"Well, you know that she didn't suddenly remember what the boat looked like, since there was no boat, and as for my father, well let's ask him how we are supposed to get him out of the tunnels."

Michael pulled his cell phone out of his pocket and began texting Chief McCrary.

I hope to hell that there's no kryptonite in underground Willow House *or else we are all doomed.*

Michael and Julie both chuckled as they read the Chief's reply.

No kryptonite, just an Indiana Jones wannabe.

Tell Julie that there is an entrance to the tunnels in Camille's old room.

I need the two of you to meet me there after dinner tonight. You can slip in while Julie helps Beatrice prepare dinner, and if we behave ourselves, maybe Julie will bring us the leftovers.

"He really is quite a character, isn't he? I can see where you get your sense of humor."

"You know, I guess I never paid that much attention to his humor, but now that you mention it, I guess I did inherit the old boy's style."

"You didn't just call your dad an old boy, did you?

Well, I guess I'm just going to have to tuck that one away for later use."

"Not even married yet and you are already threatening me?"

"Absolutely, I believe in honesty from the get go."

"All kidding aside, Julie, this rescue thing is very serious."

"I know that Beatrice is not physically dangerous to anyone; however, she is a danger, nonetheless."

"I understand that, Michael, probably more than anyone else."

"I've seen her face when she speaks of ruling underground Willow House and believe me, she will stop at nothing to make sure that this happens and should she ever suspect that anyone is onto her, she will destroy underground Willow House before we can blink."

Chapter Ninety Three

"There is something strange about the underwater springs, Zach," said Andy, as the two of them led the search for a way out.

"Andy, I have a friend in Pascagoula, Mississippi, that has an underwater spring that supplies his ice plant, so it's not really that strange."

"I realize that, but this underground spring is the main source of water for the plants, and the people, right?"

"Of course it is, Andy, what are you getting at?"

"I'm not sure what I'm getting at; I just took a page out of your little girl's imagination."

"Zach, Madison mentioned the fact that everyone down here seems quite young, for their age, and she's right. Even though you and Camille have only been down here for a year, the circumstances should have taken a toll on you, yet you both seem so relaxed and happy and Madison says that you actually look younger than you did when she saw you last."

"Come to think of it, Andy, I do feel pretty relaxed, and other than missing my children, I have never felt any panic whatsoever, in fact, I feel better physically than I ever have."

"Yeah and I'm not saying that's a bad thing under ordinary circumstances; however, these are not ordinary circumstances and I think we need to find a way out of here before Madison and I start to get too comfortable."

"Dad, are you in here?" said Michael, as he slipped into Camille's old bedroom.

"Oh, I'm here alright, Mikie, and you won't believe what I have stumbled across."

"Beatrice, do you believe in fate?" asked Julie as she was drying the dishes.

"Fate, of course I don't believe in fate, I believe you create your own fate.

Why are you asking about fate anyway?"

"Oh I don't know; it's just that I feel like I was drawn to Willow House for a reason."

"Well, Julie, maybe you were a pirate in another life."

"What do you mean, Beatrice?"

"Pirates can smell hidden treasures, can't they?"

"Beatrice, I knew you were a little cold, but I can't believe how cynical you are."

"I'm not cold, Julie, just realistic and that remark about you being a pirate was just a joke, now if you could just get a move on, I would like to do some reading before bedtime."

"You go ahead, Beatrice; I'll finish up in here."

"What, no walk on the beach tonight?"

"No, I'm a little tired tonight, I think I'll do some reading myself and turn in early."

"Just as well, I think we're in for a thunderstorm tonight."

"How do you know that?"

"Just a feeling, Julie, just a feeling."

"This from the least metaphysical person I know."

Beatrice turned and walked toward the door and just before she left the kitchen, she turned to Julie and said.

"I may not believe in fate or reincarnation or any of your other metaphysical mumbo jumbo, but one thing I do know is that I am always right about everything and when I say it's going to storm, it's going to storm."

Julie waited a few minutes to make sure Beatrice had enough time to reach the staircase, then she made her way through the dining room, into the foyer, and from there she could watch as Beatrice climbed the staircase.

She then pulled her cell phone from her pocket, turned it on and began texting Michael.

Aunt B has retired for the night- food soon.

Michael's reply to Julie was *yum.*

Yum, Michael? Is that all you have to say?

Oh, Dad says yum as well; just kidding, please be careful, and I love u oh and Dad searched the room & there are no bugs in here so we can talk freely, at least whisper freely.

Julie ran back into the kitchen and started putting the leftovers in a bag.

If Beatrice catches me with the bag, I'll just say that I'm bringing snacks to my room so that I don't have to come back down later, yeah, that's good, she'll believe me, yeah right, she'll probably stare at me until I catch on fire.

"I sure hope that Beatrice doesn't catch Julie bringing food up to us Dad, maybe I should texted her and tell her to forget it."

"Julie is a pretty clever girl, Michael; she is not going to take any chances but if you are that concerned then by all means tell her not to bother."

"Not to bother with what, Chief?" said Julie as she entered Camille's old bedroom.

"How the devil did you get here so fast, Julie?" asked Michael.

"The leftovers were still warm, so I bagged them up, threw them in a Wally World bag and raced up the back stairs as quickly as I could, I've learned a few shortcuts since I've been here."

"What will you tell Beatrice if she misses the food?"

"I'll tell her that I got hungry in the middle of the night and finished them off."

"There wasn't much left over, so she'll believe me."

"I also brought some sliced ham, cheese and bread, just in case the leftovers were not enough, and as a special treat, I brought you guys a bottle of wine and some bread pudding for dessert."

"See, I told you she was a clever girl, Michael."

"Look, I can only stay a few minutes because Beatrice just might decide to check up on me so fill me in on your plans."

Michael and the chief just looked at each other without saying a word.

"You do have a plan, don't you?"

"We have a map," said Michael, "but we don't have a plan yet."

"Julie, I have a plan, but I haven't discussed it with Michael yet because I haven't worked out all the details."

'Okay, Chief, but please text me when you have everything worked out, would you?"

As soon as Julie closed the door behind her, Michael looked at his father and said.

"You don't have a plan, do you?"

"Not even an idea for one."

Chapter Ninety Four

"Do you hear that, Mr. Bloom?"

"Andy, I told you to call me…"

"Zach, I know, I forgot, sir, but did you hear anything just now?"

"No Andy, what did it sound like?"

"It sounded like water dripping.

Let's be quiet for a minute and see if it happens again."

A couple of minutes went by and Andy heard the dripping sound again; he looked at Zach and Zach nodded and said that he heard it as well.

"What do you think it is, Zach?"

"It definitely is water dripping, but I have no idea where it's coming from."

Suddenly the alarm began to sound again and Andy knew that it had to have something to do with the dripping water.

"We have got to find a way out of here, Zach, soon."

Michael and his father had just finished eating and were going over the map when they heard the alarm sound.

"I don't think we have time to go over this map, Michael, we need to go below and try and get those people out, now."

"Bring the map along, son, something tells me that it might just be the key to getting everyone out, including ourselves."

Just as they entered the tunnels, Michael received a message from Julie saying that she was going to the computer room because that is probably where Beatrice was.

"Was that Julie?"

"Yeah, Dad, she said that she was going to the computer room to find Beatrice."

I'm texting her back to tell her that we are going below."

Julie, going below to try and rescue everyone-don't come down here for any reason, please!!!

Julie read the message from Michael just before she knocked on Beatrice's door.

"Beatrice, are you awake?"

Of course there was no answer, so Julie opened the door and immediately entered the tunnels through the closet and as she neared the computer room, she heard Beatrice's voice.

"Andy Bienvenue, this had better not be an attempt to escape because you are taking the lives of everyone else in your hands."

"Beatrice, what is going on?

I heard the alarm and…"

"Just be quiet, Julie, I'm waiting for that good for nothing private eye friend of yours to answer me."

"Beatrice, I assure you I had nothing to do with the alarm."

"Andy's telling the truth, Beatrice," said Zack, "he was with me when the alarm went off.

There's a sound like dripping water, actually it's beginning to sound more like running water now."

"What are you talking about, Mr. Bloom?"

"I'm saying that I'm afraid that if you don't get us out of here, underground Willow House will soon become *Underwater* Willow House."

"Don't be so melodramatic, Mr. Bloom, Tempest Bienvenue assured me that underground Willow House was as safe as…"

"Uh oh, that's not good," said Andy, "we just lost communication with Beatrice."

By this time, Chief McCrary and Michael had reached the entrance to the waiting room of underground Willow House.

"Andy, can you hear us?"

"Yeah, thank God for that."

"We just lost contact with Beatrice, but that might not be

all bad, at least she won't be able to listen in on what you have planned for our escape, you do have a plan don't you?"

"Now I really feel like I'm in a scene from Indiana Jones."

"Well Dad, you are the closest character to Indy I have ever known, so I'll let you answer this one."

"Andy, I don't have a plan, but I do have a map of underground Willow House. I found it in a drawer with a fake bottom in Camille's room. I have a feeling that Tempest truly believed that Camille would be the one to help him rule underground Willow House, not Rene`, that's why he had an entrance to the tunnel in her room."

"How would he have even known this before Camille was born, Mike?"

"He didn't know it before she was born but I'll be willing to bet that she was moved into that room when he decided that Camille would be the one that would rule alongside him?"

"That does make sense, that's why he tried to lure her underground, so he could brainwash her. Juliette said that Camille suddenly became afraid of her grandfather and when she asked her why, she would just say that she didn't like him very much, so Juliette made sure that Camille was never alone with him again. He must have known that Juliette was suspicious of him, plus there was always the chance that Camille would remember what happened."

"Andy, talk to Camille again and see if she can think of any…"

"Mike, I've been there and she says she can't remember anything else about that day."

"Dad, Julie just texted and said that Beatrice is headed this way."

"Andy, Mike just said…"

"I heard him, Chief, please go hide, now."

291

Chapter Ninety Five

"Beatrice, wait up, I told you I had to go to the bathroom."

"I don't have time to wait around for you, Julie, there is something going on down here and I intend to find out what it is."

"There has never been a problem in underground Willow House until Andy Bergeron arrived and if he is pulling some sort of trick in order to escape, I will make sure that he pays dearly."

"Beatrice, I really don't believe that Andy is the problem."

"Why not?"

"Because, I hear water running, as well."

Beatrice stopped in her tracks and listened for a moment.

"Well, do you hear it?"

"Yes, Julie, I hear it, but that doesn't mean that anyone is in danger."

By the time that Beatrice and Julie arrived, the chief and Michael were well hidden in a cove just beyond the entrance to the waiting room.

Though they were out of sight, they could still hear the conversation between Beatrice and Andy.

"Mr. Bergeron, are you there?"

"I'm here, Beatrice, and I have to tell you that there are a bunch of scared folks down here."

"Well there is no need for anyone to be afraid."

"I'm on my way to find out what the problem is and I will return here when I find out."

"Julie, you stay here."

"Why?"

"I am at the end of my rope with you, Julie, just wait here until I return."

"Fine, I just thought I might be able to help."

As soon as Beatrice was out of sight, the chief and Mike appeared and as Julie opened her mouth to speak, Michael put his finger to his lips.

Chief McCrary walked up to Julie, kissed her on the head and walked away.

"What is going on, Michael?" whispered Julie.

"Dad is following Beatrice."

"Trust me, she has probably disappeared by now."

"Trust me, my dad has probably already tracked her down."

"I hope so, Michael, I just want all this to be over."

"So do we, sweetheart."

Julie then turned her attention to the entrance to the waiting room.

"Andy, is everyone okay?"

"Everyone is fine thanks to you, Julie, and when this is over I think we should have a celebration in your honor."

"Not necessary, Andy, I just happened to be the one left behind."

"Thank God one of us was, sweetheart."

"Michael, have you found out what the running water is about?"

"Not yet, Andy, dad is tracking Beatrice, he thinks she may lead him to the underground operation."

"Then I guess the best thing I can do is continue trying to track the running water from inside."

"That's a good idea, Andy, oh and don't try and contact me again, just in case Beatrice is in the vicinity. I'll come back here just as soon as I find out what's going on, okay buddy?"

"Sure thing, Michael, I'll talk with you later."

Andy decided that the most productive thing he could do at this time would be to gather the residents of underground

Willow House and convince them that their lives and the lives of their children were in serious danger.

As everyone gathered in the dining room, Andy made sure that he faced the camera at all times, just in case Beatrice decided to tune in.

"Listen to me, everyone. I know that most of you have been down here for a very long time and it must be hard for you to understand that there is a world above you, but if we don't find out where that water is coming from, you may not live long enough to see it for yourselves. I'm sorry for being so blunt, but time doesn't permit me the luxury of being any other way, now let's spread out and find the problem so we can all live long enough to tell our grandchildren this story."

"Look at 'em go," said Zack as everyone ran off in different directions. "I don't believe I've ever seen anyone down here move so fast."

"That's because they've never had a reason to hurry before."

"Guess you're right about that, and speaking of hurrying, I'd better get moving myself."

"Andy, I'm really getting scared."

"So am I, Maddie, so am I."

Chapter Ninety Six

Chief McCrary stayed as close behind Beatrice as he dared, he couldn't afford to slip up and let her see him.

The last thing I need is Aunt B losing it and blowing up half of Ocean Springs.

Beatrice finally stopped at what seemed to be a dead end, reached into her pocket and pulled out a remote control.

Suddenly the wall opened up to reveal a computer room that would put any undercover agency to shame.

Holy crap, Tempest Bienvenue was one hell of a mastermind.

The chief watched as Beatrice entered the room and as soon as the door closed, he sent a message to Michael.

When this is all over, remind me to show you what a mad scientist's laboratory looks like.

Glad you're okay, Dad, and still have your wonderful sense of humor.

Thanks, Son, will let you know when she is headed your way.

It wasn't very long before the wall opened up again and Beatrice immerged.

Chief McCrary waited until Beatrice was past his hiding place, then, as quickly as possible, he headed for the laboratory, hoping the door would stay open long enough for him to make it inside.

My God that was close, he thought, *it's been many a year since I've had to move that fast.*

Michael and Julie were hiding in an alcove, just past the entrance to the waiting room.

"Can you make any sense of this map yet, Michael?" whispered Julie.

"Not much, the words beneath the drawings look like…"

"Latin?" asked Julie.

"Yeah, how did you know?"

"My grandmother was raised in a catholic orphanage when the Mass was said in Latin. She was in the choir and naturally the hymns were also sung in Latin so she would sing them to me when I was a little girl."

"I guess it felt very soothing to me when she sang those words so I took Latin in high school and actually learned quite a lot about the language."

"A women with brains, as well as beauty, how could I have been so lucky?"

"Hold that thought, Romeo, looks like your dad is messaging."

B is on her way back-tell Julie to stick close to her and keep us updated.

Without saying a word, Julie gave Michael a very passionate kiss and ran back to the entrance to the waiting room.

"What took you so long, Beatrice, I was getting very bored waiting for you?"

"Oh, forgive me, fair Juliette, I am so sorry for keeping you waiting so long."

"Forget the Juliette business, did you find out where the running water is coming from?"

"There is no running water, Julie. Andy Bergeron must be playing games with me."

Julie knew that she had to be careful not to show any concern for Andy, Madison and the others so she asked in a nonchalant manner how Beatrice knew there was no running water.

"Because Tempest told me, okay?"

There was no way Julie was about to touch that one after she saw the rage on Beatrice's face.

"Fine, so can we just get out of here, I'm beginning to get a little claustrophobic."

"Actually, Julie, you're not going anywhere."

Julie felt the needle pierce her skin and when she awoke, Madison was standing over her.

"Julie, sweetheart, are you okay?"

"Madison, is that really you? What happened?"

"The old bag drugged you and threw you in here with us."

"She told us to enter the holding room then she opened the door and brought you inside."

"What is wrong with her, she must have totally lost it."

"On the contrary, dear, you have totally lost it," said Beatrice," your treasure that is."

"You won't get away with this, Beatrice. How are you going to explain to the police where I am?"

"I doubt the police will care where you are, Julie, besides, I already told McCrary that you had to leave soon to be with your family, so if I see him again, I'll tell him that you got an emergency call and left."

"Beatrice, I don't understand, I did everything you asked."

"Yes you did, Julie, and I imagine that your friends are going to see to it that you pay."

"Don't leave anything out, Julie, like the fact that you are not a Bienvenue after all and that you had a plan to scam them from day one."

"Gotta go now, people; tell Andy that his little trick didn't work."

"Beatrice, wait," said Madison, "It wasn't a trick, everyone is running around like crazy, trying to find out where the water sound is coming from."

"Nice try, Miss Bloom, but I ain't buyin it."

"Where is Tempest, Beatrice?"

Beatrice recognized Juliette's voice, and though she was a little shaken by what she said, she answered as calmly as possible.

"What the hell are you talking about, Juliette? You know very well that he died."

"I don't think so, Beatrice."

In the first place, there is no way he would have left you

totally in charge of this place, no matter what you had on him and secondly, you know that there is a problem down here yet you don't seem to be the least bit worried about it."

"Maybe it's because I don't care what happens down here."

"Or maybe it's because Tempest told you that he would take care of it."

"That's it, isn't it, Beatrice? Tempest is still in charge, not you, he will never let you rule underground Willow House, not as long as he is alive."

"Stop it, Juliette, you have no idea what you're talking about."

"Oh, but I do know what I'm talking about, Beatrice, don't forget, I know Tempest even better than you do and now that he has his entire family down here, what does he need you for?"

Chapter Ninety Seven

Michael could hear the conversation between Beatrice and Juliette and realizing that Julie was now being held captive with the others, he texted his father to find out how much progress he was making in the master control room.

Dad, Julie is being held prisoner with the others. Are u ok?

I'm ok, little Mike, found a way out, meet me in master control room, just follow the halls to the left, the door will be open.

Little Mike? He has never called me little Mike before, thought Michael, *something is terribly wrong.*

"Dad, listen, Beatrice is still here so it will be awhile before I get there."

"I'll be waiting, son."

It was obvious that Beatrice was shaken by what Juliette had said to her because she began screaming at Juliette.

"I'm the Lady of Willow House and you will not speak to me in that manner."

"You may think you're the Lady of Willow House but if I were you, I wouldn't stay underground too much longer or you might just find yourself prisoner right along with the rest of us."

That last statement must have hit home because I could practically hear Beatrice start up her broomstick and fly through the tunnels.

As soon as I was sure she was gone, I hurried to the entrance of the waiting room and pushed the button on the wall and waited for someone to answer. I didn't want to say anything, just in case Tempest was listening in.

I heard a voice whisper, *Michael?* So I assumed that no one else could hear me.

"It's me, Julie, are you okay?"

"Yes, so far, but who knows what Beatrice is going to do now."

"She's not going to do anything, sweetheart, because she's too afraid of your great grandfather."

"My what? He's not really alive is he?"

"I believe he is, Julie, I'll explain why, later but I need to speak with Andy. I love you."

As Julie walked through the holding room into the living quarters of underground Willow House, she saw the faces of her family and tears began to pour from her eyes.

Juliette was the first to approach her.

"Don't cry, my darling, you are with your family now and we all love you very much."

"Are you really my grandmother?"

"Yes, Julie, I am your grandmother and Rene` is your grandfather."

As Rene` and Juliette held their granddaughter in their arms, Madison said she knew from the start that Julie was family."

"And how did you know that?" asked Evan.

"It's simple, really. She's so clever and quick, just like me."

Julie immediately broke out in laughter which caused everyone else to laugh. as well.

"See, I told you she was like me."

"Listen," said Andy, as he entered the room, "I really hate to break up your reunion but I need to speak with Rene` for a moment."

"Hey, no problem Andy, I will have plenty of time to get acquainted with my granddaughter once we get out of here."

"That's right, Granddad," said Julie, as she kissed him on the cheek, "You will have to put up with me for many years to come."

"Oh God, she does sound like Madison," said Evan.

As soon as Andy and Rene` entered the kitchen area, Andy quickly told him what he had heard from Michael.

"I'm afraid that Juliette might just be right, your father could very well still be alive."

"What are you talking about, Andy? My father died long ago and was cremated."

"Look, Rene` all I know is that Michael seems to think that Tempest is alive and is holding his father prisoner, so whether this is true or not, we have to assume that it is a real possibility and act on it."

"You're right, Andy, what can I do?"

"Michael believes that Tempest is holding his father in the master control room."

"You mean the computer room above ground?"

"No, I mean the brains of underground Willow House Rene`, it appears that your father has been in control all along, and Beatrice knew it."

"So how can I can I help?"

"Well, it's obvious that Tempest has been waiting all these years for his entire family to return to Willow House and apparently he knew they never would as long as he was alive, so he faked his death and has been living down here waiting for this very day, the day that the last Bienvenue was captured."

"Julie, oh my God, he was waiting for Julie."

"Yes, and now that she is with the rest of her family, he is ready to act."

"I don't think he counted on Chief McCrary and his son showing up, but I'm sure he will be happy to have them join the rest of us, especially when he finds out that Julie is in love with Michael."

"You don't mean…"

"That he will expect Michael and Julie to continue the blood line? Oh yes, just as he will expect Madison and I to present him with heirs, as well, not to mention Jack and Evan."

"This is all too insane, Andy, even for my father."

"Never the less, we have to assume the worst and I need you

to be ready to put on the performance of your life when the time comes."

"Rene`, you are going to have to convince your father that you are ready to rule underground Willow House, right along beside him."

Chapter Ninety Eight

"Tempest, you know this has to end sooner or later," said Chief McCrary."

"Why? Just because you found underground Willow House doesn't mean others will. The only reason you ended up down here is because of Julie and her relationship with little Mike."

"How did you…?"

"Know they are involved?"

"Why, Chief, I'm very disappointed in you. I thought you were a big time undercover agent."

"I saw you looking for bugs and cameras in Camille's old room and I had to chuckle. Look at what I have built here, Mike, may I call you Mike?"

"This is way beyond hidden bugs and cameras, this is technology far beyond what you have ever seen before, am I right, Mike?"

"So the running water thing?"

"Part of my plan to get you, your son, and Julie, all down here at the same time."

"You see, I was afraid that if I waited much longer, you might just decide to bring your former agency on board and I couldn't risk any outside attention. I figured it would be much easier to explain you and your son's disappearance that a whole team of government spies."

"And how do you expect to explain my son's and my disappearance?"

"You really do underestimate me, don't you, chief?"

"Did you really think that Beatrice was my only liaison in the world above?

You must know as well as I that Beatrice is an idiot and the only reason she is still alive is because she loves Willow House so much, and having her believe that she will someday reign as The Lady of Willow House has kept her right where I need her to be."

"But what happens when she realizes that you have been using her all this time?"

"You know, chief, that's my problem, is it not? You should be focusing more on yourself and your son, and speaking of your son, he should have made it here by now, don't you think?"

"Well, he did say that Beatrice was still there, didn't he?"

"Yes, he did, but she should have gone back to the computer room by now. Let's just check and see where Lady B is, shall we?"

Tempest reached into his pocket and pulled out a device unlike any that Chief McCrary had ever seen. It was about the size of a cell phone but it was round and the cover was clear.

"Another invention of mine, Chief," said Tempest, "all those little crystals look like diamonds, don't they? Oh please, don't bother to answer; you probably wouldn't know real diamonds if you saw them, now if you will excuse me, I must contact the Lady of Willow House."

Tempest then used the device to track Beatrice and when he was satisfied that she was no longer underground, he turned to the chief and began to laugh hysterically.

If I didn't know that this man was completely insane before, I certainly know it now, thought the chief, as he watched Tempest practically foam at the mouth.

"You think I'm crazy, don't you, chief? Okay, let's look at the situation for a moment. You are the one in chains here and I am the one in control so what does that make me?"

It still makes you the crazy one, thought Chief McCrary.

"Let's just text that son of yours again and see what's keeping him, shall we?"

I have got to think of some excuse to stall, thought Michael, as he read the message from Tempest.

Dad, found the treasure-meet me at the cove-no juice left in battery-come now.

"What the...."

"What's wrong, Tempest?"

"Your son, that's what's wrong. He said that he found the treasure, but that's impossible because he doesn't know what the treasure is."

"What else did he say?"

"He said for you to meet him at the cove and that his cell was dead."

"So what are you going to do now, Tempest? You can't reach him and obviously he found something."

"I guess his father is just going to have to meet him at the cove, only it won't be his father, will it?"

"Tempest, so help me, if you harm my son I will...."

"What, spit on my floor? You are chained to the wall, chief, so there is not much else you can do, is there?

Try and entertain yourself until I return."

Chapter Ninety Nine

As soon as Michael finished texting the message to his father, he returned to the waiting room entrance and pushed the audio button.

"Andy, are you there? Andy, please answer me."

"Michael, it's Jack, Andy is with Rene`."

"Jack, listen very carefully. Tell Andy that Tempest is on his way here, he thinks I have found his treasure so play along with him."

"Tempest, as in my grandfather?"

"Yes, Jack, just find Andy, I don't have time to explain."

Jack immediately ran to find Andy, and upon finding him, he filled him in on what was about to transpire.

"Guess you don't have much time to rehearse, Rene`, it's show time.

"Hello, family," said Tempest as he stood before the entrance to the waiting room."

"I know you can hear me, so you might as well answer."

"Tempest Bienvenue, as I live and breathe," said Zack, "and from the sound of your voice, I guess you're still living and breathing yourself."

"Zachary Bloom, husband to my beautiful granddaughter, Camille and my grandchildren, Jack, Evan and Madison. It's wonderful to finally meet you, Zachary; however, I must speak with my son, Rene`."

"How did you know.....?"

"That you were Zachary? Don't play dumb, son, it's beneath you, don't you think?

Just find my son and bring him here, now!"

"I'm here, father, what is it you want from me?"

"You know what I want Rene`, I want my son back."

"Which son, Father, me or Franklin?"

"Why you, of course."

"Father, I don't understand how you could have allowed Beatrice to take Juliette away from me and to hold me as her own personal prisoner for so long."

"Rene`, trust me, Juliette was safer down here than she would have been with Beatrice and you, my son. You were about to leave Willow House to join Camille and I couldn't allow that to happen."

"You are my first born, Rene`, and the rightful heir to all that I have in this wonderful underground paradise, can't you see that?"

"Father, I have no idea what you are talking about, this is a prison, not paradise."

"Please son, I don't have time to explain everything right now."

"Father, I have missed you so much, tell me what I can do to help."

"You can begin by telling me where Michael is. He says that he has found my treasure and I am asking you, my son, if what he says is true or is he just stalling for time?"

"Father, we have not heard from Michael since Beatrice threw Julie in with us, so if he really did find your treasure, chances are that he took it and ran."

"That's not even remotely possible, Rene`, he is here somewhere and I must find him before its too late."

"Then I don't know what to tell you, father, just let me out of here and we can both look for him."

"I'm sorry, Rene`, but I can't do that just yet; you see, I have to be sure that I can trust you."

"So tell me what to do to prove my trust."

"Give me Michael."

"But father, I told you…"

"You have one hour, son, I'll be back."

Michael knew that Tempest wouldn't look for him in such an obvious place like the cove past the waiting room, so he hid there until Tempest left.

"Hey guys, are you there?"

"Michael, are you crazy? Tempest just left here five minutes ago."

"I know that, Andy, I heard him, I was hiding in the cove. He thinks I found his treasure, so at least we know that it exists and that could be our saving grace."

"What saving grace, Michael? We don't even know what the treasure is."

"But I might have an idea of what the treasure is," said Juliette. "It could just be the underground spring or should I say the Fountain of Youth?"

"Think about it, Andy, aging seems to be extremely slow for the residents of underground Willow House. You said so yourself, and the only thing different down here is the water system. We water our fruits and vegetables with the water from the underground spring, we drink it and we bathe in it."

"Juliette is right, Michael, everyone looks much younger than they really are and no one ever seems to get sick."

"Hold on a second, Andy, I'm receiving a message."

Michael-meet me behind Willow House-*NOW!*

I just hope my cell is thin enough to fit under this door, thought Michael.

"Andy, look under the door and don't say another word, Dad escaped."

Michael dropped to his knees and saw an object wedged beneath the door but as hard as he tried, he couldn't seem to free it.

"Rene`, are you there?" said Tempest.

Andy stood up quickly and motioned for Rene` to answer his father.

Oh God I hope he doesn't see the cell phone under the door, thought Andy.

"I'm here, father, but what are you doing back so quickly? You said I had one hour."

"That's right, son but Michael's father has escaped and that changes everything."

"Look, father, I have been locked up for far too long to have very much compassion for anyone down here. I was chained to a bed and forced to listen to the ramblings of Beatrice while these people, some of whom are not even related to you were allowed all the comforts of home. How could you allow that, Father?"

"Rene`, Beatrice told me that you were leaving and she didn't want to put you down here with Juliette. Son, you have to understand that I needed Beatrice, at the time, so I had to make her believe that I trusted her."

"By allowing her to keep me as her personal prisoner?"

"I knew she wouldn't harm you, Rene`, and I honestly didn't plan on things taking so long."

"What things, Father?"

"The arrival of Camille and my great grandchildren, of course, they were the last of my family members living outside of Willow House and because of my Will, I had to wait for my sister to pass away before Jack, Evan and Madison arrived."

"I guess I didn't plan that part very well, son, but believe me, it will all be worth it when you see what I have planned for you."

"Fine, then let me out of here."

"I can't do that, just yet, Rene`."

"Why not?"

"I told you that I have to be sure that you will stand beside me no matter what transpires."

"Father, Juliette thought I was dead, so let's just say that she has formed a long term relationship with someone else, and though I don't blame her, the last place I want to be is down here."

"The people down here are truly happy, Father and everyone looks fantastic." Juliette looks twenty five years younger than me, and to tell you the truth, I feel that I deserve something for what I have gone through."

"Give me back the years I lost, Father, allow me to rule, beside you, after all, what else is left for me?"

Chapter One Hundred

Michael made his way through the tunnels, to Camille's room and after making sure that Beatrice was nowhere in sight, he practically flew down the stairs, out the front door and by the time he made it to the back of Willow House, he could hardly catch his breath.

"Dad?" he whispered "where are you?"

"I'm right here, son," said the chief ,as he immerged from the bushes. "Just wanted to make sure that no one followed you."

"Dad, I won't even ask how you got loose, but why did you want me to meet you back here?"

"Because the treasure is the underground spring and I believe it might just be the way to rescue everyone."

"Juliette said the very same thing, because everyone ages so slowly and the spring is where their water supply comes from, but what made you think it was the spring, Dad?"

"No more time for chit chat, son, we need to get everyone out of underground Willow House before it's too late, let's move."

As Chief McCrary took off running toward the woods, he tossed Michael a couple of tools he took from the tool shed.

"Hang onto these, Michael, just in case we need them and could you please try and keep up?"

Michael caught the tools and began running behind his dad, and as soon as they reached their destination, the chief stopped, turned to Michael and put his finger to his lips, a gesture that Michael knew meant, *don't say a word.*

The chief slowly moved forward about fifty feet, peered

through the brush, then turned and motioned for Michael to join him.

When Michael reached the spot where the chief was standing, he stood very still as his father parted the brush, revealing the most amazing sight he had ever seen.

"What the devil is that dad?" he whispered.

"That, my boy is the answer to our prayers."

Rene` held his breath for what seemed like five minutes, waiting for his father's reply to his request to set him free and allow him to rule beside him.

"My son, ordinarily I would say no to your request; however, I believe that the time you served as Beatrice's prisoner might have been the best thing that ever happened to you, yes Rene`, I think you will now be able to understand and appreciate what I am about to share with you."

"Everyone please leave the waiting area so that I can free my son, and remember that if anyone decides to try and escape, unlike Beatrice, I can wipe you all out within five seconds."

Andy winked at Rene` and motioned for everyone to leave the waiting area.

"The room is clear now, Father, you can open the door."

The door then opened, revealing a man that looked as if he could be Rene's son and as Tempest held out his arms to embrace him, Rene` had to remind himself that one wrong move on his part could mean disaster for everyone he loved; so he managed to put a smile on his face, throw his arms around his father and utter the words, "Father, I am so happy that you are alive, I have missed you so much and I can't believe how…"

"Young I look?"

"Yes and I understand that for whatever reason, everyone down here has barely aged, you seemed to have gone backwards in time, you actually look like my son, rather than my father."

"Don't worry, Rene`; soon we will look like brothers."

As the door to the waiting room reopened, Andy rushed in,

praying that Tempest had not discovered the cell phone wedged under the door.

"Thank God," he said, "I guess that when the door slid open, the phone was freed and Rene` must have moved it aside with his foot, and just in time, I might say."

The phone began lighting up and as Andy read the message from the chief, he couldn't help but smile as he read the message aloud.

Go to the greenhouse and wait for another message- 0007

Jack asked how Andy knew the message was from the Michael.

"What if Tempest was the one sending messages?"

"The message wasn't from Michael, Jack, it was from his father. I always called him triple 07 and no one knew that, except him."

As Tempest and Rene` made their way toward headquarters, Rene` asked his father if he ever found Michael.

"No, son, but it doesn't really matter because I have Michael's father and he would never do anything to endanger his life."

As Tempest and Rene` reached headquarters, Tempest pulled a remote from his pocket, punched in a code and the doors slid open.

"Welcome home, son," said Tempest.

"Father, I don't know what to say, I cannot believe this place, how could I have lived here all these years and not know about all of this?"

"Because my father started this project when I was a child, but unfortunately he died before he realized the underground spring could do more than slow the aging process."

"I was my father's protégé and I hoped that you would be mine. Your mother saw things differently and decided you would have no part of my insanity, as she called it. She arranged for you to attend boarding school in New Orleans and after high school, you decided to attend Spring Hill College, a Jesuit College in Mobile, Alabama. You said many of your friends in boarding school were from Mobile and you wanted to attend the same college as they did."

"I agreed because I believed that once you had completed your education, you would be my intellectual equal and be more than willing to help me in my lifelong quest; however, that didn't happen because you met your precious Juliette and brought her home to Willow House. There was no way I could tear you away from her or your mother, but when Camille was born, I decided that she could be my protégé."

"When she was quite young, I hypnotized her and as I was about to take her with me into underground Willow House, I heard Juliette calling for her, so I instructed Camille to forget that she had seen me and I hid before Juliette found us together."

I cannot believe this deranged old man was going to kidnap my daughter and put Juliette and I through a torture that no parent should have to go through, but I must keep a cool head.

"I never had another opportunity to be alone with Camille after that because Juliette never let her out of her sight. It was if she sensed that something was going to happen to her precious Camille."

"Father, I can see the big picture, now, but if you had taken my daughter, I would have believed that something terrible had happened to her."

"Rene`, I love my family and I would never have let you believe that Camille had been kidnapped by some psycho. I was going to have you and Juliette brought to live in underground Willow House, and though I was going to raise her, I certainly would have let her come and visit you from time to time."

My God he is a lunatic, thought Rene`.

"Father, I would have joined you if you had only asked me."

"Son, even if you had joined me, Juliette would have caused me many problems, another reason that I allowed Beatrice to take her away from you."

"I honestly thought that after you lost Juliette, you would come to love Willow House and your heritage as much as I did, so I watched and waited, but you could never seemed to stop grieving over Juliette and when Beatrice said that you were going to leave Willow House to visit Camille, well, I just couldn't allow that to happen."

"Son, I really would have reunited you and Juliette if it were not for Beatrice, you do understand that, don't you?"

"As I said before, I needed her at the time and she wanted you, so what else was I to do?"

"Now, can we please go and check on Chief McCrary?"

Chapter One Hundred One

As Andy arrived at the greenhouse his cell phone began to flash again, so he quickly opened it and read the message.

Andy, we need to stop the feed from the spring to underground Willow House – *it powers the generators-bring everyone to the greenhouse in small groups –If Tempest decides to tune in – can't have him see everyone heading for greenhouse at the same time*

"Dad, I know that you were a spy, but I'm sure you had all kinds of spy paraphernalia in those days, we have nothing now, no diving equipment, explosives, bullet proof vests, nothing."

"You really did watch too many spy movies, didn't you, Mikie?"

"To stay alive, the most important piece of equipment needed is your brain, and I have to assume that you have one of those, so please listen to me very carefully and we might just all get out of here alive, is that understood?"

Michael was taken aback by his father's words, and for the first time in his life, he realized that Michael McCrary, Sr. was a force to be reckoned with.

"Understood," said Michael. "Just tell me what to do."

"Well this is certainly an unexpected surprise," said Tempest, as he and Rene` reached their destination. "I guess Chief McCrary is smarter than I gave him credit for. It seems he has escaped."

"I really don't see that as a problem, Father, after all, we still have Julie, and Michael is not about to risk anything happening to her."

"That's true, my son, it never hurts to have hostages."

"I must say that I have a new found respect for you, Rene`,

316

being held prisoner seems to have hardened you a bit and you needed that, you know."

"I don't know that I agree that being locked up was good for me, Father; however it did change me, and more than anything else, I want those years back and knowing that you can give them back to me has caused me to release my anger towards you"

"And how do I know that you won't turn on me once I give you back your youth?"

"Because I am not as smart as you are, Father; therefore, I need you. I could never run this place without you."

"You're smarter than you think, Son, because you gave me the right answer, now shall we get on with the tour? I'll show you your quarters, first."

"But what about the leak, Father, shouldn't we be checking it out?"

"Rene`, there is no leak. I checked it out when the alarm went off and everything was fine. Alarms do go off sometimes for no apparent reason and this was one of those times."

"Father, I heard the water myself; it sounded like it was inside the walls."

"That's absurd, Son, you were just reacting to Andy's scare tactics, now let's get moving, there is much for you to see."

Andy met with Zack, Franklin, Jack and Evan and after briefing them on what the Chief and Michael were attempting to do, he asked them to help assemble everyone into small groups so that everything would appear normal should Tempest or Beatrice decided to turn the cameras on.

"What if we just covered the cameras and told Tempest that we were tired of feeling like we were on display?" asked Evan.

"Because Tempest is too smart to buy that, especially now, he would know we were up to something, so the best thing that we can do is keep our eyes on the cameras and move each group, one at a time, until everyone is in the greenhouse. By that time, if Tempest turns on the cameras, he will just assume that everyone is asleep, any more questions, men? "Then let's move."

Michael held the flashlight as the Chief reached beneath the surface of the water.

"Tempest's laboratory is positioned next to the greenhouse and the spring feeds directly into the lab, so the pipes have to be within a few feet of this spot."

"So what are you going to do if you find the pipes, Dad?"

"I'm going to do my best to stop the feed, Son."

"But what about the oxygen?"

"Well, let's hope we can get everyone out before we have to worry about that."

"Let's hope? Dad how do you know for sure that the spring feeds into the lab and…"

"Because I searched the lab before I left and I found the feed. I couldn't disconnect it inside because it would have set off the alarm and we would have all been trapped inside."

Chief McCrary continued to probe beneath the water but was unable to connect with anything.

"I guess the feed is a little deeper than I thought."

"Try this, Pop," said Michael, as he handed the chief a limb that had fallen from one of the trees.

"That did the trick, Mikie, now all we have to do is stop the feed and if I'm right, the greenhouse roof will retract; however, there could be one other problem. Tempest could close the roof manually, if he is near enough to the lab to make it happen."

"So let's just make sure he is as far away from his lab as we can get him, Pop."

"Now you're thinking, Junior."

Chapter One Hundred Two

Beatrice paced up and down the computer room, for what seemed like hours to her, before she finally decided to go downstairs and make herself a cup of tea.

Tempest said I should not turn on the audio or video until I hear from him; however, he said nothing about making tea, she thought, and as she made her way downstairs and headed for the kitchen, she found herself feeling quite lonely without Julie.

I guess the brat was beginning to grow on me.

As she reached the kitchen, Beatrice looked out the window and noticed a storm was brewing out over the sound.

Guess I need to take my tea and return to the computer room in case Tempest needs me for anything.

"I don't think so, Beatrice," said Chief McCrary. "You might be a crazy old bat, but I don't want to be responsible for your demise."

"How the hell did you get in here, Chief McCrary?"

"These old houses are a piece of cake to break into, Aunt Bea."

"Well I suggest you turn around and leave the same way you came in or I'll…"

"What, reach into your pocket, push a button and destroy Willow House?"

"How could you know about…?"

"That's not important, Beatrice, what is important is saving my friends and you are going to help me do that."

"Why should I help you, I'm the one in control here?"

"And you know what? I believed that until I found out

Tempest is still alive and pulling all the strings around here, especially yours."

As Beatrice started to reach into her pocket, the chief grabbed her wrist, reached into her pocket and seized the remote.

"Now Beatrice, I want you to step outside with me, just in case your father-in-law is listening in, although I'm sure he isn't concerned about you anymore, especially since he has Rene`."

"Don't act so surprised, Beatrice, Tempest has been using you all these years, but now that he has his entire family with him, he has no need for you."

"Now, shall we take a little walk in the woods, Beatrice?"

"What do you want from me, Chief?" asked Beatrice, as she walked with him toward the woods.

"You, my dear, are going to help me cut off the water supply from underground Willow House."

By the time the chief and Beatrice reached the greenhouse area, Michael was nowhere in sight.

"Michael, where are you," called the chief.

"Dad, I'm over here," said Michael as he flashed his light on & off. I just spoke to Andy and he has everyone in place; however there is one problem."

"Water is seeping into the underground living quarters and if we don't move fast, it may just be too late."

"Okay, Beatrice, this is where you come in," said the chief.

"We are going to send Tempest a message on your little remote. You will tell him that you shot Michael and me as we were trying to escape and you need his help to get rid of our bodies in case anyone shows up looking for him."

"And if I refuse?"

"Then you will definitely lose Rene`"

"I already have chief, he is with Juliette now."

"Not so, Beatrice, he has joined forces with his father because he found out that Juliette is committed to someone else."

"Why should I believe you?"

"If you don't believe me, ask Tempest yourself when you send the message, tell him that I told you right before I died, but if you don't hurry, Rene` is going to be the one that dies because water is seeping into the living quarters and the whole underground structure could collapse."

The chief watched as Beatrice sent the message to Tempest.

"You didn't ask about Rene`"

"No, I didn't," she said, but before the chief could ask why, Beatrice received a reply from Tempest saying that he was on his way.

"That's it, Michael, let's get these people out of there."

Chapter One Hundred Three

Andy got the signal from Michael that he had been waiting for, so he told everyone to be ready to move when he gave the signal.

"When the greenhouse roof opens up, the chief is going to lower a ladder down and we must all move as quickly as possible, women and children first, of course, is that understood?"

"Andy, I don't want to alarm you," whispered Madison, "but Jack and Evan went back to the living quarters as you instructed, to make sure no one was left behind and they said the water has broken through one of the walls."

"They sealed off the rooms as well as they could but…"

Suddenly alarms began to sound, the greenhouse roof opened and a ladder was thrust down through the opening.

"Hurry everyone," shouted Andy, as the water from the living quarters began to fill the room.

As each person reached the roof, Michael pulled them out and the chief instructed them to run as far from the house as they could get.

Beatrice watched as her subjects fled through the woods; her dream of ruling underground Willow House was over, yet she still clung to the hope that she and Rene would finally be together and find their own kingdom to rule.

Suddenly she began to scream, "Where is Rene? Where is my love?"

"Beatrice, calm down!" yelled the chief, "Rene` is with Tempest, remember?" They are probably on the front lawn of Willow House searching for you."

"Yes, I must go find them and tell them you kidnapped me

and made me send the message." And with that, she was fleeing through the woods alongside the others that had just been set free.

"Dad, go after Beatrice!" shouted Michael.

"I'm not going anywhere, Son, we are in this thing together and I'm not leaving without you."

The words had no sooner left the chief's mouth when water began to gush from the greenhouse roof. Michael was thrown by the force of the water and landed next to the chief.

"Mikie, are you okay"

"I'm okay, Dad, but I don't know where Julie is."

"We'll find her," he said, as he held out his hand and lifted Michael to his feet.

Bodies were everywhere. Some had been thrown toward the woods and others seemed to ride the wave out into the inlet of water that was fed from the sound.

"Some of these people may not be able to swim, Dad, we need to help them."

"Trust me, they all know how to swim," said the sweetest voice that Michael had ever heard.

"Julie? My God, are you okay?"

"I'm fine, Michael; we just need to find everyone and make sure that Tempest hasn't hurt any of them."

"What about the people that were washed out into the inlet?"

"All the women and children and most of the men had gotten out before the gusher came, Michael, so there should only be about a dozen men that washed out into the inlet and as I said before, they know how to swim much better than anyone I have ever been around and besides, you would only drown trying to find them."

"You're right, Julie, let's go. Are you ready, Pop?"

"Ready J…"

"Don't do it, Dad"

As the Chief, Michael and Julie reached the front lawn of

Willow house, the sun was just beginning to peek above the horizon and it seemed to Julie as if the family Bienvenue had just been created because everyone that she had come to know and love in the last few weeks appeared before her.

"Grandmother, Grandfather?" she said as she began walking toward Rene` and Juliette.

"Yes, sweetheart," said Rene` and Juliette as they opened their arms, "you are finally home."

"I think we are all finally home," said Evan, as he looked around at everyone standing on the front lawn.

"Not all of us," said Tempest, as he appeared from behind a large willow tree

"I have been cheated out of my home and I intend to right that wrong."

"As do we, Tempest," said a group of men, as they immerged from the woods.

By this time Willow House had been swallowed up, and there was no sign that it had ever even existed.

"We lost our home as well, Tempest," said one of the men in the group. "You took us without our consent and held us prisoner in underground Willow House and now that it's gone, we have no place left to go."

"I gave you life, as far as I'm concerned," said Tempest, "I took you in and gave you everything you could possibly want or need. I even gave you the gift of youth, for God's sake, what more could you have asked for?"

"Freedom, Tempest, the one thing we never had was freedom. Some of us were fortunate enough to know what a sunrise and sunset looked like, but our offspring were never able to experience the beauty of a blue sky or hear the sound of the waves from the Gulf of Mexico, the afternoon breezes, a beautiful full moon and millions of stars in the night skies."

"Our children have never fished or been on a picnic or rode bikes with their friends."

"You took their freedom, Tempest, all because you wanted to live forever."

"That's not true, I never intended to live forever; I just wanted my family to be joined together inside the only home I had ever known and to continue the work that my father started many years ago."

"I knew that once everyone was inside the walls of Willow House, I could make them understand how important it was for them to continue my father's quest."

"The underground spring has resources that seem to slow the aging process; however, I am on the brink of discovering how to use the elements in the spring to reverse aging; now do you understand why I wanted my family here?"

Chapter One Hundred Four

Time seemed to stand still as police cars surrounded the grounds of Willow House.

"No one will ever believe this story, you do understand that, don't you, Jack?"

"I do, Uncle Rene`"

"Then you must understand why we can never tell anyone about the spring?"

"Yes, but…"

"No, Jack, there are no buts, no one must know."

"He's right, Jack," said Franklin. "We must protect not only our family, but the others who have risked their lives. If the truth about the spring got out, there would be media swarming all over the place"

"I guess you're right, Uncle Franklin, it's going to be hard enough on these people once the word gets out that they were being held prisoner in underground Willow House. I guess we should gather everyone together and make sure they never mention a word about the spring."

So as Chief McCrary, Michael and Andy spoke with the authorities, Franklin, Zack, Jack and Evan made sure everyone was accounted for.

"Is everyone okay?" asked Zack.

"Everyone seems to be fine, Dad," said Madison. "Apparently, the ones that washed out into the inlet are fine, as well, because Mother said no one is missing; that is no one except Tempest and Beatrice."

"That's impossible, Madison; the police have this place surrounded. The only place they could have gone is…"

"Willow House? Dad, that place is not safe."

"I know, sweetheart, I'll let the police know they are missing and there is a possibility that they could be inside.""

"Chief McCrary overheard what Zach said and after he introduced himself, he said t he would have a crew check it out, but he had barely spoken the words when suddenly there was a loud explosion and Willow House disappeared into the ground.

"What the hell happened, Chief?"

"It looks to me like Willow House imploded."

"Tempest?"

"That would be my guess, Zack."

"Why would he do that?"

"Because Willow House was his life."

Zach, Madison and the chief turned to see Camille facing a huge void where Willow House once stood.

"I suppose he felt that he had nothing left to live for and Beatrice must have felt that way as well," she said, as she stood staring straight ahead.

"He must have had this plan in place, just in case; thank God he didn't decide to explode the building; that would have caused some casualties."

"Maybe it was his final gesture to convince us that he really did love his family, in his own twisted way, that is."

"I know I should not be making excuses for him, because he has hurt so many people, yet I really do believe he felt he was doing us all a favor, that he was taking care of his family and including us in his plan to live forever and rule the world."

Jack, Evan and Madison listened as their mother seemed to forgive this man that had tried to kidnap her and imprison her in underground Willow House, so many years ago; this man that lured her back, along with her children in hopes of fulfilling a mission his father had begun.

"What now, Miss Camille?" said Franklin, as he stood

beside her and watched the smoke surrounding Willow House disappear."

"First of all, never call me Miss Camille again, Uncle Franklin and secondly, what would you like to do?"

"Willow House was my home Mi… I mean Camille, naturally I would have liked to live here for the rest of my life, but that doesn't seem to be an option."

"And why wouldn't it be?"

"The way I see it, Uncle Franklin, Willow House was a wonderful place to live. I had many happy memories there but I blocked them all out because Tempest tried to interfere with the circle of life."

"I say we rebuild Willow House, without the underground of course, and you and Martha live here for as long as you live."

"I understand there is enough money in the bank to support Willow House for many years and if that runs out, we can always sell the water from the spring."

Everyone had surrounded Camille by then and they all stared at her with a shocked look on their face.

Camille burst out laughing and said that it was high time that everyone learn what lightheartedness was about.

"We will rebuild Willow House, bigger and better than ever; after all, we have many more people to house, don't we?"

"I'm sure we all agree that every one of us is family now and that eventually the whole city of Ocean Springs will be a descendent of the Bienvenues, Blooms, McCrarys and Bergerons"

"And what about the spring, Grandmother?" asked Julie. "It's going to be very hard to deny the benefits it has to offer."

"Who said we have to deny the benefits, my darling? After all, the spring is on the grounds of Willow House and the water is so very refreshing, is it not my dear?"

Epilogue

I do feel there is more to this story, though it may never have a sequel.

Someone is sure to take advantage of what the spring beneath the grounds of Willow House has to offer.

If you were one of the many that were kidnapped by Tempest Bienvenue, would you be content to live out your life without telling your story, having your revenge, cashing in on the revenue the spring of life could bring? Or would you be happy just to have the freedom to come and go as you please and have everyone you love by your side?

Maybe there is a sequel, Maybe Tempest and Beatrice didn't perish in the implosion of Willow House.

Could you really relax, knowing there was a spring on your property that could provide you with the gift of life and the man that could harness the energy from the spring was alive and waiting?